"You didn't think I'd bring a limo to our first date, did you?"

She did, but she didn't say so.

In the driver's seat, Shane slid his sunglasses on and revved the engine. The car rumbled like a live animal. "Ready, Freddy?"

She nodded.

"If you need a hat, there's one in the glove compartment," he said.

She decided to spare Shane her Medusa Head and pulled the baseball cap over her hair. After a few seconds of his unabashed staring, she sent him a questioning glance.

Tugging on the cap, he swore lightly. "You're too attractive for your own good, Crickitt."

Shane navigated the convertible through highway traffic with speedy caution. His hair whipped in the wind as he moved his lips to a song on the radio. He had it all wrong. It was Shane, *not her*, who was too attractive for his own good.

How about a date with a devastatingly charming billionaire? Don't mind if I do.

Shane leaned over and stole a brief kiss. Memories of last night flooded over her, the firm insistence of his lips and the feel of his hands grazing her rib cage. As if reading her mind, he shot her a primal, dangerous grin. Whatever he had planned for them today, she hoped she could handle it...

TEMPTING
the BILLIONAIRE

JESSICA LEMMON

FOREVER

NEW YORK BOSTON

This book is a work of fiction. Names, characters, places, and incidents are the product of the author's imagination or are used fictitiously. Any resemblance to actual events, locales, or persons, living or dead, is coincidental.

Copyright © 2013 by Jessica Lemmon
Excerpt from *Hard to Handle* copyright © 2013 by Jessica Lemmon
All rights reserved. In accordance with the U.S. Copyright Act of 1976, the scanning, uploading, and electronic sharing of any part of this book without the permission of the publisher is unlawful piracy and theft of the author's intellectual property. If you would like to use material from the book (other than for review purposes), prior written permission must be obtained by contacting the publisher at permissions@hbgusa.com. Thank you for your support of the author's rights.

Forever
Grand Central Publishing
Hachette Book Group
237 Park Avenue, New York, NY 10017
www.hachettebookgroup.com

Printed in the United States of America

OPM

Originally published as an ebook
First mass market edition: November 2013

10 9 8 7 6 5 4 3 2 1

Forever is an imprint of Grand Central Publishing.
The Forever name and logo are trademarks of Hachette Book Group, Inc.

The publisher is not responsible for websites (or their content) that are not owned by the publisher.

The Hachette Speakers Bureau provides a wide range of authors for speaking events. To find out more, go to www.hachettespeakersbureau.com or call (866) 376-6591.

For my husband, John, who has always believed in me and my abilities. You are a shining example of a hero.

You're right, babe, this is "our" book. I love you.

ACKNOWLEDGMENTS

Thanks to God, who knows my heart and has seen fit to "throw open the floodgates" on my behalf. You are truly awesome!

Thanks to:

My agent, Nicole Resciniti, for believing in me and working so hard to help my dream become a reality!

My editor, Lauren Plude, your love for this book is humbling. Thank you for championing me and for taking a chance on me. Who knew I could edit at lightning speed?!

Everyone at Grand Central who had a role in publishing this book, thank you for your hard work.

My critique partners: Jeannie Moon who offered helpful fashion advice for Shane such as "Black is for undertakers," and "Lime green? Really?" And for suggesting the electric wine opener—it led to a great scene. Michele Shaw, for staying up waaaay past your bedtime to read for me. I still owe you a few dollars for the clichés.

Best friend extraordinaire by day, highly fashionable beta reader by night, Niki Hughes, you ROCK! *KnowhatImean?*

"Daddio" Terry Long—seeing you proud makes me proud...I make no promises on the yacht.

Mom (Melodie) and Ted Brewer—for supporting me in all I do...sometimes, quite literally. ;)

Fellow writers at the OVRWA, for never being short on advice and support. And a special shout-out to Melissa Landers for helping me with that darn query letter!

Fellow leaders, consultants, and customers I met while in PartyLite—without each and every one of you, I wouldn't be who I am today. Thank you.

Friends and family, online and off, for your constant cheerleading. There have been a million tiny moments, a thousand kind words, hundreds of retweets and "likes," and all of them are stored in my heart.

My husband, John, who is awesome enough to get mentioned both here and in the dedication. You not only stood by me while I chased my dream but celebrated it as if it was your own. Here's to many, *many* more celebrations and life-changing moments together.

Last, thanks to you, dear reader, for taking a chance on a new author. The idea of my book being published started out as a very big, very faraway dream. That journey officially started in 2010, and now you're holding that dream in your hands. May Shane and Crickitt find a permanent spot in your hearts, and on your "keeper" shelves!

TEMPTING
the BILLIONAIRE

CHAPTER ONE

Oscillating red, green, and blue lights sliced through the smoke-filled club. Men and women cluttered the floor, their arms pumping in time with the throbbing speakers as an unseen fog machine muddied the air.

Shane August resisted the urge to press his fingertips into his eyelids and stave off the headache that'd begun forming there an hour ago.

Tonight marked the end of a grueling six-day work-week, one he would have preferred to end in his home gym, or in the company of a glass of red wine. He frowned at the bottle of light beer in his hand. Six dollars. That was fifty cents an ounce.

The sound of laughter pulled his attention from the overpriced brew, and he found a pair of girls sidling by his table. They offered twin grins and waved in tandem, hips swaying as they strode by.

"Damn," Aiden muttered over his shoulder. "I should have worn a suit."

Shane angled a glance at his cousin's T-shirt and jeans. "Do you even own a suit?"

"Shut up."

Shane suppressed a budding smile and tipped his beer bottle to his lips. It was Aiden who dragged him here tonight. Shane could give him a hard time, but Aiden was here to forget about his ex-wife, and she'd given him a hard enough time for both of them.

"This is where you're making your foray into the dating world?" Shane asked, glancing around the room at the bevy of flesh peeking out from the bottom of skintight skirts and shorts.

"Seemed like a good place to pick up chicks," Aiden answered with a roll of one shoulder.

Shane tamped down another smile. Aiden was recently divorced, though "finally" might be a better term. Two years of wedded bliss had been anything but, thanks to Harmony's wandering eye. Shane couldn't blame Aiden for exercising a bit of freedom. God knows, if Shane was in his shoes, he'd have bailed a long time ago. This time when Harmony left, she'd followed her sucker punch with a TKO: the man she left Aiden for was his now *former* best friend. At first Aiden had been withdrawn, then angry. Tonight he appeared to be masking his emotions beneath a cloak of overconfidence.

"Right," Shane muttered. "Chicks."

"Well, excuse me, Mr. Moneybags." Aiden leaned one arm on the high-top table and faced him. "Women may throw themselves at you like live grenades, but the rest of us commoners have to come out to the trenches and hunt."

Shane gave him a dubious look, in part for the sloppily mixed metaphor, but mostly because dodging incoming women didn't exactly describe his lackluster love life. If he'd learned anything from his last girlfriend, it was how to spot a girl who wanted to take a dip in his cash pool.

He'd only had himself to blame, he supposed. He was accustomed to solving problems with money. Problem-free living just happened to be at the top of his priority list. Unfortunately, relationships didn't file away neatly into manila folders, weren't able to be delegated in afternoon conference meetings. Relationships were complicated, messy. Time consuming.

No, thanks.

"I can pick up a girl in a club," Shane found himself arguing. It'd been a while, but he never was one to shy away from a challenge. Self-made men didn't shrink in the face of adversity.

Aiden laughed and clapped him on the shoulder. "Don't embarrass yourself."

Shane straightened and pushed the beer bottle aside. "Wanna bet?"

"With you?" Aiden lifted a thick blond eyebrow. "Forget it! You wipe your ass with fifties."

"Hundreds," Shane corrected, earning a hearty chuckle.

"Then again," Aiden said after finishing off his bottle, "I wouldn't mind seeing you in action, learn what not to do now that I'm single again. Find a cute girl and I'll be your wingman." Before Shane could respond, Aiden elbowed him. "Except for her."

Shane followed his cousin's pointing finger to the bar, where a woman dabbed at her eyes with a napkin. She looked so delicate sitting there, folded over in her chair, an array of brown curls concealing part of her face.

"Crying chicks either have too much baggage, or they're wasted."

Says Aiden Downey, dating guru.

"Drunk can be good," he continued, "but by the time you get close enough to find out, it's too late."

Shane frowned. He didn't like being told what to do. Or what not to. He wasn't sure if that's what made him decide to approach her, or if he'd decided the second Aiden pointed her out. He felt his lips pull into a deeper frown. He shouldn't be considering it at all.

A cocktail waitress stopped at their table. Shane waved off the offer of another, his eyes rooted on the crying girl at the bar. She looked as out of place in this crowd as he felt. Dressed unassumingly in jeans and a black top, her brown hair a curly crown that stopped at her jawline. In the flashy crowd, she could have been dismissed as plain...but she wasn't plain. She was pretty.

He watched as she brushed a lock from her damp face as her shoulders rose and fell. The pile of crumpled napkins next to her paired with the far-off look in her eyes suggested she was barely keeping it together. Grief radiated off of her in waves Shane swore he could feel from where he sat. Witnessing her pain made his gut clench. Probably because somewhere deep inside, he could relate.

Aiden said something about a girl on the dance floor, and Shane flicked him an irritated glance before his eyes tracked back to the girl at the bar. She sipped her drink and offered the bartender a tight nod of thanks as he placed a stack of fresh napkins in front of her.

Shane felt an inexplicable, almost gravitational pull toward her, his feet urging him forward even as his brain raised one argument after the next. Part of him wanted to help, though if she wanted to have a heart-to-heart, she'd be better off talking to Aiden. But if she needed advice or a solution to a tangible problem, well, that he could handle.

He glanced around the room at the predatory males lurking in every corner and wondered again why she was here. If he did approach her, an idea becoming more compelling by the moment, she'd likely shoot him down before he said a single word. So why was he mentally mapping a path to her chair? He pressed his lips together in thought. Because there was a good chance he could erase the despair from her face. A prospect he found more appealing than anything else.

"Okay, her friend is hot, I'll give you that," Aiden piped up.

Shane blinked before snapping his eyes to the brunette's left. Her "hot friend," as Aiden so eloquently put it, showcased her assets in a scandalously short skirt and backless silver top. He'd admit she was hard to miss. Yet Shane hadn't noticed her until Aiden pointed her out. His eyes trailed back to the brunette.

"Okay," Aiden said on a sigh of resignation. "Because I so desperately want to see this, I'm going to take a bullet for you. I'll distract the crier. You hit on the blonde." That said, he stood up and headed toward the bar...to flirt with the *wrong girl*.

The platitude of only having one chance to make a first impression flitted through Shane's head. He called Aiden's name, but his shout was lost under the music blasting at near ear-bleeding decibels. Aiden may be younger and less experienced, but he also had an undeniable charm girls didn't often turn down. If the brunette spotted his cousin first, she wouldn't so much as look at Shane. He abandoned his beer, doing a neat jog across the room and reaching Aiden just as he was moving in to tap the brunette's shoulder.

"My cousin thought he recognized you," Shane blurted to the blonde, grabbing Aiden by the arm and spinning him in her direction.

The blonde surveyed Aiden with lazy disinterest. "I don't think so."

Aiden lifted his eyebrows to ask, *What the hell are you doing?*

Rather than explain, Shane clapped both palms on Aiden's shoulders and shoved him closer to the blonde. "His sister's in the art business." It was a terrible segue if the expression on Aiden's face was anything to go by, but it was the first thing that popped into Shane's head.

The music changed abruptly, slowing into a rhythmic, techno-pop remix that had dancers slowing down and pairing up. Aiden slipped into an easy, confident smile. "Wanna dance?" he asked the blonde.

The moment the question was out of his mouth, the scratches and hissing of snare drums shifted into the melodic chimes of the tired and all-too-familiar line dance the Electric Slide.

Aiden winced.

Shane coughed to cover a laugh. "He's a great dancer," he said to the blonde.

Aiden shot his elbow into Shane's ribs but recovered his smile a second later. Turning to the blonde, he said, "He's right, I am," then offered his hand.

The blonde glanced at his palm, then leaned past Shane to talk to her friend. "You gonna be okay here?" she called over the music.

The brunette flicked a look from her friend to Shane. The moment he locked on to her bright blue eyes, his heart galloped to life, picking up speed as if running for an invisible finish line. Her eyes left his as she addressed her friend. "Fine."

It wasn't the most wholehearted endorsement, but at least she'd agreed to stay.

Aiden and the blonde made their way to the dance floor, and Shane gave his collar a sharp tug and straightened his suit jacket before turning toward the brunette. She examined him, almost warily, her lids heavy over earnest blue eyes. He'd seen that kind of soul-rending sadness before, a long time ago. Staring back at him from his bathroom mirror.

"That was my cousin Aiden," he bumbled to fill the dead air between them. "He wanted to meet your friend."

"Figures," the brunette said, barely audible over the music.

He ignored the whistling sound of their conversation plummeting to its imminent death. "She seems nice. Aiden can be kind of an ass around nice girls," he added, leaning in so she could hear him.

She rewarded him with a tentative upward curve of her lips, the top capping a plumper bottom lip that looked good enough to eat. He offered a small smile of his own, perplexed by the direction of his thoughts. When was the last time he'd been thrown this off-kilter by a woman? Let alone one he'd just met? She shifted in her seat to face him, and a warm scent lifted off her skin—vanilla and nutmeg if he wasn't mistaken. He gripped the back of the chair in front of him and swallowed instinctively. Damn. She *smelled* good enough to eat.

She dipped her head, fiddled with the strap of her handbag, and Shane realized he was staring.

"Shane," he said, offering his hand.

She looked at it a beat before taking it. "Crickitt."

"Like the bug?" He flinched. *Smooth.*

"Thanks for that." She offered a mordant smile.

Evidently he was rustier at this than he thought. "Sorry." Best get to the point. "Is there something you need? Something I can get you?"

Her eyes went to the full drink in front of her. "I've had plenty, but thanks. Anyway, I'm about to leave."

"I'm on my way out. Can I drop you somewhere?"

She eyed him cautiously.

Okay. Perhaps offering her a ride was a bit forward and from her perspective, dangerous.

"No, thank you," she said, turning her body away from his as she reached for her drink.

Great. He was creepy club guy.

He leaned on the bar between the blonde's abandoned chair and Crickitt. Lowering his voice he said, "I think I'm doing this all wrong. To tell the truth, I saw you crying and I wondered if I could do anything to help. I'd...like to help. If you'll let me."

She turned to him, her eyes softening into what might have been gratitude, before a harder glint returned. Tossing her head, she met his eye. "Help? Sure. Know anyone who'd like to hire a previously self-employed person for a position for which she has little to no experience?"

He had to smile at her pluck...and his good fortune.

Crickitt's problem may be one he could help with after all. "Depends," he answered, watching her eyebrows give the slightest lift. He leaned an elbow on the bar. "In what salary range?"

* * *

Crickitt scanned the well-dressed man in front of her. He wore a streamlined charcoal suit and crisp white dress shirt. No tie, but she'd bet one had been looped around his neck earlier. She allowed her gaze to trickle to his open collar, lingering over the column of his tanned neck before averting her eyes. What would he say if she blurted out the figure dancing around her head?

Two-hundred fifty thou' a year? Oh, sure, I know lots of people who pay out six figures for a new hire.

"Well?" he asked.

"Six figures," she said.

He laughed.

That's what she thought. If this Shane guy were in a position to offer that kind of income, would he really be in a club named Lace and hitting on a girl like her? Why hadn't he hit on someone else? Someone without a runny nose and red-rimmed eyes. Someone like Sadie. But he'd rerouted his friend to talk to Sadie. Why had he done that? She smoothed her hair, considering.

Maybe you're an easy target.

He saw her crying and wanted to help? It wasn't the worst pickup line in the world, but it was close.

Crickitt instinctively slid her pinky against her ring finger to straighten her wedding band but only felt the rub of skin on skin. For nine years the band had been

at home on her left hand. She used to think of it as a
comforting weight, but since Ronald left, it'd become a
reminder of the now obvious warning signs she'd overlooked. The way he'd pulled away from her both physically and emotionally. The humiliation of scurrying after
him, attempting to win his affections even after it was
too late. She lifted her shoulders under her ears, wishing
she could hide from the recurring memory, the embarrassment. Fresh tears burned the backs of her eyes before she
remembered she had a captive audience. She squeezed
her eyes closed, willing the helter-skelter emotions to go
away.

When she opened them she saw Shane had backed
away some, either to give the semblance of privacy or because he feared she would burst into tears and blow her
nose on his expensive jacket. She could choke Sadie for
bringing her out tonight.

Come to the club, Sadie had said. *It'll get your mind
off of things*, she'd insisted. But it hadn't. Even when
faced with a very good-looking, potentially helpful man,
she was wallowing in self-doubt and recrimination. She
could've done that at home.

"What experience do you have, Crickitt?" Shane
asked, interrupting her thoughts.

She tipped her chin up at him. Was he serious? Either
his half smile was sarcastic or genuinely curious. Hard
to tell. The temptation was there to dismiss him as just
another jerk in a club, but she couldn't. There was an
undeniable warmth in his dark eyes, a certain kindness
in the way he leaned toward her when he talked, like he
didn't want to intimidate her.

Maybe that's why she told him the truth.

"I'm great with people," she answered.

"And scheduling?"

She considered telling him about the twenty in-home shows she held each and every month for the last seven years, but wasn't sure he wouldn't get the wrong idea about exactly what kind of *in-home shows* she'd be referring to. "Absolutely."

"Prioritizing?"

Crickitt almost laughed. Prioritizing was a necessity in her business. She'd been responsible for mentoring and training others, as well as maintaining her personal sales and team. It'd taken her a while to master the art of putting her personal business first, but she'd done it. If she focused too much on others, her numbers soon started circling the drain, and that wasn't good for any of them.

"Definitely," she answered, pausing to consider the fire burning in her belly. How long had it been since she'd talked about her career with confidence? Too long, she realized. By now, her ex-husband would have cut her off midsentence to change the subject.

But Shane's posture was open, receptive, and he faced her, his eyebrows raised as if anticipating what she might say next. So she continued. "I, um, I was responsible for a team of twenty-five salespeople while overseeing ten managers with teams of their own," she finished.

She almost cringed at the callous description. Those "teams" and "managers" were more like family than co-workers. They'd slap her silly if they ever heard her referring to them with corporate lingo. But if she had to guess, Shane was a corporate man and Crickitt doubted he'd know the first thing about direct sales.

"You sound overqualified," he said.

"That's what I...wait, did you just s-say *over*qual-ified?" Crickitt stammered. She blinked up at him, shocked. She'd fully expected him to tell her to peddle her questionable work background elsewhere.

Shane reached into his pocket and offered a business card between two outstretched fingers. "Even so, I'd like to talk to you in more detail. Are you available for an in-terview on Monday?"

Crickitt stared at the card like it was a trick buzzer.

"I'm serious." He dropped the card on the bar. "This isn't typically how I find employees, but"—he shrugged—"I need a personal assistant. And someone with your background and experience is hard to come by."

She blinked at him again. This had to be some elabo-rate scheme to get her to bed, right? Isn't that what Sadie told her to expect from the men in these places?

"How about one o'clock, Monday afternoon? I have meetings in the morning, but I should be done by then. If the job's not a good fit, at least you looked into it."

Well. The only interview she'd managed to arrange since her self-inflicted unemployment was for a thirty-thousand-dollar salary and involved her working in a gov-ernment office. And she'd lost that job to a kid ten years her junior. She'd be stupid to pass up the opportunity for an interview with this man. Even though part of her couldn't imagine working for someone as put together as Shane. But he didn't seem demanding, or overly confi-dent, just...nice.

Which brought about another niggling thought. This was too easy. And if she'd learned a lesson from recent events, wasn't it to be cautious when things were going suspiciously well? And this, she thought, glancing in his direction again, was going a little *too* well.

"What do you say?" he asked.

Then again, as her dwindling savings account constantly reminded her, she needed to find some sort of viable income. And soon. If the interview turned out to be a sham, the experience would still be worthwhile, she thought with knee-jerk optimism.

"One o'clock," she heard herself say.

Shane extended his hand and she shook it, ignoring how seamlessly her palm fit against his and the warmth radiating up her arm even after he'd pulled away. He excused himself and made his way to the door. Crickitt watched his every long-legged step, musing how he was taller than Ronald and walked with infinitely more confidence.

A tall, confident man had approached *her*. And, okay, it may have been because she looked needy, but she couldn't keep from being flattered that Shane had taken it upon himself to talk to her.

Lifting the business card between her thumb and fingers, she studied the front. The top read "August Industries, Leader in Business Strategies." No name on the card, just an address and a phone number. She flipped it over. Blank.

Sadie returned as Crickitt hopped off her bar stool.

"Where're you going?" Sadie asked with a breathless smile. Shane's cousin stood at Sadie's side, a matching grin on his tanned face. Crickitt regarded his surfer-dude style skeptically. Cute. A departure from Sadie's usual type, but cute.

Of course, there was a good chance Sadie would never

see Aiden again given her first-date-only rule. Crickitt looked down at the business card again, chewing her lip. Maybe it wasn't a good idea to see Shane again, either. She already felt as if she'd revealed too much about herself in their short conversation. Wasn't it too soon for her to trust a man after the one she'd trusted implicitly had left her behind?

"What's with the card? Did you get a date?" Sadie asked.

"No." She laughed, her temporarily reclaimed confidence ebbing. She considered crumbling the card in her hand, dropping it onto the bar. The message would get back to Shane via his cousin, she was sure. Then she wouldn't have to worry about standing him up or canceling the interview.

Chicken.

Despite the very tempting option to stay in her comfort zone, Crickitt decided maybe it was time to take a risk. Even a small one.

"Better," she told Sadie, snapping up her purse. "A job."

$\mathcal{C}$HAPTER TWO

$\mathcal{S}$hane slowed his steps from run to walk before killing the power on his treadmill. He swiped a towel over his sweat-covered face and neck, his thoughts swimming in Gulf-Stream blue eyes, full lips, and a sea of soft curls. Since he'd returned home, he hadn't been able to think of anything other than the chance meeting with Crickitt tonight.

He faced the floor-to-ceiling mirrors while catching his breath and almost didn't recognize the guy smiling back at him. When was the last time he'd caught himself grinning about anything? He sank onto the weight bench and started unlacing his shoes, wondering at his newfound exhilaration. True, he'd been searching for an assistant, and had subsequently been drowning in paperwork, for the last month. Finding Myrna's replacement would take a load off of his mind as well as his sagging in-box.

Then he thought of Crickitt's startled expression from earlier and felt the smile spread across his face again.

Watching her go from crying to confident had been the best reward of all.

The moment reminded him of the time he'd helped a struggling bookstore owner stay in business. She'd been overwhelmed with marketing, accounting, employee issues. He'd slid the pieces into place that allowed her to focus on her love, rare first editions, while the rest of her business hummed along silently in the background. It's what he did best, and what clients paid him to do most.

Being able to share in that kind of success was the very reason he'd started August Industries and kept it going for the last decade. Feeling a similar emotion in reaction to a woman was...unnerving. He hadn't made it this far by allowing himself to be distracted by a pretty face. And she *had* distracted him.

He hoped it wasn't a mistake to offer her an interview.

Shane stood up and headed for the shower, grateful tomorrow was Sunday. Maybe he'd reward himself by sleeping in for a change. He flipped on the bathroom light, stopping short of going in when he caught sight of his mother's picture hanging in the hallway. A sad smile touched his lips, and he forced himself to look, really look, at the image now nearly twenty years old.

She smiled back at him, her gold-brown eyes open and inviting. In the photo she'd been the age Shane was now. She'd die later that year, just shy of his fifteenth birthday. The faded image showed her pressing a piecrust into a pan, her red and white apron covered in flour. Seeing it made him wish his father hadn't thrown out everything of hers after she'd passed away.

That sobering thought swept away whatever was left of his buoyant mood. His legs felt suddenly tired, his heart heavy as he spun the knobs on the large stone-walled shower.

He stepped beneath the spray considering the very real possibility Crickitt hadn't been grateful for his butting in. She could have been lying about her work experience, or about her intentions of showing up for the interview. And while he'd like to think her tears were genuine, she could have played up the damsel in distress routine for attention. If she had, she'd be no different from a handful of other women who had done the same in his presence. In a way, that might be simpler. He could handle a woman who wanted something from him. One who was genuinely interested in him was unpredictable.

As the steaming water pounded against his taut neck muscles, he thought of how being prepared for the worst was wiser than being blindsided.

That was one lesson from his childhood he didn't have to be taught twice.

CHAPTER THREE

From the moment Crickitt had landed on the August Industries website and read their motto, she had known she was going to show up for the interview—even if it turned out to be a bust. In bold blue and silver lettering, the site proclaimed "Business owners, keep doing what you love. Leave the rest to us."

The mission statement spoke to her heart. Crickitt loved entrepreneurship. Wanting to model her own career was the reason she'd gone into direct sales in the first place. No one needed to tell her she was good enough to run her own business, she *knew*. And she'd deflected her criticizers with her own hard-won confidence.

Seven years ago, Crickitt's former business started in an unlikely place. Sadie held a Celebration home party and Crickitt had gone, expecting an evening of catching up over drinks and spending a chunk of her recent bonus check.

Then the woman representing Celebration swept in

and extended a hand in introduction. She looked relaxed, successful, put together. Crickitt remembered glancing down at her own uninspired wardrobe and wondering if she had her own business whether she'd take the time to pick out coordinating jewelry or buy nicer shoes. Then later that evening the representative shared how much she earned, nearly four times Crickitt's annual salary, and the fact that she made her own schedule, and Crickitt was sold. Shortly thereafter, she'd quit her corporate climb into the ether and joined the Celebration family.

For the last seven years, she'd worn her Entrepreneur Badge with pride.

Which might explain the morsel of contention as she walked into August Industries' high-rise building Monday afternoon. She'd finally dredged up her fight, rallied her courage, and for what? An *interview*? After she'd clawed her way out of corporate America, now she was vying for an anonymous seat in a gray cubicle? She fervently hoped she wasn't here because a good-looking guy had salved a gaping wound Saturday night. Wouldn't that be lovely? Stumbling into a 401(k) because, in some capacity, a man had given her some attention.

Where was the part of her psyche that knew what she wanted, knew who she was? Was it dormant, or had she lost that in the divorce as well?

The elevator doors dinged open on the twelfth floor, and Crickitt stepped into what looked like a contemporary art museum. A woman with short black hair, wearing an A-line royal blue dress reminiscent of the days before computers, gave her a broad smile. Crickitt approached the modern glass desk, stopping short of touching the shining, fingerprint-free surface.

"Welcome to August Industries," the woman greeted in a thick accent.

Russian? Swedish?

"I have an interview with, uh … Shane for the personal assistant position," Crickitt said, praying the woman didn't ask for his last name.

"Your résumé?" she asked pleasantly.

Crickitt dug through her plain canvas bag, lamenting never having purchased a posh leather briefcase. She handed over the single sheet of paper, smoothing a creased corner as she did. A button gapped at the front of her shirt and she straightened it, wishing she had gone to Nordstrom instead of Target. She felt like a Clampett in Beverly Hills.

The receptionist glanced over her résumé before studying the sleek white computer in front of her. "One o'clock?"

Crickitt nodded.

"Have a seat. He is running a few minutes behind," she said, folding her hands neatly.

White and pale blue chairs formed an L-shape on the far wall. Crickitt took an empty seat next to a curved concrete statue of … something. She frowned up at the arced shape. Whatever it was, it was tall.

A woman in a creamy yellow suit sat in an adjacent chair flipping idly through a magazine. Crickitt twisted her mouth as she took in the matching butter-colored heels and handbag. Probably *not* purchased at a store with a bull's-eye for a logo.

As if she felt eyes on her, the other woman looked up.

"I like your shoes," Crickitt said.

She smiled. "Thank you." A moment later, the receptionist called to her and she stood, dropping the magazine onto the table in front of them. "You should check this out," she told Crickitt. "He's pretty hot." Then she sashayed away, leaving Crickitt frowning down at the periodical.

Forbes? What hot guy decorated the interior of *Forbes*?

Crickitt reached for the periodical, flipping open the cover and thumbing through the pages. Not surprisingly, she found lengthy articles interspersed with photographs of men in suits. Most of them older, with paunchy bellies and little to no hair. Then she came to a two-page spread that put her face-to-face with the man from the club. Shane. Just recalling the way his hand fit against hers had her heart ka-thumping, her palms sweating.

Wow. "Hot" was the perfect description for him.

He stood in the center of a bare room, hands in his pockets, eyes focused off to the side. His thick dark hair was the right length to be professional, but long enough to tickle the collar of his suit. Black and white treated him well, enhancing the crinkles at the corners of his eyes and the shadow marking his angled jaw. His smile was wide and genuine, and she couldn't help smiling back at the image.

Then she frowned. She remembered he'd been dressed nicely, had been pleasant and friendly. But she didn't remember him being quite so . . . hot. Then again, she'd been distracted, which was a nice way to say she was a wreck, but still, how could she have missed *this*?

Shane hadn't been a wreck. He was charming, in an odd way. His awkward conversation suggested he didn't pick up girls in clubs often. She traced the smile lines around his mouth. He certainly didn't need to.

Splashy bright orange type read: *Shane August and Everything After.* "Oh, my gosh," Crickitt breathed, and not because she was impressed by the clever play on one of her favorite album titles.

Shane didn't just *work for* August Industries. Shane *was* August Industries. She really should have shopped at Nordstrom.

"Crickitt, hi," a deep male voice sounded over her shoulder, and Crickitt nearly leaped out of her poly-cotton-blend shirt. Shane smiled down at her, the same casual hands-in-his-pockets pose as in the article between them. He wore a white shirt and pressed dark suit, paired with a coral-and-cream-striped tie.

She stood, the magazine open in her hands, her face warming as she stared up at the billionaire in front of her.

"The Counting Crows," he said, gesturing to the article.

She blinked at him. Really, how had she not noticed he was this attractive before? She was divorced, not blind. His eyes, which had looked brown in the muted club lighting, were actually warm amber with flashes of gold. And she found herself wanting to reach up and tousle his head full of thick, dark hair. Unconsciously, she curled her fingers, the magazine crinkling in her grip.

He smiled, parting perfectly contoured lips. "The article?" he said, snapping her out of her trance.

"Right! I know!" she said. "I have that CD." Caught with the proverbial canary in her mouth, Crickitt closed the magazine and dropped it onto the table. Then leaned down, flipped it over, and patted it for good measure.

"Was my picture that bad?" he asked, quirking his mouth.

"What? No! No, not at all. It's a great picture. I mean, you look really nice. Very handsome." She pressed her lips together and willed herself to shut up.

"Well, thank you." He pursed his lips, and she couldn't keep from watching them as he spoke. "You're not just saying that to butter me up before the interview, are you?"

"Hmm-mm," she answered dreamily, eyes fixed on the sexy indentation of his upper lip. Then his words hit her and she blinked. The interview! Good Lord, she'd nearly forgotten why she was here. Which was to interview for a personal assistant position. For Shane August.

The president of August Industries.

Gulp.

If she was nervous before, it was nothing compared to how she felt now. Like her adrenal glands were doing the cha-cha after a double espresso.

Shane gestured with her résumé to the short glass staircase ahead of them. Slicking her hands down her slacks, Crickitt slung her bag over one shoulder and headed up in front of him.

Here went nothing.

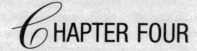

CHAPTER FOUR

 retty.

Wasn't that how he'd categorized Crickitt when he met her at the club on Saturday? But now that she was standing in front of his office windows, daylight streaming into her curls, he realized "pretty" was a gross understatement.

Horses were pretty. Sunsets, pretty. Crickitt was gorgeous.

She looked up at him, bright blue eyes at odds with her olive-toned skin. Surprise choked out his ability to speak, so he simply gestured at the guest chair in front of his desk.

Crickitt wore a boxy button-down shirt, simple pant, and plain, square-heeled shoes. A far cry from the skintight dresses and expensive pastel suits he saw around the office. Her plain-Jane neutrals may be dull, but the outfit wasn't quite able to conceal Crickitt's tempting curves. He'd bet twenty percent of his stock she had no idea how beautiful she was.

He was surprised he noticed. There wasn't a shortage of women in August Industries dressing to get attention, arguably his attention. The woman who'd graced the same chair moments ago wore a dress so short and so low cut he could practically see her navel. And she didn't stir anything within him save for irritation. Again he thought of Crickitt's blond friend at the bar on Saturday, how he'd overlooked her blatantly flashy clothing because he'd been so taken with Crickitt.

He skimmed the bullet points on her résumé before dropping it on his desk. Her work record was patchy and varied. Crickitt hadn't stayed anywhere for very long, with the exception of the last place she worked...what was it called? He lifted the paper. "Tell me about Celebration."

Crickitt shifted in her seat. "Celebration is a direct sales company with a thirty-two-year history. They specialize in in-home demonstration and high-end home décor..."

He listened, duly impressed, as she described her former career. It wasn't so much by what she said, but how she said it. Shane didn't know much about direct sales, but he knew sales. And he knew salespeople. Unlike the pompous braggarts he'd had the privilege to encounter in his ten years of business, Crickitt shared her journey from sales consultant to one of Celebration's top earners evenly, and without embellishment. She highlighted the skills pertaining to the position as his personal assistant. And while she never said it outright, Shane picked up on the ribbon of pride beneath her well-formed speech.

"Celebration might sound like a hobby, or a lonely housewife's distraction, but direct sales is a respectable way to earn an income." A note of defensiveness laced her tone, and he sensed she'd had this argument before.

Shane smiled. "Sounds like a real business to me."

Crickitt's shoulders relaxed.

"So, you made good money," he said, "and loved what you did." But she'd left out a key bit of information. "Why did you quit?"

* * *

Crickitt swallowed. Hard. She'd expected this question. Had prepared for it. There was a perfectly planned, politically correct answer poised on the tip of her tongue. But she didn't say it.

"I'm divorced," she blurted, peering through her lashes to gauge his reaction.

Shane nodded rather than comment and waited for her to go on. He was probably wondering what her divorce had to do with leaving her lucrative career. Some days she wondered the same thing.

"After he, I mean we"—she hastily corrected—"separated, I took inventory of my life." Crickitt paused under the guise of clearing her throat, but really, she was giving herself a mental talking-to. Take inventory of her life? She sounded like one of the self-help books on her shelf at home.

If she continued in that direction, she might accidentally admit the truth. That her confidence had slipped more than a few notches since she and Ronald separated. Lately she'd begun suspecting the career she'd worked so hard to build had more to do with proving she *could*, rather than because it was what she'd wanted to do.

"It's…disingenuous," she started carefully, "to continue to do something when your heart is no longer into it. And working for one hundred percent commission has its challenges."

Shane's lips tipped into a soft, utterly distracting smile, and forced herself to look at her lap instead.

"I'm not who I was six months ago," she said in a burst of honesty. She faced him. "I'm Crickitt Day, not Kitt Wachowski."

There. That speech might sound like a two-dollar fortune, but it was the truth. She watched Shane's eyebrows meet in the middle and held her breath while she waited for him to speak.

"You don't look like a Kitt." Shane grazed her with a glance, and she swore parts of her tingled wherever his golden eyes touched. "Those sound like valid reasons to change careers."

"They do?" she couldn't help asking. She'd been so used to defending herself, it was a little off-putting to hear him agree.

"Yes. And I'm going to offer you the job."

She blinked. "Just like that?"

"Just like that."

Crickitt twisted the handle of her bag, waiting for the catch. Or for the other shoe to drop…maybe both of them. It was too perfect, unless— "I'm sorry to be forward, but we should discuss salary."

Shane nodded. "Okay."

According to a book she'd read on negotiation, he who

speaks first, loses. They sat for a moment in silence. Evidently, Shane had read the same book.

"We tossed around the idea of six figures on Saturday night," she said, her heart lodged somewhere between her sternum and her throat.

"I remember."

"I'm not sure what you typically pay, but PAs, even in a starting position, can earn up to—"

Holding up one hand to halt her, he clicked an expensive-looking ink pen with the other. He scribbled a figure onto the bottom of her résumé and slid it across his desk. She took the paper, read the number, and nearly did a face-plant onto his shining office floor.

"Plus bonuses," he said.

She stared at the commas on the paper. Oh, how she wanted to sign paychecks with that many zeroes again. But that many zeroes would come at a cost. They always did. Standing abruptly, she returned the sheet to him, warning bells clanging in her head. She hoped she wouldn't regret this, but chances were if she gave him the impulsive *yes!* dangling on her tongue, she'd live to regret it even more.

Righting her bag on her shoulder, she leveled with him. "I'm going to have to say no," she said, extending her hand.

"Something wrong?"

"If this is what you're paying"—she gestured to the exorbitant amount written on the paper—"you probably expect me to work eighty or ninety hours a week. Pick up your dry cleaning. Shine your shoes." She thought about adding her mother's favorite phrase about not falling off the turnip truck yesterday, but decided against it.

Shane's eyebrows lifted. "Shine my shoes?"

Crickitt turned for the door. "Anyway, it was nice to meet you."

"Wait," Shane said, and Crickitt's hand froze on the knob.

* * *

"I'm sorry, you did what?" Sadie asked over the phone as Crickitt exited August Industries.

"I turned him down."

"Yes, I heard that," she said flatly. "What I don't understand is why. That is the closest you'll ever come to your previous income in a starting position."

"What I don't understand," Crickitt said, remotely unlocking her car and sliding into the driver's seat, "is why I let him talk me into dinner."

Sadie fell silent for a moment. "Like a date?"

"He called it a second interview."

"So, a date."

"It's tonight at seven," Crickitt said, refusing to entertain the distracting, slightly exhilarating thought.

"We should double. I have a date, too."

"You do?"

"With his cousin."

"Really?"

To the best of Crickitt's knowledge, if Sadie ever took a guy home from a club, she rarely saw him again. Ever since her fiancé opted to marry her sister, Sadie made it a point not to get too attached.

"Yeah," Sadie snorted. "I know."

"You like this guy."

"He's okay," she said, but some of the gruff edge left her voice. "Hey! Let's get ready for our dates together."

"How very preteen of you."

Four hours later, Crickitt opened her front door to find Sadie waggling a bottle in one hand. "Red wine." She held up a brown bag by the handles. "Margarita mix and champagne."

"Champagne?" Crickitt shut the door behind her.

Sadie was dressed skimpily for the warm summer weather in a denim miniskirt and pale pink tank covered with pink rhinestones. Her knee-high cowgirl boots and dream-catcher earrings hinted at where she was headed tonight. Sadie never missed a chance to theme her wardrobe to an event. And the result was rarely understated. "Are you going to a rodeo?"

"Tex-Mex restaurant." Sadie struck a pose. "What do you think?"

"You look gorgeous. But I thought we were going to get ready together."

"We are. You're going to try on outfits, and I'm going to make sure you wear the right one instead of the ultra-conservative one you'll probably choose."

"So this is a setup," Crickitt said.

Sadie paused in the middle of unloading the various spirits onto the breakfast bar. "Basically."

Crickitt propped a hand on her hip. "And where are the outfits of yours I get to criticize?"

"A, you don't criticize anyone, because you're too nice," she said, folding the empty bag. "And B, I can't change, because it would compromise my artistic integrity." Sadie screwed her mouth to the side. "Or something like that."

Crickitt laughed.

"What's your poison?" Sadie gestured to the minibar arranged on Crickitt's countertop.

"Margarita."

"That a girl."

Perhaps two margaritas before dinner was pushing it. Somewhere between trying on outfits number five and six, Crickitt's head began to spin.

"That's the one!" Sadie announced, sloshing margarita onto her shoes as she jumped up from the couch. "Ah, crap! My new boots!"

"That was a test," Crickitt slurred. "You failed." Like she would dare wear the white sundress to dinner. The swinging, flouncy material swirled around her knees with each step she took. The spaghetti straps showed way too much of her shoulders, and the black strappy sandals were far too sexy, lacing up her ankles and setting off the black sash dripping down the back of the skirt.

"You have to wear that one!" Sadie held out her hands like she was trying to get Crickitt to lay down a weapon.

Crickitt lifted the tag hanging from the armpit area of the bodice. "I bought it last year on super clearance in case Ronald took me on a cruise." She opted not to add, *for our ten-year anniversary*, which would have been this year.

"Well, that ship has sailed," Sadie said with a snort. Then she placed her fingertips to her lips. "I'm sorry. Margarita talking."

Crickitt waved her off. "I know what you mean." Sadie was entitled to be a wee tad jaded after her near miss as a bride last year. "And anyway, you're right. I shouldn't have waited for him to take me anywhere, you know?"

"Yeah, I know." Sadie offered a careful smile.

Crickitt smoothed her hands down the skirt. "It's not too much for a second interview?"

"Yes, definitely. But it's perfect for a dinner date at Triangle."

"It's not a date."

"I've never had a second date at Triangle." Sadie added, "I've never had *any* date at Triangle. I'm insanely jealous that while you are having caviar and tiramisu, I'll be hovering over a plate of nachos and a Mason jar full of beer."

Crickitt shook her head; she knew her friend too well. "No, you're not."

Sadie's face broke into a grin. "No. I'm not."

CHAPTER FIVE

Triangle, Osborn's premiere fine-dining restaurant, drew an upper-crust crowd. Crickitt had eaten here once before, with Ronald for their one-year anniversary. It was the only anniversary they celebrated extravagantly, come to think of it. She pulled into the lot, her blue Chevy Malibu out of place among the luxury cars.

She'd worn the dress. And the shoes. The prospect of air-conditioning paired with a dose of modesty had her throw a lacy black wrap over her shoulders. Sadie styled Crickitt's curly hair into an updo, leaving loose tendrils to frame her face. She adjusted a few of them in the rearview mirror and checked her lipstick as a zip of adrenaline pulsed through her.

Which made no sense. What did she have to be nervous about? She had turned down the job once already; she could do it again. Though she could blame her nerves on Sadie, who kept insisting on this being a date.

And it so wasn't.

The very suggestion that Shane August would ask her on a date was preposterous. Never mind the idea he wanted to hire her badly enough to woo her over dinner. She gulped as she rolled the word "woo" around in her head. Crickitt was woefully underprepared to date a normal guy, let alone a sophisticated billionaire.

She got out and shut the door, catching her reflection in the car's windows. Did she look like she was trying too hard? Like she had dressed for a potential lover rather than an employer? Maybe she should run home and change into sensible black pants and a blouse. She'd only be ten minutes late. Fifteen at the most.

"Crickitt, look at you."

She turned to see Shane stepping out of a long black limousine. He shut the door behind him and approached, adjusting the sleeves on his dark suit. He'd changed for dinner. And, oh, he looked good. The pale lavender shirt stretched across his chest, complemented by a plum-colored tie running the length of his torso. She dragged her eyes north before they unwittingly traveled below his belt.

He offered his elbow and she rested one hand on his forearm, pulling the shawl around her shoulders in a series of jerky movements.

"I was considering going home to change," she said, her voice wobbling.

"Why? You're stunning."

Stunning? She blinked up at him as if he'd just spoken a word outside of her native tongue. Had Ronald ever accused her of being "stunning"? Had anyone?

Forcing her train of thought back on the tracks, she rambled rather than thanked him for the compliment. "I was worried I might be overdressed, but from what I remember, the restaurant is upscale."

"I think you picked perfectly." He sent her a warm smile, one that made her mouth go dry, and led them inside. Crickitt's heart hammered her rib cage in time with their steps.

Relax, it's just an interview.

She angled her head to glance up at him. His jaw was slightly shadowed with stubble, his eyes shrouded by thick lashes. He looked dark and dangerous, and it was all too easy to imagine the scrape of that five o'clock shadow against her neck.

She licked parched lips, forcing her thoughts down a more professional road. She'd hear him out over dinner, but if the position still wasn't a good fit, she'd have to turn him down, regardless of how rich and attractive he was.

He glanced down at her, his mouth kicking up on one side.

Or maybe because of that.

* * *

This isn't a date.

Shane dragged his eyes away from Crickitt's creamy, bare shoulders. Ever since she'd uncovered them, he'd found it hard to concentrate.

Filling his wineglass to busy his hands, he dredged up another interview question for her to answer. After all, he was here to convince Crickitt to accept the personal assistant position.

That, and nothing more. He didn't believe in dipping

his pen in the company ink, especially not with a woman he'd be working with on a daily basis. It was disconcerting that he needed the constant reminder.

The moment Crickitt stepped into his office this afternoon he had known he wanted to hire her. And his instincts rarely steered him wrong. She was sharp and opinionated, charming and approachable at the same time. And attractive, he added, his eyes returning to her naked collarbone.

Not. A. Date.

The waiter arrived and delivered oval-shaped ramekins of sugar-encrusted crème brulée. Shane welcomed the distraction.

Crickitt eyed her dessert, then narrowed her eyes at him. "Bribery?"

"After you have a bite of that, you'll fold like a paper airplane."

She spared him a smile, then cracked the topping and dug out a spoonful. With a final, wary glance in his direction, she lifted the spoon to her mouth. Her eyes drifted shut and an *mmm* sound emitted from her throat. Shane watched her neck, particularly the tiny freckle on the right side, and wondered what it might taste like if he sampled it with his tongue...

"What's wrong?" Crickitt asked.

He jerked at the sound of her voice, guilty of being caught ogling his almost-new-hire. He released the stranglehold on his spoon. "Nothing," he said, brushing his thumb along his bottom lip in case his tongue was lolling out of his mouth. "There's one thing I haven't mentioned yet."

Crickitt put down the spoon and patted her lips with

her napkin. Sitting up straight, she trained her eyes on his. "Okay. I'm ready."

"Some travel is required."

She lifted her eyebrows. "Some?"

"About once a quarter. Most of our marketing and art department is in Tennessee."

"Tennessee. Art Mecca."

They shared a smile. He'd heard that before. "Angel Downey, my cousin and Aiden's older sister, is an amazing graphic designer. I hired her remotely, and as August Industries grew, so did her department. In Tennessee."

"Okay. Tennessee three to four times a year. Is that it?"

"There are occasional out-of-state trips since I'm looking to expand. Of course, you wouldn't be required to go on all of them," he added at the last second in case she was thinking of turning him down again.

She reclaimed her spoon. "Sounds great to me." With a coy smile, she added, "I think I just accepted the position."

Shane pulled his shoulders back, indescribably relieved.

Crickitt swallowed another bite and gestured with her spoon. "You're right, this tipped me. Without the crème brulée, I don't know if I would have said yes."

He'd always been good at negotiation. Nice to know he still had it. "Thank goodness I didn't order the tiramisu."

Outside, they paused in front of Crickitt's car. Shane offered his hand and she took it, and like the night at the club, his palm tingled on contact. It'd been a long time since he'd enjoyed himself this much at a business dinner...or *any* dinner, for that matter. His work was enjoyable, but it'd never before been...well, tonight had been almost...*fun*. Though he was pretty sure that aspect of the evening had more to do with the brunette whose hand was warming his.

Crickitt thanked him for dinner, pulling her fingers away a few seconds before he was ready to let go. "Company write-off." He shrugged, plunging his hands into his jacket. "One of the perks of being president."

"That and all the responsibility," she said, a hint of heaviness in her voice.

He blew out a surprised laugh. He wasn't used to anyone thinking he didn't lead a completely charmed life. Then again, Crickitt understood the pressures of running an empire. She'd built one of her own.

"How soon do you need me to start?"

"Yesterday."

A throaty chuckle poured from her lips. "How about tomorrow?" She let out a deliberate sigh. "I suppose you want me there at the ungodly hour of eight. And to think I used to start my workday at the crack of ten. And in my pajamas."

Eight? Shane nearly grimaced. His workday began between six and seven in the morning, and by eight, he was either in a staff meeting or on his way to see a client. He opened his mouth to argue, but heard himself say, "Sorry. I'm a bit of a tyrant that way."

Pulling her keys from a tiny square handbag, she turned to him one last time. "Thank you. For not letting me walk away from this opportunity. I appreciate it, Shane."

"Thanks for reconsidering," he said, meaning it.

She frowned, a little line denting the space between her eyebrows. "Do I call you Shane, or Mr. August?"

Everyone called him Mr. August. His receptionist, the janitorial staff, even his cousin Angel, who insisted on doing so to set a good example. Until now he'd agreed. So why, all of a sudden, was he having trouble justifying the formal moniker?

"Shane, please," he said, rather than mull it over. It would raise a few eyebrows at work, but he'd deal with the repercussions later. It was more important Crickitt feel comfortable around him, trust him. They'd be working closely, and the last thing he wanted was for her to feel nervous or intimidated by him.

She's your employee, came the terse reminder.

And that's all she would be. That's all she *could* be.

* * *

At home, Shane punched in the five-digit alarm code and locked his front door. An alarm system was superfluous in this neighborhood, but since it came with the house he made use of it. He'd purchased the place a year ago thanks to the former owner's misfortune. Foreclosure.

The house, with its high rounded archways and wide-open rooms, was the result of a local home show. This one, the smallest model at three thousand square feet, was more than enough space for him. He'd had one of his clients, an interior designer, furnish the modern kitchen, sunken living room, and numerous other rooms. He hadn't been much help, instructing her to "make it look less empty," but she'd done what he'd asked, filling the space with neutral, comfortable furnishings that weren't distracting.

He hung his jacket on the coatrack in the foyer, recalling the temptation to offer it to Crickitt when they stepped outside. Too bad she had worn that shawl. It was a crime to cover those shoulders.

Shane shook his head at his thoughts, which had been looping the same girl-crazy circles all evening. He liked women, especially beautiful women. And yeah, it'd been a while since he dated someone semiseriously, but Crickitt had burrowed under his skin deeper—and quicker—than most.

And as of eight a.m. tomorrow morning, she'd be his new PA.

He cuffed his sleeves and pushed them to his elbows, a wave of triumph washing over him. He didn't take no for an answer, and not only did Crickitt say yes, around a bite of dessert that had clung to her lip for one tempting second, but she'd actually thanked him for his persistence. Then nearly buckled his knees when her tongue darted out to take the sugar from her bottom lip.

But, that wasn't why he'd hired her.

He'd been interviewing for three weeks and no one came close to possessing a fraction of Crickitt's skill set. It didn't help that the position had become something of a novelty. Thanks to a poorly timed *Forbes* article, his human resources director spent most of last month weeding out interviewees who were only there to get a look at August Industries' CEO.

A bottle of Château Sedacca waited for him on the counter, and he grabbed it by the neck. Typically, he finished out his evening routine—workout, shower, an hour in his home office—before indulging. But he'd broken more than a few rules tonight. What was one more?

Shane poured the wine as the clock on the wall chimed

the hour, pulling his thoughts in an even less desirable direction.

Shane thought of his father every time he heard the damned thing.

Sean August never did come around, stubbornly depriving Shane of his forgiveness until the end, as if it cost him to give it. He'd grown accustomed to the accusations, and his father had spouted them until the day he died. The man may have disowned him, but father and son were connected by more than helixes of DNA. They shared the same tragic past. And as much as Shane wished that past had died alongside his father, it hadn't. It persisted, stymieing his breath like a lungful of accidentally swallowed bathwater.

The moment his butt hit the couch, the weight of the long day settled squarely on his shoulders. An hour ago, he'd been in the middle of the most relaxing evening since who knew when. Now his to-do list scratched at the back of his mind like a dog wanting in from the rain.

Should have known if he played hooky from his evening routine he'd pay the price. He could run, but he couldn't hide. He gave a longing look to his glass of wine. Its siren song may hum, but his regimen wailed.

Relaxation would have to wait.

He headed for the kitchen, glass in hand, reminding himself that his regimen had gotten him this far in life. He dumped the wine unceremoniously down the drain and flipped on the faucet, watching the liquid swirl from red to pink to clear.

You should have been here, not out screwing around!

The disembodied voice of his father echoed in his mind before fading into the clock's solemn ticking in the other room. What his old man didn't realize was Shane hadn't needed the constant reminders to know how greatly he'd failed.

He knew better than anyone the impact of a single choice, how a seemingly innocuous decision had irrevocably changed his mother's life.

Or, more accurately, taken it.

CHAPTER SIX

So? How's it going, Ms. Rat Race?" Sadie asked, sipping her blush-colored wine.

Today marked the end of Crickitt's first week at August Industries. Sadie had invited her to the wine bar down the road from her apartment to celebrate. The place was packed to the walls, but they managed to snag a table on the patio before it filled up.

Rather than tease Sadie for her equal participation in the Giant Maze of Life, Crickitt said, "I like it. It's different from what I was doing before, but not in a bad way. As much as I loved working for myself, it wasn't always as fun as it sounded."

Sadie gave her a dubious glance. "Yeah, working a grueling four hours a day must have been rough. And then to have to eat, drink wine you didn't pay for..." She elevated her glass and took an exaggerated drink. "I don't know how you stood it for as long as you did," Sadie finished with a teasing wink.

Her bestie may have crammed Crickitt's former career into a nutshell, but essentially, it was the simplified truth. And hadn't Crickitt described it the same way over the years? As if she was living in enviable luxury while her personal life silently crumbled down around her ears.

And, yes, part of her former workday had been spent in slouchy sweatpants. But she wasn't lounging on the couch watching daytime television. There were meeting notes to prepare, orders to enter, customers and team members to call. Errands like trips to the bank and post office were an almost daily affair. By the time most people were commuting home from work, she'd already put in a full day. There'd been plenty of evenings when she'd rather not have packed her car full of display products and headed straight into rush hour traffic.

Just remembering the hustle of those days was exhausting. Or maybe it was the memory of Ronald alongside her career that had her grousing at the basket of complimentary crackers.

"You're right, I'm being ungracious," Crickitt confessed. "But it is nice to have my evenings back. What I wouldn't have given back then to spend more—" She cut herself off, realizing what she almost said.

More evenings with my husband.

She took a hearty swig of her wine, expecting the crushing weight of loss, or loneliness, to press down on her. It didn't come. Oddly enough, life had recently struck her as simplistic. She wasn't defined by *Before Ronald* or *After Ronald*, he was simply a notch in her timeline, marking the separation from past to present. She used to have a husband. Now she didn't. And she felt...fine.

"So what do you *do* at August Industries?" Sadie asked, saying the name of the company with a deep, reverent bass and pulling Crickitt from her self-analysis.

"Mostly, I handle Shane's schedule. I thought I did a lot in my business, but he puts me to shame. I schedule his meetings, conference calls, company announcements, business dealings, pitches..."

"You call Shane August of August Industries by his first name?" Sadie asked.

Crickitt shrugged. "He's a person."

"He's a billionaire."

"He's very common."

"He's hot."

Rather than agree, which she did, Crickitt hedged. "You didn't think so that night at the club." She lifted her wineglass to her lips to keep from saying more.

The truth was it'd become increasingly difficult for her to ignore the strain of Shane's biceps beneath his sleeves. She was only a woman, after all, and *any* woman could appreciate the way his long legs stretched out into a purposeful, confident stride. But noticing him at work had led to thoughts of Shane *outside* the office...thoughts, if she wanted to continue to stay employed at August Industries, that were best kept to herself.

"That night he was just another guy trying to pick up a girl. I didn't know he was Shane August," Sadie said, lowering to near baritone to say his name.

"Well, it doesn't matter how good-looking he is. He's my boss," Crickitt said, unsure which of them she was trying to convince.

"If he were my boss," Sadie said with the rogue lift of her brow, "I'd saunter into his office, perch on the edge of his desk, and ask if I could dictate." She snorted.

Crickitt laughed, the sound not all that convincing to her own ears. For some reason the idea of Sadie garnering Shane's undivided attention made her prickle.

"I've been so busy I haven't asked about your date with Shane's cousin. What's his name?" Crickitt said, deliberately shifting subjects.

"Aiden." She lifted one shoulder in a shrug and avoided looking at Crickitt. "It was nice."

A blush crept up Sadie's neck. Crickitt never thought she'd see the day. "Sadie Ann Marie Howard."

Sadie flinched. "What?"

"You *like* him."

Again with the shoulder shrug, but a smile spread her lips. "He's okay."

"And the sex?"

"Crickitt!"

Crickitt laughed. Sadie never acted embarrassed about... well, anything. "*That* tells me everything!"

"Stop it, it's not like that," Sadie said.

"Is that why you're glowing like a stoplight?"

Sadie's jaw dropped.

Crickitt shook her head. "A dirty, one-night-stand-having stoplight."

Sadie became fascinated with the table, running her thumbnail back and forth in a scratch on its surface and fervently avoiding looking her best friend in the eye. "It wasn't one night," she murmured. "I've seen him twice."

Crickitt was stunned into silence. She didn't think

of Sadie as trampy, but she did tend to have a lot of first dates that didn't morph into seconds. Then again, this was the woman who had fed her wedding invitations into a shredder moments after her fiancé announced he was leaving her for her sister. Was it any wonder Sadie discarded her dates like tissues out of a box?

"He's not like other guys," Sadie said.

"Meaning?"

Sadie tilted her chin. "He's charming and funny in this oddly genuine way."

"He has hair down to his shoulders," Crickitt said, recalling Sadie's penchant for bulky athletes or suave businessmen.

"I know," Sadie said, a wistful smile on her face.

"Wow." This was more serious than she'd imagined. Crickitt decided to let her friend off the hook. "Keep me posted on that."

"Oh, I will."

* * *

Saturday morning, a motorcycle roared into Shane's driveway. Shane stepped out of his front door as Aiden slipped his helmet off. His hair was back in a ponytail, but several strands had wrestled their way loose.

"You need a haircut," Shane lectured.

"You need not to shave," Aiden retorted.

"Hippie."

"Yuppie."

They smiled at each other, and Shane held the door open for Aiden. "Come on in, man."

Once inside, Aiden shrugged out of the leather jacket he wore whenever he rode. "What brings you my way?" Shane asked. "Need money?"

The expression on Aiden's face suggested he might pop Shane in the mouth for even joking about such a thing. Shane expected as much. "Coffee?" Shane held up the pot after pouring himself a cup.

"That, I'll take." Aiden sat on a kitchen chair. "I was visiting Mom and thought I'd swing by."

"How's she doing?" Shane delivered his coffee. They both drank it black, no frills.

Aiden's mouth formed a grim line. "The same."

Shane nodded. "I guess that's good. At least she's not worse."

"Yeah, I guess."

"Anything else going on?" Shane asked, knowing Aiden came here to get his mind off his mother's illness, not dwell on it.

"I'm seeing your new PA's friend Sadie tonight."

Shane paused, the mug halfway to his lips. "Really? Again?"

"Don't sound so surprised."

"Well, it's just she's—"

"Hot."

"Well, okay. I was going to say she wasn't like the other girls I've seen you date." Aiden's ex-wife, and his ex-girlfriends before her, were as hippie-chick as they came. "Sadie's a little...city for you, isn't she?"

"If you ask me, she might be just what I need," Aiden said a tad defensively. He sipped his coffee and shifted in his seat. "I hate your furniture. It's like you decorated for an institution, not a house."

"Sorry, they were all out of vinyl barrel furniture and crocheted afghans."

Aiden made a rude gesture and Shane laughed.

"How's the new girl working out? What's her name, Butterfly?"

"Very funny. *Crickitt* is a fantastic assistant. I should have fired Myrna years ago."

"You couldn't. Mom would have killed you."

"True." His last assistant was his aunt's best friend. She was better suited to being a personal shopper than a personal assistant. When she announced that she was leaving because of an out-of-state move, Shane was secretly relieved. He'd put up with her less-than-stellar performance and frequent flubs for the sake of keeping the family peace.

"So, did you do her yet?" Aiden asked.

Shane coughed and settled his cup on the glass table with a *chink*. Aiden slapped him on the back. "Geez, man," Shane croaked, coughing again and clearing his throat.

"What? I thought you liked her."

"I do. She's a valuable employee."

Aiden shot him a look.

It was the truth, albeit a lame, understated truth. Shane *did* like her. He liked the way she dove in and tried to solve problems on her own before asking for help. And he liked how she blew into the office like a stiff wind was at her back. Hell, he even liked those formless button-down shirts she wore. Still— "I can't have sex with my assistant."

No matter how tempting it was.

"Suit yourself." Aiden finished his coffee and stood. "I'm going to ride down to the Brink, want to go with me?"

Shane hadn't been to the Brink since he was a teenager. A glorified creek, the wide body of water was home to a man-made sandy beach and stands selling foodstuffs and art. It was also where Aiden's ex-wife worked. "You wouldn't be going down there to see Harmony, would you?"

"Of course not." Aiden pulled a face.

"Careful," Shane said. "You know how…persuasive she can be." Aiden's ex had a way of wrapping Aiden around her henna-tattooed finger whenever she wanted something from him. Which was always. Afraid he sounded preachy, Shane glossed it over with, "I have a few proposals to write or I'd take you up on it."

"Yeah, sure you would." Aiden shook his head, seeing right through him. "It's okay to take a break sometimes, you know."

"You know me," Shane said dismissively. But did he? Shane wore his stiff-upper-CEO lip even around Aiden. Shane hadn't noticed it before, but he was starting to see another aspect of his personality that only seemed to surface around Crickitt. Whenever he was with her, his business facade slipped right off its hinges.

Aiden held up his hands. "Okay, I won't push."

Good. Because Shane wasn't anywhere near ready to make the admission he'd just made to himself. "I wouldn't listen anyway," he said.

Now *that* was the truth.

CHAPTER SEVEN

By Thursday evening, Crickitt decided she really, really liked her job. Shane gave her enough space to allow her to find her way, never losing patience when she interrupted him to ask questions or clarify how he wanted something done. Which would be exactly the kind of career she could settle into if it wasn't for her daily mini-fantasies starring Shane August, CEO of sex gods.

Crickitt tossed the empty Chinese container into the trash can and congratulated herself for avoiding dishes another night. Eating leftover takeout at 9:05 p.m. was just one of single life's perks.

Right! Single! Have at him! her errant hormones chanted.

Like that was going to happen. First of all, it was ridiculous. Shane August was a *billionaire*. Crickitt bought knickknacks from thrift stores. The idea someone like him could be interested in someone like her was...she fanned her collar, suddenly warm. Well, it was...distracting.

"Absurd" is the word you're looking for.

She reached for a dishcloth to wipe down the counters in her already tidied kitchen and distract herself from more inappropriate thoughts about Shane. She covered the minuscule space in a few seconds and, not for the first time, grieved the loss of the spacious kitchen in the house she and Ronald had built. They'd been far from wealthy. In fact, they were mortgaged up to their ears in an attempt to keep up with their affluent neighbors. Ronald's idea.

He'd kept the house, explaining that as an investment banker, he'd had appearances to maintain. Meanwhile she was Holly Hobby Homemaker who, according to him, "didn't have a real career." Funny, she'd outearned him for the last five years.

She refilled her water glass, carrying it to the living room with her. Her canvas shoulder bag sat on the corner of her sofa, a manila folder poking out of the top. Shane had dropped the folder onto her desk before he left, assuring her with one of those sideways smiles of his that she didn't have to read over it tonight. And she'd intended to leave it for tomorrow, she had. But at the last minute she brought it home. For all her declaring she wanted to watch mindless television, she couldn't make herself care who was stranded on an island or in the running for a recording contract.

And, okay, she'd admit, she was looking forward to tomorrow's meeting in Columbus with Mr. Henry Townsend. Settling onto her comfy sofa, a find from an estate sale shortly after procuring her apartment, she opened the folder and began to read about the company August Industries had been hired to represent.

Crickitt's cell phone rang, demanding her attention. She frowned at the unknown number on the screen. Maybe it was a former customer or a wrong number...It rang for the third time before she gave in and answered it. Better to handle it than end up with a voice mail she'd have to deal with later.

"Crickitt," a silken male voice said after she said hello. "It's Shane."

"Hi." The word sailed out on an exhaled breath, and she'd unintentionally added a second syllable. Maybe he'd assume the husk in her voice was because she'd been sleeping. Which made her imagine being in bed. Which made her wonder if he was. She stood and began pacing across the room. "I, uh, didn't recognize this number."

"It's my home office line," he said. "I thought I'd given it to you. Listen, I apologize for calling so late, but I forgot to tell you we need to leave early tomorrow morning."

"I thought the Townsend meeting was in the afternoon," she said, sifting through the file in search of a time.

"It is, but I have another client in Columbus scheduled in the morning and I want you to sit in on that meeting as well."

"Oh, okay. No problem." Nope. Just an entire day of one-on-one time with Shane. No problem at all. It might take extra concentration to keep her eyes from bugging out of her head, and she'd have to keep her voice from having the breathy *do me* quality it had right now, but she was totally up for it. "I'll just, um, what time do you need me to be at the office?" she asked, starting off toward her bedroom to find something to wear.

"If it's all right with you, I'll swing by and pick you up at your place. How does six a.m. sound?"

Early, she thought, grimacing. "Sounds great."

"Liar." His voice lilted, tipping her equilibrium. Was he...teasing her? She could feel the force of his smile in her stomach. "I'll need to brief you before the first meeting," he continued. "I thought we'd get to town, have some breakfast, and go over the details then."

"I'll be ready," she promised, hoping she could sit across the table from this man for a second time and not lose her cool. Not that she was all that cool to begin with.

"Great, see you then." Then he added, "Sweet dreams."

He hung up and Crickitt stared at her phone until the light went out.

Sweet dreams? If she managed to sleep at all.

CHAPTER EIGHT

Four a.m. was early. "Stupid early," as her dad called it. But Crickitt managed to rise even if she didn't shine. A cup and a half of coffee later, she was reasonably certain she'd buttoned her shirt properly.

She'd just finished brushing her teeth when a knock came from her front door. She gave her puffy reflection one last glance before swiping a dash of soft pink gloss across her lips and hurrying to get it.

Shane stood on her front porch in the waning moonlight, looking too good for six in the morning. Pressed suit, polished shoes, hair styled in damp waves.

"Good morning." He flashed her a billionaire-worthy smile, one that had her thankful for the sturdiness of the door frame. "I thought you might need this." He held out a paper coffee cup, a familiar green logo emblazoned on one side. "I called Keena to find out your regular order. Caramel soy latte with extra whipped cream."

She accepted the cup, speechless for a second. "Thank you. You didn't have to do that."

"Well, I aim to please," he said with a grin.

There was a distracting thought. "Um...do you want to come in while I grab my things?"

"Sure." Shane stepped into her apartment, and she instantly regretted inviting him in. He looked out of place among her secondhand treasures, like a fine work of art at a garage sale.

He followed her into the living room, eyeing her furniture as he sipped his coffee. She tucked the manila folder into her canvas mailbag and slung it over her shoulder. "I'm ready."

"No tour?" he asked.

She clutched the strap of her bag, flicking a longing look at her front door. "Oh, you don't want to see my little place," she said, intimidated by the idea of showing it to him. She could imagine what his house looked like. He probably lived in a sprawling mansion filled with fine rugs and leather furniture, and art costing a hundred times her salary.

"You don't want to show it to me?" He picked up a small porcelain chimpanzee covering his eyes with his hands. Gesturing to its mate, a chimpanzee covering his ears, he asked, "Where's Speak No Evil?"

"Missing," she said.

"Hmm." He set the ape back on the shelf. "Have you tried milk cartons?"

There it was again, his playful side. "Not yet," she said through a soft laugh. "They're from the seventies, I think. I found the two of them at a thrift store a long time ago, but I have yet to locate the third. I check eBay every once in a while, and yard sales, but"—she shrugged—"no luck."

"Why not toss them and buy a new, complete set?"

Crickitt lifted her chin. "They're not worthless just because they're incomplete." Besides, they'd been with her for a dozen years, had survived three moves and any clumsy attempt she'd made to dust around them. Which was more than she could say for her ex-husband. She plucked the figurine from Shane's hand, ignoring the tingle in her fingers as she brushed against his skin. "I'll find him one day," she murmured quietly.

Shane took a leisurely gander around her living room before stopping on her face. She shifted on her feet but refused to look away. "We have a few minutes," he said. "You sure about that tour?"

Ten minutes later they were in the limousine on their way to Columbus. "I don't get it," Shane said. He sat in the seat facing her, his back to the privacy panel shutting out the driver.

"What don't you get?" Crickitt wrung her hands. What comment would he have about her hodgepodge apartment? Her decorating style ranged from contemporary to country, the embodiment of a patchwork quilt. There was a charcoal sketch of a bowl of fruit in her kitchen, an oversize black-and-white James Dean poster in her bathroom, and her guest bedroom was a homage to wicker furniture. She'd bet he couldn't choose which room to be most appalled by.

"You get a soy milk latte with whipped cream," he said.

"Yes," she said, taking a moment to shift gears. "I do."

"Why do you do that?"

"I don't like milk, unless it's whipped cream."

He chuckled, shaking his head. "Well, I got a strange glance from the barista this morning."

She blinked at the cup in her hand. "*You* picked up the coffee?"

"Yeees."

"I thought you had people to do that for you." Isn't that what rich people did? Hire others to run their errands?

"People?" he asked, bemused. "Well, every once in a while I stoop to do my own bidding."

Great. Now she'd offended him. "Oh, I didn't mean—"

"Relax, Crickitt, I know you didn't." He watched her for a beat, lips twitching, before he popped open his brief-case and extracted a pile of paperwork.

They lapsed into comfortable silence, Crickitt watching out of the tinted windows as Shane worked. Every once in a while he'd make a deep sound in his throat. It usually paired with him pinching his eyebrows together. Then he'd make a few scratches on the paper in front of him and continue to read, his thumb and finger pressed on either side of his bottom lip.

Watching him made the ride worthwhile. How often could she stare at him without worrying a coworker might catch her ogling? Not often enough. He lifted his head and she flicked her eyes away.

Busted.

Fidgeting with the strap on her bag, she watched the buildings and cars pass by her window.

"You're making me feel self-conscious," he said. "Am I doing something strange?"

Her eyes widened. "What do you mean?"

"Weren't you just looking at me?"

She shook her head. "No, not at all."

"You'd tell me if I had any weird habits, right?"

"Uh..."

The limo came to a stop, and Shane ducked his head to look out the window. "We're here."

After a small-town-diner-worthy breakfast and more coffee, Shane reviewed the details for their first meeting. "We don't have to go over the file here if it's too distracting. We can get a coffee to go, read it in the car if you like."

"Can't," she said.

"You can't what, read?" he joked.

"Not in the car," she said.

"Ah. Well, in that case, let's hang out and make the waitress's day."

At first she thought he was being facetious. "Hanging out" would clog up the young girl's table. She'd miss tips from new customers. Crickitt opened her mouth to tell him so, when the waitress stopped to refill their coffee mugs.

"Excuse me, Debbie, is it?" Shane asked her.

"Yes," Debbie said, pointing at her name tag.

Shane made small talk, asking Debbie about her job, how long she'd worked there, if she liked it. Crickitt watched as the young waitress succumbed to his charm. By the time Debbie had divulged that her full-time job made it harder to be a good mom to her three-year-old, Crickitt could see he'd won her over. Debbie couldn't be more than twenty, twenty-one, tops. And while Crickitt guessed single motherhood was difficult at any age, she couldn't imagine going it alone that young.

"Bear with me." Shane flashed Debbie a heart-melting smile. "This is a personal question, but I'm an investor and I'd love an honest answer."

"All right." Debbie gave him a small smile that suggested if her heart wasn't melting, it was at least warming. She rested her free hand on her hip, elevating the coffeepot in the other. "Shoot."

"Do you rent or own?"

Debbie rolled her eyes. "Own? I wish. I don't have the credit, or the cash, to buy a house. I rent an apartment."

"And your rent per month is...?"

"Six seventy-five."

"Nice place?" Shane asked.

"Not really," Debbie said with a humorless laugh.

"Roommates?"

Her smile vanished. "Not anymore," she bit out.

Crickitt wondered if her former "roommate" was her son's father. There was definite determination in the way she shot out her chin. "It's just me and my son," Debbie said with an assertive nod.

"I appreciate it, Debbie," Shane said after mentioning he'd enjoyed breakfast. "Thank you for the coffee and for your honesty. You've helped me a great deal with my next endeavor."

Debbie left their table and Crickitt waited for Shane to explain. He didn't, only tapped the open file in front of her. "Come on, you've got another forty-five minutes to bone up." Then he leaned back in the booth and sipped his coffee as if he hadn't just had an odd and slightly invasive conversation with a total stranger.

When the check came a half hour later, she was surprised to see Shane pull out cash.

"Shouldn't you charge that and write it off?" she asked, having been accustomed to doing so for her own business.

"Not today." His mouth lifted mischievously as he counted out ten one-hundred-dollar bills and one twenty. He folded them into the black book on the table and slid it to the edge.

Their breakfast and a twenty percent tip would have been more than covered by the lesser bill. A moment later, Debbie came by to pick up the book. "Change?"

"No, thank you. Keep it. You know, for that nice apartment of yours," Shane said with a smile and a wink that would most likely be the most charming Debbie would see all day. Maybe all week.

Debbie laughed and rolled her eyes, probably imagining an extra four or five bucks hidden behind the vinyl cover, then she headed to tend to her other guests.

"So you weren't just taking a random poll?"

"I don't do anything randomly," Shane said with a lift of his brow. He slid out of the booth, stealing a glance over his shoulder. "Let's go."

"But..." Crickitt looked down at the scattered papers.

"Hurry," Shane whispered, helping her fill the manila folder as swiftly as if they were fleeing the scene of a crime. Crickitt shoved the folder and pen into her canvas bag as Shane grasped her free hand and towed her to the door. As they walked through it, Crickitt turned to catch a glimpse of Debbie standing statue still in the center of the restaurant, her hand pressed to her chest as she stared at the "tip" Shane left her.

"Come on." He tugged her to the limo parked out front. The second they were outside Crickitt registered Shane's long fingers wrapped around hers. Warmth between their palms sizzled her nerve endings. She squeezed his fingers, savoring the opportunity to be close to him, the excuse to touch him. Shane spared her a glance as they descended on the limo, slowing his frantic pace long enough to flash her a wry half smile. Was he thinking the same thing?

The driver poked his head out the driver's-side door, but Shane waved him off. "I got it, Thomas."

He held on to Crickitt's hand until she was safely inside, then climbed in and took the seat facing hers. Shane rapped on the privacy glass and Thomas pulled into the light traffic.

At first, Shane looked like a kid who dropped off a tire swing into an ice-cold lake. But as the restaurant grew farther away, his grin emerged. Lifting thick eyebrows in a show of relief, he said, "That was close."

"She would have thanked you if you hung around," Crickitt said, barely repressing a chuckle. "I saw her face, she was—"

"No, don't tell me." Shane held up a hand. "The goal is *not* to be thanked."

"There's a goal? Is this, like, a game?"

"Sort of. Ever heard of Dine and Dash, where you go out to eat and run out without paying your tab?"

"No," Crickitt said, appalled. "Do people do that?"

Shane offered a somber smile. "My mom was a waitress when she met my dad, happened to her a few times. Anyway, I like to do what I call Dine and *Cash*, where you run out after paying someone's rent."

"Much better."

He shrugged, but his smile was genuine.

What Shane had done for a perfect stranger was beyond sweet, it was downright admirable. But the seed of doubt that had recently taken root in the back of her mind had begun to flower. She had to know, had to be sure he hadn't hired her only so he could tick off a box under the Charitable Giving section of his tax forms.

"Do you only do it for waitresses?" Crickitt asked before she could rethink it.

Shane cocked his head. "Sorry?"

She swallowed. Cleared her throat. "Is that why you helped me?"

"No." He answered immediately, the look on his face intently serious. "And by the way, *I'm* the one who needed help, not the other way around."

She allowed herself a shaky smile at the idea of being needed. Maybe because she'd been overlooked for so long.

He leaned his elbows on his knees and met her eye. "I hired you because you're qualified. You're paid well because you deserve it. Never let anyone tell you differently."

She looked at her lap, unable to hold his unflinching gaze. "I believe you."

"Good." He reached forward to pat her hand before settling back into his seat.

She lifted her head. "That was pretty impressive, by the way."

"Well, you're lucky," he said, lowering one eyelid into a wink that sent her pulse racing. "I only do that to impress my new assistants."

CHAPTER NINE

Their morning meeting was with a man in his late forties launching a tattoo shop. And if Crickitt thought Shane was too polished to talk to a goateed, bald, bare-chested man in a leather biker vest, he proved her wrong in the space of a few minutes.

Crickitt had already assumed Shane was passionate about entrepreneurs, but seeing him in action was like watching a bird take flight. Natural, easy. Shane's enthusiasm shone in every hand gesture, every answer, and through every assurance he made. When Shane vowed to do what it took to help the man become successful, all three of them knew he meant it.

After the meeting, they stepped outside the shop and Shane lifted his ringing cell phone to his ear. "August."

Crickitt paused, taking in the truncated exchange.

"Yes. No problem," he said, gazing in her direction. "Absolutely. See you then."

He pocketed his phone as the driver opened the door for them. "Thomas, I'll need you to work late tonight. Does Darcy have you booked?"

Thomas gave Shane a pained smile. "Tango lessons. I'd be glad to stay and work late."

Shane chuckled and palmed the older man's shoulder. "Excellent. Find a place we can loiter for a bit, will you?"

Shane ushered Crickitt into the limo. Once inside, he said, "Townsend pushed our meeting to five thirty. I realize you expected to be done working by then. I can have Thomas take you home. If we leave now, I can still make it back in time for the meeting."

Crickitt frowned. It was a superfluous amount of driving simply to see her home. "I'm sure a four-hour round-trip isn't the best use of your time."

"I can read in the car. There's no shortage of what I could learn," he said with a grin. "It's your call. I don't expect you to stick around. You wouldn't get back to Osborn until late tonight and I don't want to break up your plans."

Plans. Yeah, right. Her big Friday-night plans involved pajamas, a DVD, and eating out of a paper container of some sort. No, she'd prefer to spend the evening with her impressively capable boss, even if her reasons were bordering on unprofessional. Or stalkerish. "I'd like to stay," she said, tacking on, "and meet Townsend."

"Good," he said, and she could swear he looked relieved.

* * *

Shane was relieved.

Henry Townsend was an important, if not *the* most

important, client August Industries had. But as much as Shane loved the thrill of landing a new account, of helping a business owner see his dreams come to fruition, the lengthy drive and downtime were significantly less thrilling. He usually filled the hours with solo lunches or reading dry stock reports.

It was nice not to be alone, and Crickitt was good company. She pushed a curl away from her face and pinned him with serene blue eyes. Okay, she wasn't *just* good company. He liked her. Liked the way she asked questions and was genuinely interested in his answers. Liked the way she waited for the right moment to interrupt him when he was deep in thought. She was good for him.

As his assistant, he reminded himself, glancing down at his folded hands.

Now that he thought about it, he doubted she'd want to spend the afternoon pinned up in the limo reading bland reports. He was already tying up her evening. "What would you like to do today?" he asked. "Art museum? Shopping? We have several hours before Townsend."

He'd surprised her. Her eyes widened and her brows elevated in the cutest, startled expression.

"Or we could work?" he said, wondering if he'd miscalculated her after all.

"You're paying me. It's your call."

Shane nearly flinched. He hoped she hadn't stayed out of some misplaced sense of obligation. He wanted her to want to be here with him. Which wasn't something he should allow himself to want at all. This was a business trip. He was her boss. It wasn't a weekend trip filled with sightseeing, shopping, and dinner at Skyview.

Man, he'd like to take her to dinner again. A real dinner, one without interview questions and ending with a kiss good night.

You hired her. You can't date her.

Tamping down his out-of-place disappointment, he tried again. "Since you'll be working late, you have the middle of the day to yourself. Thomas can drop you off somewhere. Like the mall, or... a shoe store?"

Crickitt twisted her lush lips into a grimace. "Ugh. I hate shopping."

A woman who hated to shop? He'd never met one. "What do you like to do?"

She shrugged, considering his question. "Watch movies."

He recalled her apartment, the stacks of DVDs in her living room, the pile of plastic cases next to the TV in her bedroom. "Okay," he said. "Let's go to a movie. Anything out you'd like to see?"

"Seriously?" Her eyebrows rose even higher. "You're taking me to a movie? And letting me pick?"

"Oh, no. You're going to drag me to a girly movie, aren't you? Like..." He was reaching here, trying to grasp the title of the last movie he'd seen with a woman. "*Steel Magnolias* or... *Beaches*?"

"It's been a while since you've seen a movie, hasn't it? Both of those are nearly as old as we are."

"I admit I don't watch a lot of movies."

"Too busy being successful, I guess," she supplied.

She was right. Unless it promoted a healthier bottom line, he didn't do it. And a movie midday when he could be on the phone with clients? Unheard of.

But it was important Crickitt enjoy herself today. And he wasn't about to suggest she go to a movie theater alone. It would be good for him to loosen up, have a bit of unscheduled fun.

Fifteen minutes later, Thomas pulled to a stop in front of Regal Cinemas. Shane and Crickitt stepped out as a passing mother and her young daughter paused to gape at the limo.

Crickitt didn't seem to mind the attention, waving at the towheaded girl. "Neat, huh?"

The girl smiled, then hid her face in her mother's skirt.

Inside, he perused the movie titles on the marquee board, each one as foreign as the next.

Crickitt studied the board carefully, as if choosing a stock for her investment portfolio.

"What looks good?" he asked.

She turned to him, her face flushing. "Truth? I really want to see *Creep*."

"*Creep*," he repeated, clueless. "What is that about? Abusive boyfriend? Maniacal ex-husband?"

"No," she said, drawing out the word. "It's about these snakelike creatures that live in a lake and eat the locals."

He didn't hide his shock. "Horror movie?"

"I'm sort of a junkie."

"If you're sure you won't have nightmares, let's do it."

He followed Crickitt to a row midway up the theater. She pushed the seat flat, juggling her drink and purse as she sat. Shane sat next to her, cradling an enormous bucket of popcorn he'd insisted on buying since he hadn't been in a movie theater in years. But as he eased into the seat, it wasn't the buttery snack that dominated his senses. It was Crickitt's edible body spray that made her skin smell like dessert and heaven all rolled into one. He hadn't been close enough to her today to notice, but he did now. Her neck was *right there*. Along with that little freckle he'd singled out the night they were at Triangle.

"Thanks for the popcorn, boss," she said, reaching over to scoop up a handful.

Boss. There was a rude awakening.

He should stop staring, and salivating. Using the bucket as a chaperone, he shoved it between them. He hadn't thought this through. A movie theater midday? He and Crickitt were alone in the darkened room, save for the few souls scattered several rows behind and in front of them. If that wasn't bad enough, she brushed his fingers with hers as she reached for another handful of popcorn.

She slanted him a glance, but the lights dimmed before he could think of something to say.

For the next hour and a half, he had a hard time keeping his eyes up front. And not because the on-screen monsters had three rows of razor-sharp fangs and, by some imaginative twist, moved as fast on land as they did in water. No, Shane had a hard time keeping his eyes focused on the screen because the woman next to him, who smelled like the sexiest birthday cake on the planet, had clutched his arm twice. *Twice.* She'd offered a whispered apology both times, blaming the movie, but he hadn't minded.

He hadn't minded at all.

By the end, she'd curled into the fetal position, heels on the edge of her seat, arms around her knees. The look of utter terror on her face made him want to comfort her, but he stopped short of wrapping his arm around her shoulders. That would be...wrong. And weird.

He should've tried to talk her into the pirate movie.

The credits rolled and lights rose. Crickitt finally unhinged her shoulders from her ears.

"I thought you *liked* horror movies," Shane said, gauging her reaction.

She spun on him, eyes wide. "I do." She dropped her feet to the sticky floor as her face split into a childlike grin. "Wasn't it great?"

He gave her a bemused chuckle. "Great?"

"Yeah. Half the fun is being afraid. Did you like it at all?"

"It was...okay."

"Were you scared?" She lifted one eyebrow in challenge.

"No way." He tilted his head. "Then again, they did remind me of a team of lawyers I used to employ," he said, deliberately shuddering.

Her warm laugh tugged at the center of his chest. He could get used to that sound, especially if he was the one to draw it out of her. When was the last time being around a woman was this effortless?

"I can't see you being intimidated by lawyers," Crickitt said, standing from her seat. "You," she gestured to him, "are Shane August, saver of lost entrepreneurial souls."

He grinned, flattered. "Funny, I just ordered a plaque with that on it."

He let her go ahead of him, following her down the narrow staircase toward the exit. He raised his palm but stopped short of pressing it against her back. Side by side, they entered the lobby, her hand brushing his as she crossed her arms over her chest. She mumbled an apology, her cheeks going a pretty tinge of pink.

Had she done it on purpose?

He found himself wanting to take her hand like he did earlier today, just to feel the warmth of her skin...but that kind of intimacy crossed the line from professional to really-bad-idea.

He balled his hand into a fist and returned it to his side, but it didn't keep him from wanting to reach for her, bad idea or not.

CHAPTER TEN

Townsend flew in from Miami to his Columbus headquarters named, fittingly, Town Ventures. Crickitt had learned that his newly acquired company, MajicSweep, wasn't his first rodeo. Which, according to Shane, was good news for August Industries. Repeat business was a rarity.

"So," Shane said, ushering Crickitt into the air-conditioned lobby, "this could be huge for us." He worked the buttons on his jacket through their holes with the fingers of one hand. "Ready?" If he was nervous, it didn't show. He was pressed and poised, not a hair out of place. She allowed her gaze to slide down his jacket and pants, taking in the sleek lines and the way his body filled out his suit.

"Ready," she said, dragging her eyes from his broad shoulders and trying to mimic his Fonzie cool.

On the eighteenth floor, they stepped out of the glass elevator. Shane introduced himself to the receptionist, a pleasant-looking blonde who returned his smile and directed them to the conference room. When Shane thanked her and turned, the woman perused the length of his body with hungry eyes. She noticed Crickitt watching her but only offered an unapologetic shoulder shrug as if to ask, *Do you blame me?*

And, no, she didn't. Shane's attractiveness was undeniable.

A young man wearing a brown suit gestured for them to go into the conference room where light poured in from the floor-to-ceiling windows that ran along one long wall. Townsend's staff each gave them an acknowledging nod before turning back to murmur among themselves, their voices echoing off the high, bare ceilings.

"Mr. August." Townsend entered and his staff cut their conversations off midsentence. Townsend extended a palm, standing a few inches over her Shane's six three. His tanned skin contrasted dramatically with his white, cropped hair, and his suit looked as if it'd been stitched together while he wore it.

"This is my assistant, Crickitt Day," Shane said.

"Nice to meet you," Townsend said with a scowl suggesting the contrary. Crickitt kept a smile on her face and echoed his greeting, determined not to be intimidated by his powerful presence.

With staff introductions out of the way, Crickitt followed Shane's lead and took a seat at the long mahogany table. Henry's six staff members waited until Townsend took his seat before collapsing into their chairs like dutiful soldiers. Already this felt more like her divorce hearing than a team meeting. Didn't Townsend's employees know they were all on the same side?

Mr. Townsend opened the meeting by pointing in Shane's direction. Shane handed over a leather portfolio filled with plastic-protected linen pages and began the informal presentation. Henry stared him down, but Shane remained unflustered. He outlined the plan for MajicSweep, referencing the charts and forms when necessary.

"Do you have a wholesale supplier for MajicSweep's cleaning products?" Shane asked.

Townsend looked to the woman on his left. "Carrie?"

Carrie blinked from behind a pair of tortoiseshell glasses and did her best to answer, all the while quaking like an overcaffeinated chipmunk. Crickitt offered her a reassuring smile, but the woman sank into her chair, trying her best to blend in with the upholstery.

Crickitt felt the frown dent her brow and quickly hid it. There was no reason for the man to be so brusque, but she wasn't all that anxious to be on the receiving end of his steely glare, either.

Townsend reached for one of the water pitchers in the center of the table and refilled his glass. He took a long drink, idly flipping through the portfolio while everyone, Crickitt included, held a collective breath. When he turned to the last page, he paused, and Crickitt caught a glimpse of MajicSweep's new mascot. The idea was mentioned in the file she'd reviewed last night, but this was her first look at—

"Sweepy the Broom," Mr. Townsend grumbled.

"Our art department took your suggestion to create a mascot," Shane explained. He lifted his notes before continuing, "Carrie Dillard worked closely with our head graphic designer on the concept."

Carrie swallowed with an audible *gulp*. Shane nodded at her. "I agree with Carrie. A mascot is a great tool. Potential customers may choose MajicSweep over Company X because they're familiar with your cartoon from billboards or television ads."

Crickitt eyed Shane, trying to discern if he thought this *particular* mascot was the best representative for a corporate cleaning service. While she agreed a mascot helped with company recognition, she doubted if Sweepy, a cartoon broom with wide, round eyeballs, would draw the kind of high-paying clientele Henry Townsend intended to attract.

"What about you?"

Crickitt looked up to find Mr. Townsend grousing at her.

"Me?" she asked, her voice higher than she would have liked.

"Yes, you. You look like you have something to say. What is your opinion about"—he held up the full-color grinning broom—"Sweepy, here?" He rattled the page when she didn't answer.

All eyes were on her. "Well…" She flicked a look at Shane who dipped his chin in encouragement.

"To be perfectly honest…"

Carrie's eyes widened behind her glasses.

"I think it's…"—Crickitt cleared her throat and forced herself to continue—"silly."

* * *

Shane was silent during the elevator ride to the ground floor, watching the numbered buttons rather than face

Crickitt's reflection on the doors. But, oh, she could feel his eyes boring into her now as they strode toward the visitors' parking area.

Thomas rounded the limo and opened the door for them. Behind her, Shane muttered, "Can you give us five minutes?"

"Certainly," Thomas answered. "I'll just grab a cup of coffee. Can I bring you back anything?"

"No, thanks," Shane said.

"Miss?" Thomas asked.

Crickitt shook her head, wondering if she'd even be allowed in the limo when he got back. Maybe Shane would put her on a bus back to Osborn. Or make her walk. She doubted he wanted to ride home with the woman who tanked his reputation in the span of a few seconds.

"Get in," Shane instructed, one hand on top of the car door.

She did as requested, grateful Thomas had left the AC running. Shane climbed in behind her, and heat infused the space between them. And this time, not because of the taut cord of attraction she felt whenever he was near.

Wrestling with the cuffs on her shirt, she pushed the sleeves above her elbows, then fanned her collar over her damp bra. The door slammed as Shane settled into the bench beside her. Before he opened a can of "You're fired," Crickitt turned toward him and made her plea.

"I know what you're going to say, and you're right. It wasn't my place to speak so boldly in there. Mr. Townsend is a consummate professional. Like you," she added, figuring a little sucking up never hurt. "I should have deflected his question, or at the very least answered with a bit of finesse. It wasn't my intention to undermine your authority or insult our design staff. And I embarrassed poor Carrie who suggested the mascot in the first place." She took a breath to give him a chance to comment.

Silence greeted her.

"If you keep me on at August Industries, the next time I promise..." She trailed off as Shane's lips tilted into a smile.

"You through?" he asked.

"I guess so." Crickitt clasped her hands and awaited the blow. "Am I fired?"

Shane barked a laugh. "Fired?" He shook his head, looking more bemused than frustrated. "I underestimated you," he said. "You know how to handle people." He leaned against the armrest, propping his head in his hand. "You're an asset, Crickitt. You saved my ass in there."

She blinked at him. "Really?"

"Hell, yes, really! Townsend is one tough customer. He didn't appreciate my 'kid gloves' approach. He asked for your opinion and you gave it to him. He liked your honesty."

"But he said 'We're through here,' and then he left the room."

"Did you notice I stopped to talk with him on the way out?"

She didn't. Reeling from embarrassment, she'd made a mad dash for the elevators in her sensible shoes.

"Henry told me to get my best people on an entirely new concept for the company," Shane said. "He also said that the team had better include you. He gave us one week."

"He did?"

"I should probably give you a raise."

"You should?"

His smile widened, crinkling his eyes at the corners. "Yes, Crickitt. You were amazing in there."

He pointed to her as she opened her mouth, cutting her off. "And don't you dare say otherwise."

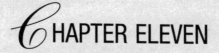CHAPTER ELEVEN

The calm didn't last.

Shane's easy demeanor had slipped during the drive back to Osborn. And since it was because of Crickitt's assessment that Townsend had requested a new marketing plan, she felt mostly responsible for Shane's mood swing.

Which was probably why she'd offered up her rudimentary art skills. Well, that and the fact Shane had mentioned he'd be working late in his home office tonight. What did Shane August's lair look like? She'd admit, curiosity had gotten the best of her.

Shane's house was more like the Bat Cave than Bruce Wayne's mansion. There were no expensive paintings, no ornately carved wooden furniture, no butler. A wide blank wall stood behind a black fireplace and cream-colored chaise longue in the open foyer. Beyond, a massive black wraparound couch dominated the sunken living room, which connected to a monochrome kitchen.

"Not much for color, are you?" she asked, toeing off her shoes.

"Oh, well, I don't give it much thought." He dropped his jacket on the chaise and she followed suit, laying down her bag.

Crickitt took the three stairs that led to the kitchen and scanned the floor plan, which was beautiful, open, and inviting. But the color scheme—if it could be called that—didn't fit its owner. She glanced over at Shane who unbuttoned his cuffs and shoved his sleeves over his forearms, his warmth in contrast with the cold backdrop.

"Hungry?" he asked, bracing his arms on the counter.

Yes. But not for food. Crickitt swallowed, her throat suddenly tight. She shook her head.

"Yeah, me, neither," Shane said.

A chime sounded, pulling her attention back to the living room. Next to a television mounted above another fireplace was an aging wall clock, its gold pendulum swinging. The wood was worn, the glass scratched. The brown-stained wood was definitely outside of the monochrome palette, but it didn't look antique or expensive. Just old, and out of place.

"How about wine?"

Crickitt flexed her tired feet on the cool ceramic tile. "Oh, wine sounds great."

"Normally, I force myself to work out before indulging," he said, placing two balloon-shaped goblets on the breakfast bar between them. "But we're in for a late night as it is."

"Rules are made to be broken." Especially the one about how a PA shouldn't be standing barefoot in her boss's kitchen, eyeing him from across the room.

Shane knelt in front of a narrow cooler on the far wall, his shirt molding to the muscles on his back. She followed the line of his shoulders, running her eyes down his defined arms to his torso, and finally to the pants that hugged his remarkable backside.

When he turned, bottle in hand, Crickitt averted her gaze, though she did peek under her lashes to watch him peel the wrapper from the neck. He opened a drawer and extracted a black gadget, cylindrical in shape and nearly as tall as the wine bottle itself.

"What is that?" she asked.

"Electric wine opener."

She lifted an eyebrow. "Fancy."

"Want to try it?"

"That's okay."

"It's fun," he teased, dragging out the word.

Well, who could resist that? "Oh, all right."

Shane rested the device over the neck, and Crickitt grabbed hold of the bottle. "There's a button," he murmured, enclosing her hand with deft fingers and sliding hers to the opener. He was leaning a hairbreadth away, his brows pulled down as he arranged her fingers over the round rubber circle she couldn't see. Then he pinned her with a hooded gaze, his lips kicking up in one corner. "Just push," he said.

Crickitt stared at his pursed lips.

"You'll hear when the cork pops."

She depressed the button that sent the opener whirring to life, unsure if the shock waves were coming from the reverberation of the equipment in her hands or from Shane's fingers. She met his eyes over the bottle, pulse pounding in her neck, palms dampening under his.

How had she managed to turn this into an erotic experience?

Look at him. He is *an erotic experience.*

A subtle *pop* sounded, and Crickitt dragged her eyes from his face as he released her hands.

"You're a natural," he said, pressing another button to release the cork and catching it in one hand.

A lump of lust formed in her throat. She put a palm to her cheek. Her face felt hot. Actually, her *everything* felt hot. Shane disposed of the cork, his every move as fluid and smooth as the wine he poured into their waiting glasses.

"You okay?" he asked.

She dropped her hand. "Yep," she answered a little too loud. "I'm great."

He handed her a glass and raised his for a toast. "To kicking ass."

She released a laugh and, hopefully with it, some of the tension knotting her intestines.

"I know what you're thinking," he said after they took a drink.

Lord, she hoped not.

"You're wondering if I have any personality at all."

Way off. Way, way *off.*

She swept her hair from her neck, hoping a dose of cool air might domesticate her Girls-Gone-Wild hormones. "No, I don't think that," she said, gesturing across the room in an attempt to change the subject. "Anyone with a clock like that has to have a personality."

He didn't laugh with her as he moved from the breakfast bar to stand next to her. He frowned at the clock, his emotions receding like he'd backed into a dark corner. "It was my father's."

Crickitt's heart squeezed. *Was.* The clock was a family heirloom, and from the sound of it, not a good one. She'd singled out the one personal item in the room and learned that it held a secret he wouldn't share. One that he *shouldn't* share with a colleague. Taking a giant mental step away from the line she'd crossed, Crickitt said, "I like it." Before tacking on a lame, "It's nice."

"We should get started," he said. Brushing by her, he headed down the hallway.

CHAPTER TWELVE

Two hours later, Crickitt stifled a yawn and nearly poked herself in the eye with her pencil.

"I've kept you too late," Shane said from his desk. Crickitt was stretched out on the leather couch on the other side of the room, sketches and pages of handwritten notes scattered at her feet.

"No, I'm fine." The image on the page blurred in front of her. "Well, maybe I am a little tired."

"Yeah, so am I."

For once Shane looked tired; no less attractive, but tired. His hair was disheveled from pushing his hands through it one too many times, and his five o'clock shadow had struck twelve. Which made her worry what she must look like. She doubted *haggard* looked as good on her.

He'd abandoned his starched button-down shirt in favor of the white V-necked tee underneath. He rolled a shoulder, and the rumpled cotton sculpted to his pectorals. She couldn't keep from staring. Until now, she hadn't had to contend with the distracting view. He'd been perched behind his computer screen for most of the evening.

He stretched his arms overhead, revealing his tanned abdomen. Seeing that flash of skin made her want to yank his shirt over his head and explore the rest of his amazingly contoured torso with eager hands.

She dragged her eyes, kicking and screaming, from the flat planes of his stomach, reciting a lecture about how she needed to stop objectifying the stacked, ripped, delicious man across the room. She refocused on the sketchbook in her lap, a far less satisfying view.

"I'm relieving you of your duties," Shane said, approaching the sofa. "Before I get accused of being a slave driver."

Aware she was sprawled on his couch like she owned it, Crickitt moved a pile of sketches to a nearby chair and put her feet on the floor. Shane sat at the other end with a huff, the warmth from his body drifting across the cushion, his nearness causing her heart to pound.

He dropped his head onto the back of the sofa and closed his eyes. "Are we going to be able to come up with anything he'll like?"

She didn't reply right away. She was too busy watching the low groan work its way from his throat to his lips.

Snap out of it.

She wasn't being paid to check him out after-hours. They had a job to do and had very little time to do it. Shoving away teenage tendencies, she finally managed to speak. "Of course we will."

He opened one eye. "Don't patronize me."

Crickitt smiled. He could be funny with a straight face. She *really* liked that about him.

Focus!

She cleared her dry throat and clutched the notebook against her chest. "Actually, I may have something," she said, rerouting her attention to the task at hand. She lowered the notebook and examined her drawings. For the last half an hour she'd been working on a new concept while Shane pecked away on his keyboard. And, if her worn-out synapses weren't misfiring, she thought her idea had potential.

Shane sat up and scrubbed his face with both hands. He moved closer, his shoulder and hip brushing against hers. "All right, let's see it."

She showed him.

He muttered her name, the deep timbre of his voice gliding along her ribs like a mallet on a xylophone. "This is really good."

"Really?" she asked, lifting her chin.

He looked up at the same time, bringing their noses inches apart.

She froze like a butterfly on a board, pinned into place by his golden gaze. Shane's eyes dropped to her mouth for the briefest second before he emitted a low grunt of approval, and she could swear he leaned in just the slightest bit closer. And then it was as if every cell in her body moved in conjunction with his. Like a magnet being pulled to metal, she breached the distance between them and touched her lips to his. His mouth was firm, warm, and tasted every bit as good as it looked. The low moan rumbling between them came from her this time. Her eyes flew open.

What had she done—or, more accurately, since her lips were still fused with his—*what was she doing*? She pulled back, their lips making a smooching sound as she did.

Crickitt stood, the notebook on her lap clattering to the floor. "Oh, my gosh." A smudge of lip gloss decorated his bottom lip. "Oh, my gosh," she repeated.

She bolted from the room, and somewhere beyond the sloshing heartbeat in her eardrums, registered Shane calling her name.

* * *

Shane stood in the middle of his office, hands on his hips, and stared down at the sketchbook at his feet.

"Oh, my *gosh*," he repeated, chuckling. He wiped his lips, noticing faint sparkles from her lip gloss on his fingertips. *Man.* He wished he would have been ready, he'd have loved to taste those lips a while longer. His entire body hummed like a transformer about to blow, and from what? A chaste, closemouthed kiss.

A zillion shouts of encouragement came from the direction of his dormant hormones. It'd been a long time since he'd been kissed, even longer since a woman initiated it. He stepped to the doorway and poked his head out. A slice of light shone under the bathroom door and bisected the hallway.

Obviously, she regretted doing it. And wasn't that a shame? Hadn't she said earlier that rules were made to be broken? He was beginning to agree.

He'd been too aware of propriety and his position as her employer to lean in any closer. Remembering the feel of those plush lips set off a string of thoughts like fire-crackers…and a warning siren he couldn't ignore. As amazing as it was to feel her warm and willing against him, he was pretty sure it shouldn't happen again.

"Damn."

Given the fact she was hiding in his bathroom, she must feel the same way. With no idea what he'd say when he got there, he stalked toward the door. As it turned out, a conversation started without him.

"Maybe it's hormones," he heard her say, which almost made him laugh out of solidarity. "Or maybe I'm lonely." Her voice grew farther away, then closer, like she was pacing the floor.

"Or desperate," she continued.

Well, that wasn't very flattering.

"It was bound to happen," she said. "Could have been anyone. Given the chance, I may have kissed Townsend."

Shane cringed. "I certainly hope not," he said through the door.

Silence. Then, "You weren't supposed to hear that."

He smiled at the floor and leaned a palm on the door frame. Could she be more adorable? "Open the door, Crickitt. You can't hide in there until morning."

"Actually, I could," her muffled voice pronounced. "It's plenty big, and I can make a bed out of these fluffy towels."

"Crickitt," he scolded. She really was regretting it, wasn't she? Well, he wouldn't let her. She had nothing to be embarrassed about. He'd been right there, too, letting it happen. "What if I promise not to bring it up?"

More silence was followed by the snick of the lock disengaging. Crickitt peeked out of a narrow gap in the door, her wide, doelike eyes brimming with innocence. "Really?"

"Yes."

Careful not to touch him, she slipped into the hallway, making him feel as if he'd been the one to take advantage of her instead of the other way around. Not that he felt at a disadvantage, he thought as he swaggered toward his office. When he got there he found her hastily shoving papers into her canvas bag.

"Just so you know"—he straightened a stack of drawings and offered it to her—"I wanted to kiss you, too."

"You promised!" She pointed the papers at him accusingly.

"I know." She turned and he caught her elbow. "How about we deal with it now and we won't be uncomfortable later?"

She looked at him like he'd offered her a liver and Limburger cheese sandwich.

Finally, she said, "Okay."

He gestured to the sofa and she sat. He kept his distance, sitting on the opposite arm. The situation would only get messier if they didn't just say the truth. Here went nothing.

"I find you more attractive than I should given my...position," he said reluctantly. She squirmed. "But I promise it won't interfere at work." He dipped his chin. "Your turn."

"My turn to what?" she asked, eyes wide.

He blew out a soft laugh. She was entirely too appealing when her cheeks pinked with embarrassment. "Your turn to be honest. Come on, hit me. I can handle it."

She clenched the strap of her bag, and for a second he

wondered if she'd taken him literally and was about to brain him with it. Then a sober look crossed her face.

"I think you have the nicest lips I've ever seen," she said. "And felt."

He gulped. Her blush deepened. He struggled to keep his expression neutral as his hormones lined up to do the conga.

"But I can control my impulses," she finished.

He tried to speak but couldn't. His tongue was Gorilla-Glued to the roof of his mouth. He repressed the sudden urge to dump the water bottle on his desk over his head. *You have the nicest lips I've ever felt.* And here he was, getting her to agree never to do it again.

Moron, party of one.

"See?" His voice cracked on the word and he cleared his throat. "Now we can put it behind us."

$\mathcal{C}$HAPTER THIRTEEN

$\mathcal{C}$rickitt made it through the next several days without locking lips with her boss. By then, she had labeled The Kiss as circumstantial, ebbing from sleep deprivation and/or proximity. Shane was a distraction, a *preoccupation* she hadn't counted on, and becoming increasingly hard to resist.

They opted not to work in his home office over the weekend. The August Industries building was much more convenient…and far less distracting. Since then, he'd seemed remarkably unaffected. Which was a little disconcerting. Did rogue kisses from new employees happen often? Was it outlined in the employee handbook?

Shane breezed into her office, wavy hair styled against his head, his face cleanly shaven. Cool, crisp cologne wafted around her, and Crickitt pressed her knees together under the desk.

"I'm late," he announced, sliding one sleeve aside to look at his watch.

"No, you're not. Your meeting with Ms. LaRouche is at ten."

He lifted his eyebrows in challenge. "She called late last night and bumped it to eight thirty."

"Oh." Crickitt yanked her eyes from his face to check the clock on her computer screen. "You're right. You're late."

"Tell me you know enough to give me a five-minute breakdown?"

She did. Last night after work, she read all about Lori LaRouche's line of mineral makeup and skin care products. Crickitt gestured for Shane to sit. He did, but only after another nervous glance at his watch.

"LaRouche Skin Care is a complete line featuring everything from alpha hydroxyl cleansers to easy-to-remove mascara." Crickitt paused in her reading to look up.

His brow furrowed.

"Do you need me to come with you?" she asked, the offer more appealing now that she'd said it aloud. "Being a woman, I'm quite familiar with products like toner, glycolic gel, and day-to-night moisturizer." And, being a woman, she was also quite familiar with the way Shane attracted members of the opposite sex like static cling.

He shook his head. "No, thanks. I can handle it. Makeup or motor oil, business is business. But I will take your notes," he said, standing.

His cell phone rang and he extracted it from a pocket. After a clipped "August," he eased into a smile. "We were just talking about you," he said, charm bubbling over like a brimming glass of champagne.

Crickitt twisted her lips. *Lori LaRouche.* Shane's tone had changed from all business to cotton-candy sweet. He offered a warm laugh, one she'd prefer he didn't share with clients, and explained he was running "a tad behind."

A tad. *Really?*

Her reflection on the screen of her idle computer frowned back at her. She wiggled the mouse to wake it up. Anyone who didn't know her might think she was jealous. And she was *not* the jealous type, especially over a man she wasn't even seeing. Heat speared the center of her chest as she reconsidered. Maybe she didn't used to be the territorial type, but something about Shane talking to another woman had definitely raised her hackles.

What if he was flirting with Lori? It wasn't any business of hers. They'd agreed on Friday they would be professional, despite a shared attraction. Scowling at the back of his head while he talked to another woman was definitely *not* professional.

Crickitt tried to focus on something else, but honestly, wasn't his voice "a tad" too sensual to be discussing directions?

Giving up, she slouched in her chair in time to see Shane move his jacket aside to stuff a hand in his pant pocket, the movement revealing one well-formed butt cheek. Was admiring her boss's derriere considered inappropriate if he didn't know about it?

She perused the intricate stitching of the material hugging his perfect butt, too wrapped up to notice he'd hung up the phone. He turned so suddenly she didn't have a chance to avert her eyes. She was staring directly at the fly of his pants.

She redirected her gaze to the design of his tie, staring at it for a good long while before daring to look up at his face.

"I'm…going to go," he said, capping his statement with a hoisted brow.

She peeled her lips back into what she hoped resembled a smile and not a mortified grimace. "Okay, I'll just"—*stop ogling your crotch*— "finish up…"—she gestured at the screen—"…here." Fingers on the keyboard, she began pecking Lord-knew-what onto the screen while he made his way to the door.

After he left, she buried her head in her forearms. Or she would have if the file Shane needed wasn't right under her nose. "Crap."

Snatching the folder, she ran across the waiting room, catching up to him as he pressed the call button for the elevator.

"Shane!" She held up the folder.

"Ah," he said, reaching for it. His fingers brushed hers and he held her gaze a second longer than necessary. Or maybe she was the one who couldn't look away. She let go of the folder as the elevator dinged, its doors sliding open. "Thanks."

Crickitt waved a hand as he disappeared behind the door, then slapped it to her forehead.

"Tempting, isn't he?"

She flicked a look over at Keena, who was grinning and waggling a pen between her manicured fingers.

"Excuse me?" She'd forgotten she wasn't in a bubble. And if Keena had noticed her eating Shane up with her eyes, he probably had as well.

"Shane August," Keena said in that mystery accent of hers. Czechoslovakian? Welsh? "He's *tempting*."

Crickitt offered a tight nod. She really didn't want to know if Keena spoke from personal experience.

Back in her office, she returned to her e-mail. After ten minutes of channeled focus that could have caused a nosebleed, she leaned back in her chair. A single thought continued to gnaw at her.

Did Shane make it a habit of romancing his coworkers?

Had Keena once been the shy new girl? Had Shane urged her out of her shell and into his bedroom? According to Sadie, some men could plant ideas in a woman's head without her knowing it. Like a kind of masculine superpower. Maybe kissing Shane wasn't even her idea. How convenient that they'd ended up at his house on Friday. How did she know those files weren't tucked in his briefcase the entire time?

She shook off the budding conspiracy theory. If Shane wanted to seduce her, he wouldn't have insisted Thomas take her home. He wouldn't have suggested the no-kissing policy.

Come to think of it, that last bit bothered her.

Maybe he doesn't want you to kiss him. Ever think of that?

She had. As well as she remembered the feel of his lips, she couldn't recall a second when he'd kissed her back. He just sat there while his personal assistant made out with him. Then he asked her to promise not to do it again, as if she were the loony new hire bent on seducing him.

No, that wasn't exactly true. He wasn't appalled by her. He even admitted being attracted to her. She pulled her shoulders back. And why not? She was attractive. Maybe not va-va-voom-Sadie attractive, but she wasn't exactly a can of Spam, either.

So if she liked him, and he liked her, why the boundaries?

The digital purr of her office phone answered her question. Because office romances rarely worked out. That was why companies had no-dating policies.

And sexual harassment laws.

"Crickitt Day," she answered.

"A few of us are going to Kung Chow's. Would you like to go?" Keena asked.

"Um, no, thanks, I brought my lunch today." She didn't need fried rice. What she needed was a slap upside the head, a reminder of what was important. She said good-bye to Keena but instead of returning the handset, she punched a button for an open line and dialed Sadie's cell phone number.

What she needed was her best friend to set her straight. If anyone knew how to *not* get distracted by a man, it was Sadie Howard.

* * *

Shane would choose a Novocain-free dental visit over Lori LaRouche's nasal voice any day of the week. He managed to smile through their meeting; that is until she teased his lapel with one red talon and invited him back to her place. He begged off through gritted teeth, claiming he had another meeting.

Lori was beautiful, he'd add "for an older woman," but that wasn't fair. Lori was beautiful, period. He'd had dealings with Lori in the past, and as much as he wished they were strictly business dealings, they weren't. He had been twenty-one, with shaky confidence and a rocky bank account. Lori had been an in-her-prime thirty-five and had taken an interest in him. *Thirty-five*. That's how old he was now. He couldn't imagine having an interest in a twenty-one-year-old. Especially one as immature as he'd been.

Back then, Shane hadn't yet learned to control his impulses. Too flattered to say no, he'd seized Lori's offer with both hands. The affair was short-lived, a handful of dates mostly at her place. Lori was the one who taught him sex was sex and love wasn't worth considering. He'd been on his way to arriving at the conclusion anyway, but Lori cemented it.

On the limo ride back to the office, Shane jotted down a note to talk to Crickitt about Lori's account. Maybe he should have them sit down together. He twisted his lips. Maybe not.

It was hard to conceive how he'd ever become intimately involved with a predatory woman like Lori. She'd dressed to kill today in a tight black dress, tall heels, and patterned stockings likely clipped to a pair of lacy garters. And yet, Shane found himself barely tolerating her attempt to get his attention, leaning away any time she moved to touch him. On the other hand, he hadn't been able to get Crickitt out of his mind since the moment she'd inadvertently tugged her bottom lip with her teeth. He pictured her again, arms folded on top of her desk, curls tumbling around her face as she looked up at him. He shifted discretely, his pants suddenly tight. Geez. If the woman only knew how crazy she made him…

Yeah? And what if she knew you'd slept with a client years ago?

Bet she wouldn't kiss him then, he thought with a derisive chuckle. If Crickitt was anything, it was genuine.

He may not have known her for very long, but there was a blatant earnestness in Crickitt he couldn't deny. If he wanted to prove she said just what was on her mind, he need look no further than Henry Townsend. And he knew from personal experience she *did* what was on her mind, too. She was the one who kissed him, wasn't she?

"Yes, she was," he said aloud, waving off the glance Thomas threw at him from the rearview mirror.

No, Crickitt may be smack in the middle of restarting her life, but he knew enough about her to know that "arm candy to a sugar daddy" wasn't anywhere in her agenda.

The limo came to a stop and Shane got out, waving good-bye to Thomas. As he walked into the building, his stomach clenched. On the elevator up, his heart rate increased with the floors, the handle on his briefcase slick with sweat. He felt almost...nervous. Which made no sense. How many times had he walked this same route to his office? Hundreds. *Thousands.*

Stepping into the waiting area, he waved hello to Keena and crested the short staircase leading to his and Crickitt's adjacent offices. The closer he drew to her door, the more edgy he felt. Perspiration beaded his lip and he wiped it away, bemused. The last time he had a case of nerves around a woman was junior prom.

He'd tried to keep a professional distance, but trying *not* to notice Crickitt only made him notice her more. He'd enjoyed discovering her little tics when she didn't know he was watching. Like whenever she moved from notebook to keyboard. She didn't drop her pen, instead resting it between her plush lips while she typed. Or what about the way she wound the writing utensil through her curls when she talked on the phone? Last he checked ink pens weren't erotic. But as with the clunky mailbag she carried or the square-heeled loafers she wore, Crickitt had a way of making bland look damn sexy.

And he wasn't the only one of them struggling with boundaries. This morning she'd been salivating over a part of his anatomy well outside the "friend zone." Even now, the memory made parts of him stand taller. At her door, he raised a fist to announce his arrival, stopping just short of knocking. Her door was closed? Crickitt never shut her door.

Since she'd started working for him, he found himself following her lead, propping his door open more often than not. When he asked her why the "open-door policy," she claimed the barricade would only slow her down. To her point, she did run around this place like her hair was on fire. He blamed the complimentary coffee bar down the hall at first, but seeing how quickly she fled after kissing him, he'd concluded warp was her normal speed.

He lifted his hand again, but this time, Crickitt's raised voice stopped him cold.

"How can you say that?" she spat in a tone accusatory and hurting at the same time. "I buried nine years of marriage because you wanted out. You stopped loving me first. Don't forget that."

Whoa. Shane retreated from the door, even as he felt a surge of protectiveness for her well up within him. But he didn't dare go in. It was a private conversation and none of his business. He backpedaled to his office, watching her closed door for two more seconds before pulling his door to as quietly as possible.

Forget you heard any of it, some part of him silently warned.

At his desk, Shane leafed through his mesh in-box and found a stack of phone calls to return. He reread the same one four times without comprehension before tossing it aside and slumping in his chair. He couldn't forget her words or the painful undercurrent in her voice when she said them.

You stopped loving me first.

The words echoed in his head once, twice, and just for kicks, looped a third time and kneed him in the nuts. Something about the phrase sent a graveyard chill over his skin, made him want to ignore the emotions that came with it. Ugly, banished, and best left in the dark.

You stopped loving me first.

It wasn't as if he'd been close enough to a woman to commit the same crime as Crickitt's jerk of an ex-husband. Shane made sure not to get to the point where deep feelings came into play. And because he always set expectations, the women he'd been involved with in the past hadn't left brokenhearted, just pissed off.

So, why were her accusatory words eating at him?

Then he thought of his dad, and a shiver of hair stood on the back of his neck.

Bingo! I think we have a winner.

Shane shrugged, tried to dismiss the thought. But he couldn't. The truth was he'd felt *exactly* the kind of betrayal Crickitt was feeling right now. He knew too well the consequences of love unreciprocated. And if his father was here, and Shane blurted out those same words, they'd ring as true and hit as hard.

The fact was his dad couldn't handle losing his mom, and after had turned into one rough, mean sonofabitch. Since his father's death, he'd struggled to reconcile his father's accusations. Surely, the man had known what happened when Shane was a kid was an accident. All Shane wanted back then was to hang with his friends. How was he supposed to know that the one day he left his mother unattended she'd have a seizure?

"Shane?"

He jerked out of his thoughts and focused on Crickitt's curly head peeking through his door.

"Didn't you hear me knock?" she asked.

Shane busied his hands stacking the notes back into his wire in-basket. He muttered an apology and put on a fake smile. "Come in."

"Is something wrong?" She scanned his face, her brow furrowing.

"Oh, uh…headache," he lied. He never traipsed down briar-filled memory lane. Not at home, and certainly not at work. Thankfully, Crickitt interrupted his full-on nosedive. He could practically smell the ozone burning around him.

"Lucky you." Crickitt clapped her hands and rubbed them together Mr. Miyagi style. "I can help."

"With what?" he asked as she crested his desk.

"Your headache, silly."

"Right." His imaginary headache, which, ironically, was developing this very instant.

Crickitt placed her hands on each of the arms of his chair and spun him to face her. As she hovered close, he couldn't escape the sugary scent of her. His mouth watered. She didn't look like a woman who'd minutes ago gone a few rounds with her scumbag ex. Her eyes were bright and clear, her face relaxed.

She leaned in, feathering his hair away from his temples and placed the first two fingers of each hand on either side of his head. Her touch was expert, tantalizing. He felt her breath on his forehead as she muttered, "You are going to thank me *so hard*." His gaze traveled to her lips, where she wore the most adorable cheeky grin. He forced his eyes away from her mouth before he hauled her into his lap and kissed her senseless.

Then a strangled groan escaped his lips.

Speaking of hard.

"Told you," she said.

Her voice sounded a mile away. Probably because all he could hear was the thundering of his blood supply as it traveled from his brain to his lap. He should tell her, or at least avert his eyes. But no amount of self-talk enabled him to look away.

Either she'd purposely undone it, or a button had wriggled free of its closure, because when she'd leaned over him, her shirt gapped open, giving him an eyeful. He clamped on to the armrests on his chair, eyes delving into all the smooth skin laid out before him like rolling fields and amber waves of grain. He had no idea of the bevy of femininity she'd been hiding beneath those poly-cotton shirts of hers. But now he had proof.

Two handfuls of C-cup proof.

Crickitt continued to caress his temples, completely unaware that with each stroke, she sent his blood pressure rising.

Shutting his eyes, he took a deep breath and tried to

think of something, *anything*, else, but the persistent image of her breasts encased in a—God help him—black lace bra had burned into his retinas and was currently playing on the screen of his eyelids.

"Better?" she asked.

"Mm-hm," he grunted, wondering if steam was billowing from his ears.

"Give it five minutes." Her voice was low, husky, *sexy*. She slid her hands away to rearrange his hair, the innocuous touch sending a drove of blazing hormones straight to the Promised Land.

He spun out of her touch and promptly pulled his chair to his desk to hide his now obvious reaction to her.

"You look better already," she said, propping her hands on her hips.

The opening in her shirt was far less exaggerated but no less erotic.

"Thank you," he said, finally finding his voice. It took every ounce of willpower he owned to keep his eyes on her face. She'd gone beyond driving him crazy, he was there. Fit-me-with-a-straitjacket-and-call-me-Patsy mad about her. But what, exactly, could he do about it? She was standing in his *office*. He was in no position to act on any of his impulses.

She turned to the guest chair and lifted a manila folder. "I didn't come in here to massage your head, believe it or not."

Or sleep with me, he thought numbly. "Of course not," he said, grateful he hadn't blurted out the thought. "What do you have for me? I mean, to give me? I mean... to show me." He pointed at the folder rather than attempt to rephrase.

"MajicSweep notes from this afternoon," Crickitt said, smiling, blessedly clueless to the lust-monster hiding beneath his desk.

"Hey, okay. Great. Thank you," he bumbled, his brain still off-line.

"You're welcome."

He sensed an ellipsis. He hoped she didn't bring up her phone conversation. If she started sharing, some of his discombobulated thoughts might accidentally burble to the surface.

"If you don't mind," he said, gesturing toward his office door. "I do have a few things to prepare before the meeting."

"Oh." She glanced at the door, back at him. "Of course you do. Sorry to interrupt." She waved her hands in a flustered manner as she walked away, making him feel like a complete jackass.

Which he was.

"Crickitt?" he called after her.

She turned, raising her eyebrows. "Yes?"

"You're a lifesaver," he said.

She smiled. "Glad I could help."

"I mean it," he mumbled, flitting his eyes away. She'd reached into the muck and pulled him out, fished him from the refuse floating in the dingy waters of his soul. It was no small feat, and she hadn't even been trying. And there was no way to tell her that without sounding certifiable. So instead, he pointed at his scalp. "Good as new."

"Well, if it comes back, you know where to find me," she said, then stepped out of his office.

He shook his head and opened the folder on his desk. "Yeah," he muttered to himself, "I do."

CHAPTER FOURTEEN

The afternoon meeting with "Team Townsend" went smoothly.

And Shane had successfully pulled out of the cloud fogging his brain earlier. Not that Crickitt was ever a far-off thought. He'd seen her blurry figure rushing down the hall a couple of times. It'd taken some doing to focus on the projects littering his desk, but once he dove in, thoughts of his father receded into the distance, leaving him feeling more in control than he'd been earlier.

"'Night," Crickitt called as she passed by his office.

Shane's eyes went to the clock. *Six already?*

"Wait!" He thrust out of his chair and walked over to her, trying to come up with a valid reason for what he was about to ask. "Are you available this evening?"

She stopped in front of his office, eyes widening as her hand went to her chest. "I'm sorry?" she asked, trying to act natural while clutching the front of her shirt for dear life.

He pretended not to notice, it was the least he could do, but the relentless vision of her cleavage snapped into his memory all the same. *Sexual harassment suit, here we come.*

"I didn't have a chance to go over Lori LaRouche's account with you earlier." He palmed his neck in embarrassment. First eavesdropping, then looking down her shirt. What was he, fifteen?

"Oh." Crickitt's forehead bunched as she looked over at her darkened office. "I didn't expect to work late. I sort of made plans."

With whom? Her ex? He clenched his jaw at the idea of her with that bozo.

"I guess I can reschedule," she said, reaching for her phone.

"No, don't." Shane pushed her phone aside. He'd asked her to stay under the guise of work when what he really wanted was to be near her a little longer. Even for a useless fifteen-minute meeting. It was selfish. Dangerous. Like picking a fight with Temptation and betting on himself to lose.

"No need to change your plans," he said, sorry the second he said it. He tucked his hands into his pockets, trying to look nonchalant.

"If you're sure?" She held up her phone again. "It's just drinks with a friend."

A male friend? Worry ate at him as he considered that upsetting possibility.

"Thank you. I'm sure." But he wasn't sure. About anything. He shooed her off anyway. "Go. Enjoy."

Sending him a tentative wave, she headed into the empty reception area. If not for the guard on the door after five p.m., he would have walked her down. But the afternoon had sent his normally reined emotions all over the place as it was. It was probably better he stayed put.

He stood over his desk and blew out a long-suffering sigh. Where he would normally dig in with renewed vigor once the building was quiet, tonight he found himself distinctly unmotivated.

Making a snap decision, he picked up the desk phone and speed dialed a number. His cousin answered on the third ring.

"Wanna grab a beer?" Shane asked.

"Who is this?" Aiden asked. Then with a smile in his voice added, "Name the place."

* * *

Crickitt picked the greasy wings-and-fries joint near her apartment instead of a wine bar or equally stuffy atmosphere. She'd been spoiled lately with catered lunches, breakfast quiche from the high-end cafeteria, and caramel soy milk lattes from an in-house espresso machine. Crickitt worried she was losing touch with her less-refined self, who indulged in flat beer and gnawed chicken directly from the bone.

"I almost didn't make it tonight," Crickitt said to Sadie after they decided what to order. "Shane asked me to stay late. No wonder he's a billionaire. He's a complete workaholic."

There it was, her attempt to segue into, *By the way, I jumped him the other night, and this morning he caught me staring at his second in command.*

But Sadie didn't bite. "What happened to your shirt?"

Crickitt looked down where a not so strategically placed paperclip held her shirt closed. "I lost a button." Thankfully, she had discovered the button missing before the Team Townsend meeting this afternoon. To think how close she'd come to flashing her boss. She *so* did not need the added pressure. As it was, her attraction for him was teetering on a thumbtack's edge. Thankfully, Shane's killer headache kept his eyes tightly shut. She didn't need him thinking she was a shameless hussy on top of everything else.

"Last week, we went to Columbus for an account, then back to his home office to work until midnight," Crickitt said, attempting to steer the conversation back to her brewing confession.

Sadie sighed.

Crickitt slouched in the uncomfortable wooden booth. "I give. What's wrong?"

Sadie met her eyes, and Crickitt felt the force of her anguished expression all the way down to her trouser socks. Her best friend looked like she might burst into tears in the middle of Wings n' Things.

"Aiden saw her the other day," Sadie said, her voice barely audible over the bar hubbub.

"Who?"

Sadie rolled her eyes. "Who do you think?"

Like her, Crickitt knew Aiden was recently divorced. "His ex?"

Sadie nodded.

"That happens," Crickitt said carefully. She and Ronald got together several times after their split, either to discuss division of property or exchange items mixed up in the boxes when she moved out.

"Do you think he still loves her?" Sadie asked.

Crickitt would do anything to comfort her friend. Anything except lie to her. Aiden and his former spouse could be reconciling right this minute for all she knew. Marriage inextricably linked two people. As much as she hated to admit it, if Ronald begged her back during the painful and emotionally draining separation, Crickitt would have said yes. At the time, the familiarity of even an unhappy marriage would have been more appealing than the great unknown. Now she couldn't even imagine being with him, knowing what she knew.

"I don't know," Crickitt said softly.

The waitress brought a pitcher of beer and filled two glasses. Sadie studied her lap until she was gone.

"You really like him, don't you?" Crickitt asked.

"We have a connection."

Wow. That was almost...romantic. And coming from her tough-talking friend, a little frightening.

"I don't want to lose him," Sadie said, her voice cracking.

Crickitt reached for her friend's hand over the table. The gesture must have snapped Sadie out of her melancholy. She blinked several times as if coming out of a trance.

Sadie raised an eyebrow. "I think I need a drink."

They hoisted their mugs and, in a tradition years old, banged them together and agreed, "Toasts are lame."

Half the contents gone, Crickitt refilled both their glasses.

"Is that shirt...pink?"

Crickitt tucked her chin to examine her wardrobe. "Um...peach. I think. Why?"

"You usually wear neutrals. You look really pretty. Girly."

Crickitt shrugged. "Thanks."

"Okay, Kitty-cat," Sadie said, the only person on the planet allowed to call her by that ridiculous name. "You called me. Spill it."

Well, bringing up Shane now would just be insensitive. Sadie was uncharacteristically torn up over his cousin. Before she could speak, their food arrived, a BBQ chicken pizza and plate of fries smothered in cheese sauce. Crickitt moved a slice of pizza to her plate to cool.

"I'm waiting," Sadie said.

She'd have to tell her something…and she knew just what. With a wince, she blurted, "Ronald called me today."

"What the hell did he want?" Sadie spat. "Lose his balls again?" She snorted and munched on a fry. On anyone else it would have been unattractive.

"He—uh…" Wow. She didn't expect this to be so difficult to say out loud. "He told me he missed me and said he made a mistake."

Sadie sat slack-jawed, half of a French fry in one hand. And that wasn't the worst of it.

"He wants us to get back together. And start a family."

* * *

Aiden took a slow sip of his beer, taking care to line it up on the square cardboard coaster on the bar.

Shane stared down at his own, unable to take a drink. "When did you find out?"

"On the way over. They don't know for sure. But all of her symptoms are like they were."

Aiden's mother had been suffering from cancer on and off for the last five years. Until now, she'd been in remission for eight months.

"She's going to see her doctor tomorrow." He shrugged.

"Maybe it's not back," Shane said carefully.

"Yeah. Maybe." Aiden took another drink of his beer.

Shane wasn't buying his own empty reassurance. If Uncle Mike and Aunt Kathy told Aiden, chances are they already knew the worst and were planning on breaking it to him in person tomorrow.

"If Mom's sick again," Aiden said, "Harmony's coming back."

The walls of the bar practically shook from that bombshell. "What do you mean 'coming back'?" Shane asked. When Aiden had divorced, Shane had been tempted to throw a parade in his honor. He hoped his cousin wasn't contemplating getting involved with her again. If he did, he'd be setting himself up like a ten pin.

Aiden angled a glance at him. "Mom doesn't know we're divorced, Shane."

"Why the hell not?"

"Because we didn't want her worrying herself sick. Literally." Aiden's eyebrows slammed together.

Shane worked to process the new information. Aunt Kathy may have cancer again, *and* still believed Aiden and Harmony were lawfully wedded? Worse, Harmony might actually worm her way back into Aiden's life?

"She's not living with me."

Thank God for that.

"I called Harmony. She's agreed to meet us at the doctor's office tomorrow." Aiden's face twisted. "She's going to be around a lot if this doesn't shake out the way we hope."

"What about Crickitt's friend? I thought you two were hitting it off."

He didn't miss the flash of guilt on his cousin's face. "I have to do what's best for my mom right now, Shane."

Selflessness. One of Aiden's finest qualities. Shane spent a lifetime arming himself against that kind of vulnerability, and here Aiden was, putting himself last with hardly a second thought. It was admirable...and frustrating.

"Have you talked to Sadie yet?" Shane asked, wondering, *Does Crickitt know?*

"Not yet." Aiden shifted on the bar stool.

After a moment, Shane couldn't help but mutter, "It's not good, man."

"Right, because you have so much experience seeing relationships through," Aiden snapped.

Shane started to argue but decided against it. What Aiden said was harsh, but it was also the truth.

"Sadie and I just met. Do you think she's going to stick around while I'm scrambling to help Dad care for Mom? Think she'll come with me to the waiting room while Mom has chemo? Do you think Sadie wants to be around the drugs, the sickness...the utter depression of watching someone die?" On that final word, Aiden's voice cracked. He brushed the heels of his hands over his eyes, then polished off his beer.

Shane gave his cousin some space, signaling for the bartender to bring a refill.

Aiden had made a good point. And he'd probably prefer to stop making it. If the news was bad, who could blame Sadie for walking away? And knowing Aunt

Kathy, she would take the news of Aiden's divorce—and the fact that Aiden had lied to her for the last several months—hard. Aiden was right. His mother didn't need the stress.

Shane opened his mouth to change the subject to how well Angel was doing on the Townsend project, but "Crickitt kissed me" tumbled out instead.

Aiden's mug hit the bar with a thud. "No shit? When? Why?"

"Last Friday. And what do you mean, *why*?"

"I thought you had this 'I don't have sex with my assistants' rule you follow."

"I don't sound like that."

"Yeah. You do. You need to loosen up. It's okay to give yourself a break sometimes."

Did Crickitt see him that way? Some stiff, stuffed shirt who sat rigidly still while she moved her luscious mouth over his?

"I know you like her. From the second you pushed past me at the club," Aiden said, stabbing the bar top with one finger, "I knew."

"Well, it was an accident. I don't even think she meant to do it," Shane said, suddenly worried by how true that sounded. "We agreed to keep things professional for the good of our working relationship."

"For the good of your— Do you hear yourself, man? When was the last time you let yourself have a little fun, anyway? Even when you dated what's-her-name—"

"Sara," Shane supplied.

"—you were miserable. Already, Crickitt's had a positive effect on you. You've been acting like the old you instead of Robo-Shane."

Shane pulled a face, not sure which name to be more offended by. "The old me?"

Aiden gestured around them. "You're in a bar. On a weekday."

He had a point. Since Crickitt started working at August Industries, he'd felt more relaxed than he had in years. He'd thought at first it was because of her efficiency, but lately he could see it was something more.

"Well, she's good for you, whatever she's doing," Aiden said.

"We're not doing anything."

"Whatever," Aiden said, his lips quirking.

They sipped their beers in silence for a few minutes before Shane spoke. "I'm sorry."

Aiden nodded.

"Let me know if there's anything I can do." It was the most useless sentiment ever, but what else could he say?

"Thanks," Aiden said. He sounded sincere.

Shane found himself wanting to bring up Crickitt again. But hadn't Aiden just proved there were more important things going on in the world than the flirtation Shane was having with an attractive coworker? Besides, if they did broach the topic again, what did Shane have to add? What he knew about relationships could fit in the bowl of peanuts resting at his left elbow.

He turned his attention to the televisions blaring overhead and commented on the game. Aiden cheered his approval, content to focus on anything but the topic at hand. Shane obliged, settling back into his chair and whooping alongside him.

CHAPTER FIFTEEN

Henry Townsend perused the fresh artwork before him in flinty silence. Crickitt fidgeted as she waited and watched. Though she was confident the meeting wouldn't end with Shane firing her, she didn't have as much faith in Townsend.

The new logo was almost identical to the one she'd sketched that night in Shane's office. The same night he'd moved to sit next to her, then brushed his shoulder against hers. The memory snapped like flashbulbs in her mind.

Fiery, amber eyes flicking to her lips.

A guttural sound escaping his perfect mouth.

The heat of his lips searing hers.

She risked a look over to Shane, who happened to look over at her at the same time. He nodded his head in reassurance, and for the first time in a good long while, she didn't feel alone.

"No mascot," Townsend growled.

Carrie straightened, perched on the edge of her chair like a nervous canary.

Shane and Crickitt kept quiet.

Townsend slapped the portfolio full of artwork, business plans, and ad pitches closed and slid it across the conference room table. It skidded to a halt in front of Crickitt.

"Let's do it," he said.

Crickitt and Shane exchanged glances. "Which part, Henry?" she asked.

His lined mouth tilted into what she guessed was supposed to be a smile. "All of it, Ms. Day. All of it."

With that, he pressed his gnarled hands onto the table's shining mahogany surface and pushed himself up. His cronies followed him single file out of the room. The moment the door swung shut behind them, Crickitt turned to Shane. He startled her, grabbing her up and lifting her off her feet. Instinctively, she wrapped her arms around his neck.

"You did it!" he said, giving her a squeeze and pressing her against a wall of hard male chest. He set her down, but his cologne continued tickling her nostrils. He smelled *so good*. Downright edible. She slid her arms from his neck, letting him go, even though every part of her anatomy protested.

"You really did it," he said.

"We did it," she corrected as they took an awkward step away from each other.

Shane palmed the back of his neck. "Yeah, I guess we did." Then he smirked. "And you didn't even have to make out with him."

Crickitt flushed. "Lucky me, I guess." She busied her hands packing the portfolio into her bag.

Shane gathered his briefcase. "Do you have plans tonight?"

She didn't. And more than anything she hoped that Shane was asking because he wanted to make plans with her. She shouldn't hope that at all. Not after they promised to keep things between them platonic. Not after Ronald's confusing phone call.

"Why? Feel like treating your PA to a congratulatory dinner?" she blurted anyway.

"You've earned it."

A thread of pride caused her to lift her chin. She had earned it. And more than that, she deserved to spend the evening the way she wanted. And she wanted to spend it with Shane. "Okay," she told him. "I accept."

* * *

Crickitt stood on the sidewalk in downtown Columbus beneath a building that resembled the space needle in Washington. She craned her head, shielding her eyes from the warm summer sun. Skyview was practically perched in the clouds, rotating too slowly to notice, giving its diners a three-hundred-and-sixty-degree view of downtown. "I've always wanted to eat here."

Shane took his eyes from the skyscraper to look at her. "Me, too."

He'd never been here before? And he'd brought her, which made their coming here instantly more meaningful.

Inside, the hostess sat them at a coveted window seat. Crickitt studied the Matchbox-size cars below before focusing on Shane's reflection in the window. He was watching her, the sun highlighting the line of his jaw, his perfect lips.

"Madame?"

Crickitt turned to find their wine waiter, *sommeliers* she remembered they were called in five-star restaurants, a bottle of wine propped onto a white cloth over his forearm. "Château Sedacca." He placed the bottle on the table and opened it with a manual wine service. Shane watched her through twinkling eyes, which made her remember the electric bottle opener, his fingers gliding along hers. Was he remembering that, too?

The waiter splashed the slightest bit of red into the bottom of her glass. When she only smiled up at him, he raised an eyebrow.

"Oh, right." She lifted the wine and sipped, allowing the liquid to slide on her tongue before trickling down her throat. It was the same wine she'd had at Shane's house. She remembered the burst of fruitiness, the soft tannins in the background. And the hint of it on Shane's lips when she'd kissed him.

She put her glass back on the table, unable to look Shane in the eye. But he watched her. She could feel his stare from across the table.

"Madame?" the sommelier asked again, bottle poised to pour.

"Oh. Yes, um, it's perfect." He filled her glass, then Shane's, and finally retreated. "That was stressful," she mumbled, only half kidding.

Shane chuckled, drawing her attention.

"What?" she asked, unable to keep from smiling over at him. "Did I do that wrong?"

He cradled his glass in one large palm. "You did not do

anything wrong. I just..." He shook his head as if arriving at a conclusion that surprised him. "You're refreshing, do you know that?"

"I am?"

He kept his eyes on hers as he took in some of the red liquid and pursed his lips, sucking in air as he rolled the wine around on his tongue. She simply stared, utterly distracted by the contours of his mouth.

"Completely," he said. "I like that you're not intimidated by"—he gestured at the five-piece band and flock of well-dressed diners—"any of this."

"I'm following your lead," she said honestly. "You're the most grounded billionaire I've ever met."

"Know a lot of us, do you?"

She waved a hand. "Tons."

He laughed, a deep, rumbling sound that made her stomach pitch. "To us." He lifted his glass. "We kick ass."

* * *

After she ate the finest meal to ever touch her tongue, and they'd emptied the bottle of wine and refused a second, the conversation shifted from work to family.

"My parents live in Missouri, though they do visit me several times a year." She pretended to look at her invisible watch. "They're about due for their quarterly butt-into-my-life visit, as a matter of fact."

Shane smiled. "Siblings?"

"One brother," Crickitt said, pushing her plate away before she stuffed herself beyond repair. "He's in Missouri, too."

"What does he do?"

"He works for the phone company. He's a repairman. What about you? No wait, let me guess," she said pressing her fingertips to her temples and pretending to read his mind. "You are an only child."

"Very good."

"And I'll bet you were first in your class when you went to college."

"I wasn't first but I was close," he said with a crooked smile.

Fingers to her temples again, she narrowed her eyes, concentrating. "Your parents bought you your first Mercedes when you were sixteen. Your dad taught you everything you know about business."

Shane's smile faltered. Like the moment she mentioned the clock on his living room wall, she sensed she had crossed a line.

"I'm sorry."

"No, it's okay," he said, but his smile was polite. "My dad was a machinist at a factory." He spun his wineglass, the liquid swirling against its sides. "And my mom was a schoolteacher."

"And they are no longer living," Crickitt said, picking up on the obvious. "I'm sorry I brought it up."

"Don't be. Dad died a year ago. It wasn't easy, but I've recovered."

"And your mom?"

He averted his gaze, spinning his wineglass on the tablecloth. "When I was a kid."

The waiter descended with a tray of desserts. Crickitt waved him off, having eaten too much of the five-star cuisine to make room for caramel-chocolate cheesecake.

Shane settled the bill, and they rose to leave. As she

stepped around tables and dodged an incoming waiter with a tray of food, Shane briefly pressed his palm on the small of her back. A fiery trail licked her spine, and she inadvertently tensed. By the time they'd boarded the empty elevator, Crickitt was clutching her purse with strained fingers.

Shane leaned against the wall on the opposite side, regarding her from beneath thick lashes. He was so tall and broad and handsome, being under his scrutiny made her nervous. Or maybe that was excitement. It was getting easier and easier to forget this man was her employer, that he wasn't attempting to seduce her, that he was treating her because of a job well done. She turned her eyes to the digital display and counted down the floors, hoping the gesture would tame her hijacked hormones.

Outside on solid ground, the night air welcoming and cool, Crickitt sucked in a quiet, clarifying breath. Shane easily kept pace, his long legs eating up the same distance in half the steps. He reached for the door of the limo and popped it open, gliding his palm along her back again as she slid inside.

If he made her body hum by raking her with the briefest touch, what could he do if he really took his time? She clambered inside, straightening her curls and her clothing in one nervous gesture after the other. Shane climbed in and sat beside her, at a respectable distance, but still, too close. Heat leaped to the surface of her skin, burning her cheeks, flushing her neck and chest.

His aftershave had long faded, but the crisp fragrance of his laundry soap combined with his pheromones mingled in her senses. Twice she heard an intake of breath and twice she turned in anticipation, but each time his breath ended on a sigh as he focused on the landscape whizzing by the window. Crickitt spent the remainder of the ride staring out her own window, the dead air between them stifling.

The limo door opened in front of her apartment. Shane got out first, offering Crickitt his hand. She took it, shuddering as his long fingers grazed her bare flesh.

"I'll walk you up," he murmured, taking her canvas bag and slinging it over his shoulder.

Heart thundering in her chest, she fumbled with the keys, grateful to have something in her hands. At the door, it took all of her willpower to keep the key steady as she pushed it into the lock. She could feel Shane standing behind her, the heat radiating off his big body surrounding her like an embrace.

Finally, the key slid home and she turned the knob. If she faced him, he'd see every ounce of desire on her face, every bit of longing reflected in her eyes. She kept her back to him and focused on opening her front door. "Thank you for dinner."

But he didn't let her get away with it.

"Crickitt?"

She took a deep breath, tried to mask her expression in nonchalance. But when she turned, she found Shane close enough to touch, his face bathed in the pale porch light, his perfectly formed mouth edged in a day's growth. Moving her eyes from his face didn't quell the urge to devour him where he stood.

His suit was creased, his collar open, giving her a generous view of his bitable neck. His tie, harmlessly dangling from his jacket pocket, filled her head with fantasies she'd never had before.

Tempting. The word echoed in her ears, making her wonder how long Eve was able to resist before caving in and sampling the apple.

She finally managed to dredge up her voice. "Did you forget something?" she asked.

He scanned her face, his nostrils flaring. Her heart sped and she sucked in a breath and held it, waiting for his answer.

"Now would be the perfect moment," he said, leaning a palm on her door frame and causing her to press her back against the door, "for me to say yes." He reached out and toyed with a button at the top of her shirt. "And kiss you good night."

Her fingers convulsed around the doorknob.

Please. Please do that.

"But . . ." He pushed away from her, his fingers leaving her shirt. "I wouldn't want to be the first to break our pact."

"Our pact?" she squeaked, her voice tight with longing.

Shane stepped away, and Crickitt's breath left her as if he'd taken it from her lungs. The moment evaporated, lost in the span of that single breath. Shane handed over her bag and she took it, unable to hide the shake of her fingers.

"Let me know," he said, watching her as he backed down each of her porch steps, "if you want to revisit that agreement." Rolling one shoulder, he added, "Make an amendment."

She opened her mouth, then closed it ineffectually. At the moment her muddled brain couldn't recall what, exactly, an amendment was. She knew it had something to do with the Constitution.

At the limo, Shane tortured her with one final sexy grin before sinking into the limo. "Sweet dreams, Crickitt," he said, then shut himself inside.

When her brain sent the message to her hand to wave, the limo had pulled out of her street and disappeared behind a thatch of trees. She wrestled her keys from the knob and shut the door, pressing her forehead into the solid wood until it ached.

Let me know if you want to revisit that agreement.

She pushed herself upright and let out a groan that sounded like a mix of longing and defeat. Trudging to her bedroom, she tossed her bag aside and collapsed onto her multicolored comforter.

She should be relieved. There were a hundred reasons why getting physically involved with her boss was a bad idea.

But she couldn't think of any of them. The only images flooding her mind were the things she would have done to him if he'd leaned in the slightest bit and closed his mouth over hers. She would have hauled him into her foyer by his collar and put those lips to good use for the next hour.

Rolling over, she smothered a groan into her frilly decorative pillow.

Bad idea, her brain reminded her. But she couldn't get a single other part of her body to agree.

CHAPTER SIXTEEN

Crickitt ignored the purr of her desk phone and continued filing the papers stacked in the crook of one arm. It was nearly seven o'clock, and she was more than ready for a relaxing weekend away from the office. It'd been impossible to relax around Shane this week. The almost-kiss at her front door left her flustered and sexually frustrated. Though she hadn't actually been around him much since then. Which made her wonder if she'd squandered the moment.

Her desk phone rang again, and Crickitt growled under her breath. She stalked to her desk and answered, trying to sound neutral. "Crickitt Day."

"Hey," came the gruff greeting over a din of other voices.

"Ronald." She wasn't able to keep the shock out of her voice. The name of a local pub lit the caller ID screen.

She lowered herself into her chair. Of course he hadn't called from his cell phone. He knew she wouldn't have answered.

The last time they'd spoken, Ronald had insisted on them getting back together, proclaiming he was wrong and begging for her forgiveness. By the time he'd mentioned the word "remarried" and claimed he still loved her, Crickitt had heard enough. The last thing she wanted was a repeat of that conversation.

She heard a slurping sound as he took a drink, vodka tonic if she had to guess, and the clink of ice cubes against the edge of the glass. "I was thinking," he slurred, "about you and me."

"I'm busy," she grated, raising every internal shield in an attempt to protect herself.

"You haven't changed," he said with a derisive grunt. "Still ignoring life outside of work?"

"Ronald—"

"No wonder the sex was so bad."

A hot wave of anger blasted through her limbs, leaving shock waves in its wake. She rummaged around her head for a comeback that wasn't littered with profanity but came up empty-handed.

"You should have been thinking about me instead of your precious career," he continued, oblivious to her emotions. "Maybe then I would have let you stay."

She squeezed the phone so hard her fingertips tingled. She loosened her grip and forced herself to breathe. "You're drunk." But acknowledging his state didn't erase his accusations.

"The sex schedule was a little impersonal."

Her stomach pitched.

"But you wore that lacy thingy, which I guess kind of made up for it."

"We were on a schedule because I was trying to get pregnant." The words bubbled up from some deep, dark place she would have preferred not to acknowledge. "You weren't complaining at the time," she added, tears flooding her eyes.

"Well, whatever." He crunched an ice cube. "It worked out for the best."

Thick emotion blocked her throat as she tried to digest the truth behind his statement. Yes, she was glad she never had children with Ronald, but it didn't change the fact she still wanted them.

"I was thinking," he continued rather than wait for her reaction, "about how you never bought the bread I liked, only the multigrain. And you know how much I like to get the mail, but you always ran out to the box first."

She shook her head, trying to understand how he could follow a callous statement with one so pithy. "What are you even—"

"I loved you, Crickitt, I did," he said in the condescending quality he'd perfected over the years. "But, more like a friend. Or a sister."

She gave herself a moment to regroup, for the sting of his statement to dull. "Just because you're angry," she said, feeling her blood boil, "doesn't give you the right—"

"Angry doesn't change the fact that I can't, in good conscience, be with you any longer."

"I don't want to be with *you*!" she shouted. Without waiting for a response, she slammed the phone onto the cradle. She stared at it, daring it to ring again. It didn't.

And though she'd have rather died than cry over Ronald's harsh accusations, the tears came. And wouldn't stop coming.

* * *

Shane rubbed his eyes, but the computer screen stayed blurry. He leaned back in his chair and scrubbed a hand over his face. Maybe he'd been putting in too much computer time this week after all. In order to avoid his assistant—his incredibly sexy, distracting, kissable assistant—he'd been e-mailing her across the hall rather than walking the ten yards to speak with her in person.

You're being ridiculous.

True. But he was also being practical. If she knew the wayward direction of his thoughts, she'd make a suggestion involving a bridge and a flying leap. And he wasn't about to bring up the comment he'd thrown at her feet like a gauntlet. He thought he was playing it cool by suggesting she be the first to break their friendship pact.

Why hadn't he just winked and pointed his finger like a gun while saying, *Ball in your court, babe*? What was he thinking, trying to pull off that Pierce Brosnan crap? He should have kissed her or not, and left it at that.

If Crickitt noticed his reclusive behavior, it was news to him. While he didn't want her to feel pressured or awkward, her disinterest was making his ego sting. How could she be unaffected while he tried—and failed—to think of anything *but* her?

Then again, maybe she was struggling. There was a moment earlier in the week when he'd leaned on the door frame of her office, and while he'd given her an update on the Townsend account she'd given him a generous eye-sweep from head to toe. It was difficult, but he'd managed not to smile. And then there was yesterday. In the break room, he poured her a cup of coffee, teasing her about her unusual penchant for soy milk and whipped cream. She couldn't meet his eye, twirling one short curl around her finger while studying her filling mug.

A few more weeks of intense office flirting and they'd both spontaneously combust under the pressure. And, for a change, he was all for it.

Opting to talk to Crickitt in person rather than finish the e-mail he'd started drafting, he stood from his desk. He steeled himself with a breath and opened his office door. The lobby to the right was dark, Keena's desk abandoned. Not that he'd expected to find her there. No one stayed late on Friday evening, save for him. And Crickitt. He could hear her shuffling papers in her brightly lit office.

He strode through her open door to find her in her chair, bent over a bottom drawer. Taking advantage of the curls that hid her face, he admired the curve of her thighs and bottom as she sat rummaging through the files.

"Milking the clock?" he asked. "Just so you know you're not going to get any overtime out of…"

The words died in his throat when she lifted her head. Her eyes were puffy, her nose red, her face tear-streaked. In two steps he rounded her desk and knelt next to her chair.

"Crickitt, what happened? Are you hurt?" In a panic, he reached for her shoulders, searching for signs of injury even as he reminded himself she couldn't have suffered anything more serious than a paper cut.

"You could say that," she said, her voice choked with tears. She rubbed her fingers under the hollows of her eyes and sniffed, looking everywhere but at him. "I had...an unwelcome phone call."

"From your ex-husband," Shane guessed.

Crickitt gave him a searching look. "Yeah."

That one word was full of longing. Desperate for camaraderie. And he'd gone and kicked open the door, practically inviting her to talk to him about it.

Shane released her shoulders and stood too quickly, causing his head to swim. Oh, how he wished it had been a paper cut. Then he could leave in search of a Band-Aid and escape the emotions pressing down on him from every angle. He was ill equipped to handle his own personal issues, let alone help with hers. He should leave. For both their sakes.

"I'm sorry to barge in," he started, shooting a longing glance at the doorway. Crickitt wiped her hands over her face, looking small and alone. And just like the night he spotted her in the club and felt the pull to comfort her, he couldn't walk away.

Settling awkwardly on the corner of her desk, he plucked a tissue from the box next to him. When she accepted it, he offered her another, not sure what else to do. He reached for a third and she waved him off.

He should say something. But what? Your ex is a jerk? I'm sorry? Everything will be okay? Shane drummed his fingers on his knees, his thoughts racing. He couldn't write a check to solve this problem, and, frankly, he wasn't sure if anything he said or did might make it better.

Crickitt stilled his jittering hands with her palms. "Don't feel like you have to stay, Shane. I'll be fine."

Her words were strong, but her voice was wobbly. "I just"—she looked around the room, lost—"need to go." She tossed the tissues into her wastebasket, gathered a few files into a stack. "I need to get home," she muttered again, rising from her chair.

But she didn't move. Just stood there staring at her hands while tears pooled in her eyes.

Ah, hell.

Acting on instincts he wasn't sure he could trust, Shane pulled her into his arms. She stiffened against him. He did his best to remain calm despite the fact that wrapping his arms around a crying woman was a completely foreign concept.

"It's okay," he murmured to both of them, smoothing a palm over her back. Before his insecurities took flight, she lifted her arms and looped them around his neck.

Shane stroked her back, then her hair, the movements coming more naturally than he expected. Crickitt clung to him, the cries wringing from her lungs causing his heart to lurch.

A wash of anger came over him, directed toward her jag-off ex and whatever he said to make her cry, but he forced his irritation to the side. Crickitt didn't need his anger; she needed his friendship. He held her until her cries ceased, until her breaths evened out.

She didn't loosen her grip but stayed positioned between his legs, her breasts smashed into his chest. Ignoring her soft curves was downright torturous, but he forced himself to focus on giving her what she needed. Moving his palm in lazy circles on her back, he offered assurances of "I'm here" and "You'll be okay."

When she finally shifted, he tried to back away, to give

her space. She was probably embarrassed and wanted a moment to herself to—

The slow upward thrust of Crickitt's fingertips along his scalp stalled his thoughts in their tracks. As each follicle fell back into place with agonizing sluggishness, a new pattern of gooseflesh cropped up on his forearms.

It's an involuntary reaction, he thought, struggling to keep his palms flat on her back rather than crush her against him. *She probably doesn't even know she's*—

A hot breath fanned over his neck, and Shane sucked in one of his own, the muscles in his thighs going as rigid as rebar. Before his rapidly fading self-control hijacked his brain, Shane gripped Crickitt's upper arms to pull her away. He'd offer to get her a glass of water, then find a chair and whip to tame the drove of hormones busily turning him into a horny teenager.

"Sweetheart . . ." His voice was strained, tight.

Crickitt moaned what sounded like "no" before knotting her hands into his hair, tugging his head back and searing the side of his neck with an openmouthed kiss.

Shane's nerve endings tripped like breakers. Without his consent, his hands hauled her closer as she devoured and nipped his neck. Then suckled his earlobe, her breaths coming out in short pants. By the time she blazed a mind-numbing path to his jaw, leaving his skin damp and cool, Shane's good intentions were a far-gone memory.

Until he opened his eyes and took in their surroundings. The fluorescents overhead hummed quietly, a light blinked on her phone to show a waiting voice mail. And here he was, *the boss*, sitting on his personal assistant's desk, taking advantage of her vulnerability.

Using the sprinkler system overhead as a focal point, he gripped her arms and firmly but gently hauled her away from his body. Stormy blue eyes met his, heat and sincerity and tenderness mingling in their depths, and whatever practical, pragmatic argument he'd cooked up dispersed like steam from an overheated kettle.

Her plush, full lips crashed into his, and with a low moan of defeat, Shane threaded his fingers into her crown of curls and tugged her mouth to his.

This. This is what he should have done the first night she tentatively pecked him on the lips. He'd allowed guilt to hold him back, resisting with everything he had, but now that he'd given in to the temptation eating him alive, he couldn't stop. Her hands rested on his thighs as she tilted her head back, her lips pliant and soft beneath his. She silently conceded control and he took it, sliding his tongue along her lips, begging for entrance.

One taste. Just one taste.

She obliged and his tongue swept into her mouth. She tasted of peppermint and thick, hot passion. She gave as good as she got, gripping his tie and dragging him closer, her teeth scraping his bottom lip. She freed the knot with a sharp yank, and he heard the rasp of silk as she slipped the tie through his collar and tossed it aside.

He grabbed for her shirt with both hands, untucking it even as Crickitt worked the buttons on his shirt with shaky, impatient fingers. Her hands were everywhere, and his abdomen clenched, muscles tightening under the nip of her short nails.

Returning the favor, Shane slid his hands under the hem of her shirt, over her contracting and expanding rib cage, and closed his palms over her breasts. A breath hissed between her teeth, and her mouth was on him again, tongue dipping into the hollow of his throat. Beneath his hands, her nipples hardened and Shane plucked them with eager fingers.

Crickitt snapped to attention, mouth leaving his with an audible pop as she straightened her spine.

Too far, Shane realized a second too late.

Moving his hands to her waist, he inhaled a ragged breath, lust fogging his brain and stalling his thoughts. The heat in Crickitt's eyes dimmed, replaced by shuttered, shell-shocked awareness. He licked his lips, an apology forming in the depths of his throat.

She beat him to it.

"I—I'm so sorry." Touching her kiss-swollen lips, she surveyed his open shirt before turning mournful eyes up at him. "I—there's n-no excuse—," she stuttered, fussing over his shirt buttons.

She was apologizing to him? Shane watched her jerky movements, amused by her clumsy attempt to dress him and regain her composure. He tamped down a budding smile as his hands left her baby-smooth skin. Couldn't she see there was no way to go back? Not now, not after that game-changing kiss. Brows meeting in the middle in deep concentration, she tried but failed to pull the last button through the hole. He stilled her hands with one of his, pressing them to his chest. His heart gave a dangerous leap as she met his eyes. She looked cute and slightly muddled with her hair tousled in the pattern of his fingers. And again, he felt powerless to resist her.

"Shane," she whispered.

He didn't let her finish, trapping her words with his lips. He caught the back of her neck with one palm but held her gently, giving her every opportunity to pull away. She didn't. He swept his tongue into her mouth in triumph, stroking her for long, breath-stealing seconds, until he felt her go limp beneath him, her hands bunching the front of his shirt weakly.

He pulled away and found her looking up at him drowsily, her eyelids at half-mast. "You're a great kisser," she murmured. Then a hue of pink stole her cheeks, and her eyes went wide. "Sorry."

Shane allowed himself to laugh. "Would you stop apologizing? You're making me feel bad." He placed a final, full-lipped kiss square on the center of her mouth. "I should have done that a long time ago."

A vision assaulted him: her beneath him, naked, willing, tangled in his bedsheets. Reluctantly, he pushed the thought away. She could be brimming with regret for all he knew. He was her boss, signed her paychecks, made her schedule...special-ordered the desk he was sitting on. And while it would only take the slightest nudge to convince her to come home with him, he didn't want her regretting that, either.

"I...guess I should get home," Crickitt said, straightening her clothing and glancing around as if she was lost.

He heard the question in her voice, felt the longing mirroring his own. She was *asking* if she should get home. Giving him every opportunity to suggest she come home with him. And he wanted to, so badly. Wanted to pretend there was nothing standing between them. But if they were going to do this, it had to be handled delicately. He scanned her face, her soft features. She needed to be handled delicately.

"Yeah. Me, too," he said, sympathizing with the flash of disappointment in her eyes.

With superhuman strength, he left her side, taking one leaden step after another. Away from her, he didn't feel stronger, only weaker. And filled with so much regret he could hardly breathe.

You're doing the right thing.

"I'd better be," he growled under his breath.

CHAPTER SEVENTEEN

$\mathscr{S}$econds turned into minutes as Crickitt came to the slow realization that Shane was giving her some space. Soon she'd have to face him again and relive the moment she jumped him like a cheetah on a baby gazelle.

She pressed the heel of her hand to her forehead. *That would be twice now. Twice you've thrown yourself at your boss.*

Only this time, she'd lost her composure at work. *At work.* The one place she should be able to control her emotions.

If not for Ronald's poor timing she would be at home, nuking a frozen dinner and settling in for a *Texas Chainsaw Massacre* marathon. Despite what had just happened between her and Shane, Ronald's final words before she hung up reverberated around her like a Sunday-morning church bell. She didn't know if she could forget it or ever forgive him for saying it.

"Still reeling, I see?"

She jerked her attention to the doorway. Shane leaned against it, strong and solid, his black leather bag hooked on one shoulder. Faint red scratches decorated his neck, and a thread missing its button poked from the collar of his shirt.

My gosh. I attacked him.

Feeling a swell of guilt, she opened her mouth to apologize but swallowed it. Still, she couldn't keep from muttering, "Your neck..."

"Love bite?" He rubbed at the spot, making it redder. "Good thing tomorrow's Saturday. This would have been fun to explain in the Townsend meeting."

She gaped at him, a humorless laugh eking out of her throat. "You're impossible."

"You started it," he reminded her with a lopsided grin.

Shane stepped into her office, reclaiming his perch at the corner of her desk and choking the atmosphere with his overwhelming presence. Was that shame or lust burning a hole in her stomach? Hard to tell.

It wasn't her fault Shane's arrival happened to be perfectly in sync with her pending nervous breakdown.

"We should talk," he said, his voice a low husk.

He sounded so serious, her heart stalled, then pounded extra hard to make up for the missed beat. The last thing she wanted was to talk. She wanted to pretend the kiss had never happened, to be in blissful denial. She wanted to—

"I'd like to take you on a date."

Crickitt felt her eyebrows rise.

"You've left me no choice," he continued. "Since you singlehandedly nullified our friendship pact."

She gaped at him. Was he saying she'd seduced him? Hadn't Ronald just accused her of being lackluster in the bedroom? Yet Shane, a potent mixture of masculinity and sex appeal, wanted to take her on a date?

How could two people see her so differently? And who would she rather be? The barely tolerated wife of a banker, or lover of a primal, potent man whose knees she'd weakened with just a kiss.

There was a heady, downright delicious prospect. Shane wanted more. Shane wanted *her*.

Shane's mouth twitched in what she recognized as him barely holding back a smile. He stood abruptly and walked into the hallway. "How about tomorrow?"

She didn't answer right away. The idea excited her as much as it intimidated her. Was she even equipped for a date with someone like Shane August? Shouldn't she have a few practice dates with men who weren't billionaires? Her gaze flickered over his body. Or built like underwear models?

He lifted his brow at her silence, holding out a palm. "Well?"

Crickitt had never been a fan of futility, and no amount of stalling would change the answer pressing against her lips. She reached for her mailbag and extinguished the light in her office before stepping forward and putting her hand in his.

Shane intertwined their fingers, and their steps automatically aligned as they walked through the abandoned waiting room. He stopped to press the call button on the elevator, and the doors slid open.

She cast one final glance at the threshold, her mind whirling. Crossing the literal line from lobby to lift would, in a way, also be crossing the one drawn between coworkers and lovers.

"I promise to stay on my own side of the car," Shane said at her hesitation. "Think you can keep your hands to yourself, Ms. Day?"

A burble of laughter burst from her lips at his challenge. How did this man make her feel powerful and confident when Ronald made her feel exactly the opposite? Shane dropped her hand to press the button for the ground floor, and Crickitt took a bold step in his direction.

Startled, Shane flattened against the wall, an amused expression on his face as Crickitt poked a finger into his lapel.

"The next move, *Mr. August*," she said, issuing her own dare in a low voice, "is yours."

CHAPTER EIGHTEEN

Crickitt frantically searched her sparse, bland closet in search of something to wear for her date with Shane this morning. He'd promised to pick her up at eleven, instructing her to "wear something comfortable." Rows of "comfortable" clothes greeted her. All dull-colored and more function than form. Then she came across the peachy-colored blouse Sadie had complimented her on the other day.

And suddenly, she knew just what to wear. Digging through her dresser drawers, she finally found the bright coral-colored tee and white shorts Sadie bought her for her birthday. She ripped off the tags and put them on, admiring herself in the bedroom mirror. The color gave her cheeks a rosy glow, and the shorts did wonders for her butt. And, for a change, there was a chance of someone other than her noticing both of those details.

She slipped on her tennis shoes and watched for her date out the kitchen window. A gentle breeze blew the leaves on the trees and sent puffy clouds sailing across the late June sky. Instead of Thomas's limo, a sleek, topless black sports car growled into a guest parking space.

Shane unfolded himself from his car, looking wind-tossed and casual in a pair of plaid shorts and an olive shirt. Crickitt lapped up the sight of him as he strode to her door on long, strong legs leading down to a pair of sturdy leather sandals.

Unbelievable. Even his feet were attractive.

She pulled the door open before he had the chance to knock. His T-shirt strained the width of his chest, and it took her a few seconds to redirect her eyes to his face. He gave her a toothy grin.

"Keep that up, we won't make it off this porch." He brushed her body with his eyes. "You look gorgeous."

So do you, she thought, gawking at him hungrily.

"Thank you." She slid her hands down her shorts self-consciously. Were they this short when she put them on earlier? Palming a small purse, she stepped outside and closed the door behind her.

Shane didn't reach for her hand or move to kiss her, and Crickitt couldn't decide if she was glad about that or not. He opened the passenger door.

"You drove," she said, sinking into a butter-yellow leather seat.

"You didn't think I'd bring a limo to our first date, did you?"

She did, but she didn't say so.

In the driver's seat, Shane slid his sunglasses on and revved the engine. The car rumbled like a live animal. "Ready, Freddy?"

She nodded.

"If you need a hat, there's one in the glove compartment," he said.

She decided to spare Shane her Medusa head and pulled the baseball cap over her hair. After a few seconds of his unabashed staring, she sent him a questioning glance.

Tugging on the cap, he swore lightly. "You're too attractive for your own good, Crickitt."

Shane navigated the convertible through highway traffic with speedy caution. His hair whipped in the wind as he moved his lips to a song on the radio. He had it all wrong. It was Shane, *not her*, who was too attractive for his own good.

How about a date with a devastatingly charming billionaire? Don't mind if I do.

"What are you smiling about?" Shane yelled over the music.

She shook her head. Shane snapped his attention to the road and cars around them, gauged his speed, then leaned over and stole a brief kiss.

Memories of last night flooded over her, the firm insistence of his lips and the feel of his hands grazing her rib cage. As if reading her mind, he shot her a primal, dangerous grin. Whatever he had planned for them today, she hoped she could handle it.

Ten minutes later they pulled into John Adams Reserve. Crickitt held on to the door handle for stability as Shane whipped into a parking space. He killed the engine and she tossed the hat into the backseat and tousled her hair into some semblance of shape. "A park," she said, taking in their surroundings as he opened her door for her.

Picnic areas were alive with smoking grills, their inhabitants milling around ice-filled coolers or lounging at brown wooden tables. Kids and adults dotted a lake in the distance, some fishing off the dock, others from boats. A few dogs chased balls and Frisbees along the water's edge.

"Hope you like the great outdoors," he said.

"I do." She accepted his hand and he helped her out. "Kind of surprised you do."

"You underestimate me." He tsked. "I like that in a woman."

After nearly an hour of traversing a rocky hillside, navigating around logs and boulders and through dense brush and trees, Crickitt realized Shane was right. She *had* underestimated him, and *overestimated* her level of physical fitness. Her calves screamed, her steps slowing as they came to yet another incline.

She leaned against a tree trunk to catch her breath, remembering too late she'd worn white. Stepping away, she dusted the back of her shorts.

"Let me know if you need help with that," Shane offered.

"Are you always this forward?" she asked, but her reprimand held little threat.

"Not always."

"I think I need a break."

He grimaced as he approached. "But we're so close."

She looked over his shoulder where a hill as steep as the side of a pyramid loomed.

Giving her a brief assessment, he turned away and squatted down. "Get on."

She took one look at his broad back and shook her head. "No way."

"Why not?"

She crossed her arms. "Because…" She stopped short of the litany of obvious references. She was five five, not exactly petite, and she had a healthy curve to her hips and backside. She was far from overweight, but neither was she rail thin. "Because," she repeated.

"Lame," Shane said, standing to face her. "You're underestimating me again. Tell you what, you can either get on my back, or I'll toss you over my shoulder and carry you the rest of the way." He flashed her a smile. "I dare you to call me on that." He bent down and patted his back with both hands.

She believed him. Believed he'd carry her off into the woods like Tarzan while she kicked her legs uselessly. Putting her hands on his shoulders, she said a prayer and hopped, throwing her legs around his waist.

He locked his arms beneath her knees and stood easily, muttering, "Lightweight."

Arms hooked around his neck, Shane ponied her up the trail, sidestepping a low-hanging branch. "Watch your head," he told her. She ducked, pressing even closer against him, feeling the rumble of his voice in her stomach when he spoke again. "Don't want to add clotheslining to our first date."

Their first date. The night she met Shane at the club, she never could have imagined riding on his back in the woods or kissing him until he stole the oxygen from her lungs.

"Here we are." He lowered her to the ground. She landed not-so-gracefully, and he grasped her arm to steady her. The force of his charismatic smile shook her to the core.

They crested one small bump of a hill, the sound of flowing water growing louder as they approached. A waterfall stood in the distance, cascading over a rocky ledge of moss and smoothed rock before breaking into a shallow pool below.

"It's beautiful," she said.

It was also hard to believe the Kodak-worthy spot wasn't teeming with sightseers. Then a man stepped out from behind a tree and she understood why. Apparently, the falls were guarded by Andre the Giant.

"Leo," Shane greeted him. "Meet Crickitt."

Leo stepped forward and swallowed Crickitt's hand in his, his smile lighting his oddly large features. "I like your name," he told her, releasing her hand. He nodded to Shane. "It's ready."

Then Leo stepped past her, a roll of yellow Caution tape in one beefy mitt, and began stringing it around the trees.

"What's he doing?" she asked Shane.

Shane clasped her hand, leading her closer to the falls. "Giving us some privacy."

CHAPTER NINETEEN

Sunlight streamed through a maze of tree branches down to a sprawling red-and-white-checkered blanket in a clearing near the water. A traditional woven basket sat in its center, and next to it a sweating ice bucket holding a bottle of wine or champagne.

"See what your slogging through the wilderness has earned you?" Shane sat and reached for the bottle.

"A bit early for cocktails, isn't it?" she asked. "If we finish that I'll never make it back to the car."

There was a sound of cracking plastic as he twisted the cap. "From grape juice?" He spun the label toward her. Sure enough, the contents of the bottle were an innocuous blend of white grapes and carbonation.

He handed her a flimsy plastic wine cup and she drank, the bubbles dancing on her tongue, sweet and tart.

"Next you're going to tell me you don't want to eat lobster and caviar," he said.

Crickitt fought the grimace dying to produce itself on

her face. She didn't want to appear ungrateful. Or picky. "I'll eat whatever you brought," she said diplomatically.

Shane narrowed his eyes, pausing with one hand in the basket. "Really?"

"Yes." She wasn't sure which of them she was trying to convince. Oceanic arthropods and eggs from a fish made her stomach clench, and not in a good way.

He lifted her offering out of the basket. A cellophane-wrapped sandwich sat in the center of his palm.

"Ham and cheese?" she asked.

"Peanut butter and jelly," he answered.

Along with PB&J, he'd packed potato chips and carrot sticks with ranch dressing for dipping. Dessert was a container filled with chocolate chip cookies. Crickitt expected to like them—they were chocolate chip cookies, after all, nature's perfect food. But "like" wasn't a strong enough word for the moist, chewy morsels.

Swallowing the last bite, she reached for another, holding it between them. "Where did you get these?"

"There is a bakery in New York City called—"

"You had these shipped from New York City?" She eyed the cookie with newfound reverence.

"No. But it is their recipe."

She took another bite, savoring the subtle nutty flavor beneath the bold richness of the dark chocolate. "Think you could ask your house staff to whip up a batch for me?"

He chuffed. "I baked those myself, thank you very much."

She couldn't square the image of Shane in an apron with flour on his hands with the sleek, suited powerhouse he portrayed at work. And yet, the homier vision of him held just as much sex appeal.

"You're full of surprises," she said.

"My mom taught me how to bake." He fell quiet the way he did whenever the subject of his parents came up, then turned his head and squinted into the sunlight.

"Well, you're lucky, my mom is a terrible baker," she said, smoothing over the awkward moment. "I once had a birthday cake made entirely of stacked Little Debbie Oatmeal Pies."

Shane smiled.

"Which would have been fine, had she taken them out of their plastic wrappers first."

He had a great laugh, and she couldn't help joining in, feeling a mix of relief and pride that she'd cheered him up.

She polished off the last bite of her cookie, unnerved when she noticed him staring at her mouth. She touched her lips self-consciously. "Do I have chocolate on my face or something?"

"Let me get it."

Before she could wipe away the incriminating splotch, Shane stopped her hand. Leaning in, he swiped the corner of her mouth with the tip of his tongue, then covered it with a kiss. She allowed her eyes to slide shut, savoring the feel of his mouth as he repeated the action on the other side and then moved to her top lip, then the bottom.

Crickitt opened her eyes drowsily.

"Sorry," he murmured, pulling away. "I lied. You didn't have chocolate on your face. I just wanted to kiss you." He hoisted an eyebrow. "Hope you're not mad."

Mad? Not quite. Drunk from his potent kisses, maybe. Wildly turned on, definitely. She found Shane downright irresistible whenever he dropped his guard, which he seemed to do a lot around her. At work and with clients she'd noticed this "consummate professional" side of his personality. But when he was with her, away from office obligations, he was relaxed. Open.

Shane rested his elbow on one elevated knee, demonstrating her point. His eyebrow lifted the slightest bit, and she knew he was about to tease her. "Your move," he said.

The lingering taste of Shane and chocolate mingled on her lips. And she wanted more.

Lifting from her cross-legged position on the blanket, Crickitt knelt in front of him, holding his eyes with hers. Heart leaping to her throat, she leaned in and kissed him. He returned her kiss with gentle pressure. Scooting closer, she clutched the hair at his nape and captured his lips again.

When his warm fingers gripped her waist, her breath hitched. Shane moved his hand away. "Sorry."

She moved it back, continuing to tease him with her tongue and convince him he had nothing to be sorry for. He didn't need to be told twice. Wrapping her in his arms, he hauled her onto his lap where he continued his slow, intentional exploration of her mouth.

She'd missed this. Mutual attraction. Being held, pampered, adored. Being kissed by a man because he wanted her, rather than out of a sense of marital duty. She'd forgotten the excitement of being new to someone. The way it caused her heart to swell against her rib cage as if it were ready to burst. Settling onto Shane's lap, she enjoyed the luxury of it, allowing her own hands to travel. The sounds of nature slowly grounded her, and she ended the lengthy lip-lock in favor of much-needed oxygen.

He peered at her under thick, dark lashes, his lips

parted and damp from her kisses. She moved in for another taste—she couldn't help it—and shifted on his lap. Then she tensed as his hard length pressed into her inner thigh. Drawing away, she met his eye.

Shane's lips tipped into a rueful grin. "You weren't supposed to notice that." He clasped her hips.

"Kind of hard to miss."

He threw his head back and laughed. "I'm glad I hired you," he said, tucking a curl behind her ear.

His light comment brought with it a heavy reality. Crickitt winced.

"Poor choice of words," Shane said. He slid another curl away from her eye and watched her for a second. "Your brain's working some overtime, there."

Overtime. Another poorly chosen word. It was easy to suspend reality while they were hidden beneath a cage of trees, the waterfall splashing behind them drowning out any pragmatic argument. But what about after? When she returned to being his subordinate and he was in charge of giving her an annual review? What about her coworkers, who would soon notice their lingering gazes or whisper about how often she and Shane were in one another's offices?

Instead of denying the obvious, Crickitt fixed him with a look and asked the question marinating in her brain. "What are we doing?"

* * *

This conversation came sooner than he preferred. Like never. Never would have been better.

Shane chased her question around his head and tried to

figure out what, exactly, she meant by it. Was she trying to backtrack? Did she think they were moving too fast? Was she trying to define what happened, or what was going to happen?

Crickitt faced the falls, chewing her lip and arriving at a God-only-knew-what conclusion.

He'd been hell-bent on keeping his attraction to her to himself…until last night, anyway. Crickitt tearing at his clothes and devouring his mouth had him tossing his restraint out with his good sense. And now that he knew how good it felt to be close to her, to hold her, to kiss that luscious pink mouth of hers…well, he had no interest in backing off. But he wouldn't press forward if it wasn't what she wanted.

Crickitt opened her mouth to speak, her eyebrows bowing.

Please don't say you regret it.

"Is work going to be weird?" she asked.

Shane sighed, a sound of pure relief. "It doesn't have to be."

Something flashed in her eyes. Shane wished he could read her expressions, or her mind. That would be handy. It wasn't as if he'd never had a conversation like this before. He preferred to outline expectations before getting involved with a woman. It was okay to have some fun, or in Crickitt's case what he suspected would be *a whole lot* of fun, just as long as neither of them expected something permanent. Even if that's what he wanted, he knew he couldn't live up to the promise of forever.

He watched her for another beat, coming to an uncomfortable realization. She might say no. And wouldn't that suck?

"Say it. Say whatever it is you're thinking," Crickitt said, clasping his hand. "Before I go nuts."

He was thinking how he didn't want to miss the opportunity to continue what they'd started. "Don't worry about work," he said instead.

Her eyes downcast, she stroked his hand in both of hers. "And outside of work?"

For a second, no words came. He knew what she was asking. She was asking if they would be exclusive, eventually move in together. Meet each other's families, give Christmas gifts with both their names on them. He couldn't continue to let her assume that's where they were headed. If he was a different man, with a different past... but he wasn't. And telling her would risk losing her, but she deserved to know.

"We'd keep it casual," he hedged.

"Casual." She dropped his hand, moved away from him as if being near him was suddenly undesirable.

His stomach sank. *Way to go, jerk.*

"I don't think it would be a good idea..." Shane swallowed thickly. There was no good way to say it. He'd just have to blurt it out and hope for the best. "I want to be with you, Crickitt." He reached out to her with his eyes, too afraid if he touched her she'd recoil. "But I can't... I'm not able to make any promises about the future."

Shane pressed his lips together, wanting to take every word of it back. It was ugly and graceless. It was also the truth.

"I see," she said, her voice hard.

She gave him a hot look. But not one filled with passion, more like fury. Or like she was attempting to burn a hole through his head using only the power of her mind.

"I don't consider sex casual," she said. "Ever." She stood in a rush, and Shane jumped to his feet. She glared up at him as she spoke. "I'm good enough to sleep with, but not if messy feelings get involved? Sounds eerily like my marriage."

Pain like a thousand sharp needles pierced his heart as he realized he'd not only hurt her, but hurt her in the same way her ex-husband had. The fact was Crickitt was good enough; it was Shane who was lacking. How could she not see that? "Let me rephrase—"

"Don't bother." Crickitt stood. "It's better I know up front."

It sounded far less noble when she said it. But what choice did he have?

Shane gathered the picnic supplies while Crickitt folded the blanket in silence. He took it from her, carrying it down the trail as they walked back to the car. She didn't speak, only trotted several feet ahead of him, eyes straight ahead.

Already he missed her closeness, her willingness to touch him, even casually. But he'd efficiently removed that possibility, and while disappointed, he shouldn't have been surprised by her reaction. That he was only gave merit to what he'd told her. He was not equipped for a relationship.

At the car, he deposited the basket and blanket in the trunk before sliding onto the seat and shoving the key in the ignition. He didn't start it, only sat there, watching the back of Crickitt's head as she focused on a spot off in the distance.

Finally, the words that had been simmering in his gut during the walk back boiled over. "I'm sorry."

She looked surprised to hear his voice. "Like you said last night, I started it."

"That's not what I meant." He'd played this all wrong. Crickitt wasn't some shallow girl looking for a fling. And he hoped she didn't think that's how he saw her. She was transparent and vulnerable. Honest and complex. Qualities he wasn't sure how to handle...especially when rolled into one woman. Was it any wonder he'd royally blown it back there? "I should have—"

"Shane? Let's not autopsy what happened, okay? Monday things will be back to normal."

He nodded, accepting the loss, and put the car in reverse.

Normal. Whatever the hell that was.

* * *

Pride goeth before the fall, Crickitt thought, recalling her reaction on Saturday. Like it or not, Shane was honest with her. And that was more than she could say for herself. Not that she'd been dishonest, per se, but she'd certainly been inconsistent. One minute, she'd climbed him like a cat on a curtain, the next she was oiling the lock on her chastity belt.

Shane breezed into her office, the scent of his aftershave whirling around her and causing Crickitt to swallow a lump of regret. Why did he have to look so good today? His sleeves were rolled casually to his elbows, showcasing corded forearms, and his face was shaved smooth.

It was torturous to think of what could have been, but she'd thought about it anyway, succumbing to a weekend's worth of self-imposed manual labor. She'd been scrubbing her refrigerator's shelves lamenting the action her prim lacy duvet *wasn't* seeing. Then she'd shined every window inside and out and wished her muscles were sore for a far naughtier reason.

Shane folded the day's agenda and stuffed it in his pocket. As if in tune with her thoughts he asked, "Do anything fun this weekend?"

You mean besides what I did with you?

"If you consider housework 'fun,'" she said.

"Housework, huh? I baked."

His comment brought with it thoughts of unrushed chocolate kisses...the ones that came from Shane's lips rather than tiny foil wrappers. Her heart sped beneath her breast, desire taking the place of good sense.

"Baking is a great way to burn off sexual frustration. Like housework," he added with a wink. Hoisting a thumb over his shoulder he said, "Pies and cookies in the break room."

How did he do that? Look so disarming while admitting he'd entertained the same fantasies she'd had about him over the weekend. This was her chance.

Eat crow or forever hold her peace.

She was tired of being pragmatic and practical. So far all her careful plotting had gotten her was divorced and temporarily jobless. If an incredibly attractive, single man wanted to take her to bed—an idea that made her hair curl even more—why shouldn't she be allowed to say yes?

"I've been thinking," she said, eyes on the pen in her hands. "I'd like to have some more of those cookies." In case he missed her double entendre, Crickitt looked up and reiterated, "I may have been remiss on Saturday... when I said no." Her heart tapped out an SOS, but she refused to take back her words.

On second, third, and *fifteenth* thought, what Shane had offered at the waterfall wasn't all that unreasonable. He was a busy CEO working five to six days a week. That didn't leave much time for a girlfriend. And, if she were being honest, it was too soon after her imploding marriage to consider a relationship. Keeping things casual didn't have to mean they didn't care about each other, only that they wouldn't have impractical expectations.

Shane came to the corner of her desk and sat, reminding her of the passionate kiss they'd shared. How he'd held her while she cried. How it felt to have his arms around her. How charming and funny he'd been.

Shane touched her arm, sending a rush of warmth through her body, buoying her hopes. Then he spoke, sinking them.

"No, Crickitt, you were right." He spread his hands. "And hey, look at us, practically back to normal already."

He gave her a friendly pat. "It'll pass."

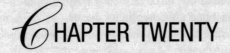

CHAPTER TWENTY

 It'll pass?

It wasn't what he wanted to say. What he wanted to say was, *Yes, Crickitt, you were wrong. Let's take the rest of the day off so I can show you how wrong you were.*

Okay, that wasn't quite it, either. But some-thing...something other than agreeing that their sleeping together was a bad idea.

Which it was.

Shane growled and stood from his desk, pushing his hands through his hair in frustration.

It wasn't like him to waffle over decisions. He weighed the options, came to a conclusion, and never looked back. Instinct and life experiences granted him a solid gut he could trust. Even in the most difficult of situations.

As he'd been so often lately, Shane was hit with a memory of his father.

It was a Friday afternoon when Shane learned of his father's lung cancer. He may never have found out if it wasn't for his father losing his house. Sean August called to ask Shane for a loan to "float him through to the next month." When Shane asked what happened to the last loan, he found out through a series of shouts and swearwords that it had gone to pay for chemo.

Angry that he hadn't known sooner, Shane was half tempted to ship the old man off to a care facility and let him be a belligerent pain in someone else's ass. Over the last twenty years Shane saw his father exactly twice a year, and only because Shane insisted.

Despite their virtually nonexistent relationship, Shane had relented, opening his house to his father, inviting him to live the remainder of his days with him. If Sean appreciated it, he never said. Shane avoided Sean's side of the house as much as possible, until his father's cancer progressed. Once he was too weak to speak, Shane sat by his side. Accusations and apologies clogged his throat, but Shane said none of them. His father's clouded, watery eyes held judgment until the end.

It hadn't been the easy thing and sure as hell hadn't been the convenient thing, but it was the right thing. And Shane knew it.

Like hiring Crickitt was the right thing. And subsequently, preserving their professional relationship was the right thing. It was his first decision, the right decision, and he should have stuck with it.

He sat in his chair with a huff and keyed in his computer's password. "I'm an idiot," he grumbled.

"You have your moments."

Lori LaRouche stepped through his open office door and shut it behind her, walking through his office like a model on a runway. She lowered herself into a guest chair and gingerly crossed one lithe leg over the other. "Have a minute?" she asked, her painted red lips parting into a predatory grin.

"You could make an appointment."

"You could make time for an old friend," she countered.

He'd never been good at letting people down, especially women. It was one reason he didn't get into relationships. He didn't have to end them, or worry that they might end in abject tragedy, if they never started. But Lori was the one to let him down not so gently all those years ago. Lately, he worried he'd have to return the favor.

"I'm here on business, peanut," she teased with a wink. "You can relax. I won't pull a Mrs. Robinson cougar thing on you." She sent an admiring gaze down his body. "Not that we both wouldn't enjoy it."

"What can I do for you?" Shane asked, adding, "Professionally speaking."

Lori's smile was at odds with the sadness in her eyes. Shane knew she'd never married. And he'd never seen her with a regular companion. He wondered if she was lonely, and if in fifteen years, he'd be just like her.

"Good boy, get down to business," she said, pulling a notebook out of her handbag. "I have a few ideas regarding my makeup line."

CHAPTER TWENTY-ONE

The warm trill of female laughter followed by the rumble of Shane's voice wafted through his closed office door. Crickitt paused on her way back from the fax machine, tempted to press her ear to the wood and find out what was so darn funny. Whoever she was, she sounded dazzled. Shane had his charm-o-meter dialed up to ten.

Another ripple of laughter permeated the air.

Maybe eleven.

Crickitt curled her lip, nearly hissing at the door before stomping into her own office. But she'd had her chance, hadn't she? She'd been kissing him, and he'd kissed her back. So pleasantly distracted by his clever mouth, she willingly stepped over the line before remembering she'd been the one to draw it.

Besides, she justified, stacking a pile of papers and stapling them with inflated importance, she'd likely spared herself the humiliation following an office fling. Who knew how Shane defined "casual"? Casual to him might mean Crickitt in his bed one night followed by a revolving door of other women.

She rejected the visual of Shane as a billionaire playboy the second she thought it. His little picnic speech never hinted at the fact he wanted to sleep around. He just didn't want her getting too comfortable. Maybe so he wouldn't have to dredge up the courage to dump her a decade later like Ronald had.

Her cell phone rang and she latched on to Sadie's incoming call like a lifeline. "Tell me to stop worrying incessantly."

"Stop worrying incessantly," Sadie parroted. "Is this about your hot boss?"

Crickitt needlessly lowered her voice. "I'm not answering that question."

"Don't waste your time," Sadie said, a hard edge outlining her normally hard voice. "All men are bastards."

She was tempted to agree.

"Did something happen between you and Aiden?" Crickitt asked.

Sadie was quiet for so long, Crickitt checked to see if her phone dropped the call.

"I called to tell you I can't do drinks tomorrow," Sadie said.

"Is everything okay?" Crickitt's Spidey senses were tingling.

"Of course. I have to work, that's all," Sadie snapped.

Concern overtook her need to be polite. "And you and Aiden...?" she pressed.

"Are no more," Sadie said tersely. "It had to end sooner or later."

Crickitt knew her best friend was hiding something. There was a ribbon of sadness beneath Sadie's attitude, she could feel it. Shane stepped into her office before she could quiz her further. She uttered a quick apology and promised, "We'll talk later."

She placed the phone on the cradle as Shane introduced the woman at his side. "Crickitt, this is Lori LaRouche, owner of—"

"LaRouche Cosmetics," Crickitt finished, standing to extend a palm.

Lori removed her hand from Shane's arm, almost reluctantly, and shook Crickitt's hand.

"I'm familiar with your brand, Ms. LaRouche. All natural, no animal testing, chemical-free. It's an impressive line of skin care."

Lori curled her lip, assessing Crickitt as she would a spider skittering across her vanity.

"Lori has some ideas for her marketing campaign," Shane said.

The request was unusual. Established clients were typically filtered to specialized teams within the company. Shane's expertise was in landing clients, and he'd made it clear time and again that was his primary focus. Evidently he was making an exception for Lori LaRouche.

"Certainly," Crickitt said, giving no hint she found the request odd. She gestured for Lori to sit in the chair across from her desk. "Ms. LaRouche, should I call down for coffee?"

"Lori," she corrected. "No coffee," she said, and then added with a feral curve of her lips, "but I'd love a martini."

"I'll leave you to it," Shane said, patting the door frame before heading back to his own office.

Crickitt lifted her phone and rang Keena's desk. She wasn't sure how easy it would be to scrounge up a bottle of gin, but surely Keena could—

"Front desk," Keena answered.

"Hi, it's Crickitt." She sent a smile at Lori, but the meticulously dressed client was busy examining her nails and ignoring Crickitt entirely. "Is there any way I could get a—"

"Three blue cheese olive martini, extra dirty, straight up?" Keena finished.

"Um, yes, actually."

"Coming right up."

Minutes later, Keena arrived in the office balancing a very full glass in one hand. She placed a black cocktail napkin on Crickitt's desk and rested the glass on top of it. Lori watched her every move, somehow managing to slide a look of disgust down her nose even though Keena was standing over her. Crickitt was beginning to think it was the way she looked at everyone.

"Thank you, Keena," Crickitt said when it was apparent Lori wasn't going to.

"You are welcome, Ms. Day." Keena flashed one of her dazzling smiles, not looking the least bit bothered or intimidated, then turned to leave.

Maybe it's just me.

After Keena had gone, Lori took a leisurely sip of her drink and let out a harrumph. "This will do," she said on a heavy sigh.

Clearly, Lori LaRouche was used to getting what she wanted. A thought that made Crickitt scowl when she thought of Lori and Shane.

"Now," Lori said to Crickitt, "let's talk."

Crickitt dutifully pulled a yellow pad in front of her and clicked her pen.

"Number one," Lori began. "The labels look cheap. Get rid of the gold. Simple black and white. Number two, the bags. Earth-friendly and hideously ugly should not be synonyms. Kraft brown is for grocery bags, not LaRouche Cosmetics."

"Got it." Crickitt scribbled the information onto the pad. They sounded like simple requests but would require several quotes from alternate suppliers.

"Last," Lori said, pausing to drink down half of her martini. "Home shopping. I'd like to be on QVC by the end of this summer."

"Home shopping," Crickitt said. "Who's handling that aspect of your marketing?"

"Why, you, of course. I wouldn't hire a company other than Shane's for my baby. He's the best."

"We appreciate your business," Crickitt said, ignoring the suggestion lacing Lori's voice. She jotted a note on her yellow pad to Google how to negotiate a television deal.

"You're pretty."

Crickitt lifted her head and met the older woman's shrewd, dark eyes. "Um, thank you." Crickitt could have paid her a similar compliment. Lori was beautiful.

"I always wanted Shane to settle down with a nice girl," she said in a motherly fashion.

"Oh, we're not—"

Lori made a rude noise and waved one bejeweled hand dismissively. "Don't even. That boy has been mouthwatering for ten years," she said, her voice trilling in a *not-so*-motherly fashion. Then Lori said something that drove Crickitt's suspicions home. And parked them in the detached garage. "He'd be worth it, you know. Even if you lose this job. Although, I suspect if he found the right girl"—she speared Crickitt with a look that made her want to fidget—"he'd forget about being so damn formal all the time and allow himself to finally enjoy life."

After their meeting concluded, Crickitt saw Lori as far as her office door. Lori promenaded down the corridor and ticked down the stairs in her pointed, heeled shoes. Crickitt felt as if she'd been visited by the ghost of Katharine Hepburn. Or Mae West. She still didn't know if Lori was someone she liked, but she did have an undeniable "I am woman, hear me roar" quality Crickitt could appreciate.

"She's really something, huh?"

She turned from Lori's retreating figure to see Shane leaning on his door frame, his arms crossed over his chest. It wouldn't have surprised her to see interest, even blatant appraisal for Lori, reflected on his face, but as much as she tried to imagine it there, it wasn't. What she saw was admiration. Respect.

It didn't keep a catty remark from tumbling out of her mouth. "She thinks you're *something*, too."

Shane's eyebrows went up and with them the corner of his lips. "You think so?"

Ignoring his fishing, she spun toward her office and tore a page from the legal pad where she'd been making a list of Lori's requests.

Shane stood in front of her desk. "That was a long time ago."

"I don't know what you're talking about," Crickitt said, avoiding his eyes to make unnecessary notes on the paper in front of her.

"Yes, you do."

She forced herself to look at him.

Shane crossed his arms over his chest and regarded her. "There's nothing between us now," he said.

Bristling, she clutched her pen. Was she this transparent? "It wouldn't matter to me if there was."

Shane stared down at her, a scowl on his cleanly shaven face. Crickitt felt her face warm under his scrutiny, abruptly reminding herself that she was his employee. She was *way* overstepping her boundaries. And not in a fun-roll-around-on-a-picnic-blanket way.

"I'm—I didn't mean for that to come out that way," she said. "Your past and Lori's is none of my business. I was out of line. It was…"

She stalled, even though she knew exactly what it was. A surge of jealousy paired with regret. Lori knew what Shane meant by "something casual," and Crickitt was far too unadventurous to find out.

"…unprofessional," she finished.

Shane held her eye for so long, heat crept along her collar. Just when she was sure he'd call her out, he said, "I'm leaving for a meeting in a few minutes."

Instinctively, she glanced at her desk calendar.

"You don't know about it. I'll be out of the office the remainder of the day."

"Okay," she said. She should be relieved Shane was discussing his agenda instead of whatever continued to brew in the air between them. She should be. But she wasn't.

"Feel free to take off early if you need to. You work too much."

She didn't respond, studying his blank face for signs of anger. Or desire. She saw neither.

He peered at the floor for one endless minute before concluding the conversation with a clunky, "Okay, I'll, uh, let you get back to it."

"Okay," she repeated, her chest tightening as he left her office.

Why did she feel like an adolescent whose steady boyfriend just dumped her? She needed to go back to thinking of Shane as her boss, and *only* her boss. Then everything would be fine.

Just fine.

* * *

A prickle of awareness crawled up Crickitt's spine as she stood in the break room stirring soy milk into a fresh mug of coffee. *Shane.*

She started to offer a neutral "good morning," but the words hovered unsaid in her throat.

He approached slowly, taking each step as intentionally as a jungle cat stalking his prey. Which might have sent her hormones into a tizzy if it wasn't for the serious expression on his face. The pleat in his brow matched the crease running down his starched sleeves.

Something was wrong.

"I've arranged a meeting with a firm in Georgia," he said, voice as rigid as his posture.

"Okay."

"They're interested in opening another branch of August Industries."

"That's great." She'd been expecting bad news. Expansion was a good thing, wasn't it?

He clenched his jaw, then concentrated intently on the

task of filling his mug. Without meeting her eye, he mumbled, "It requires a week's worth of travel. Overnights, hotels."

Oh.

Understanding dawned like puzzle pieces sliding together. She'd wondered why he'd been acting weird. He'd ducked out of her office yesterday after the awkward exchange over Lori, and this morning he'd avoided her. Now she understood why. They were going out of town together. And if his body language was anything to go by, he was just as nervous about it as she was.

He leaned a palm on the countertop behind him and stared down at her. When his eyes met hers, they softened, inviting her to him, drawing her in.

Like a moth to the flame...

She took an impulsive step toward him.

Laughter sliced through the air behind her as Keena, and Brigit from legal, stepped into the break room. Their voices hushed as they flicked glances from Crickitt to Shane, who straightened and donned a practiced smile on what Crickitt had come to know as his "business face."

Crickitt pivoted on her heel and busied herself putting the soy milk back into the refrigerator.

Whatever conversation Keena and Brigit were having had died since they walked into the room. They refilled their coffee and tea mugs exchanging forced good mornings while Crickitt and Shane stayed on opposite sides of the room from one another.

When the women left, Crickitt blew out a tormented breath. She hadn't missed the deliberate look Keena had exchanged with Brigit, or the knowing brow Brigit had lifted in response. No, those two definitely hadn't missed the tension crackling in the air between August Industries' CEO and his personal assistant.

Shane had told her not to worry about work if they did embark on a physical relationship, but how could she not? Who knew what Keena and Brigit had said to one another—were already saying to other coworkers—about Crickitt and Shane?

Shane had moved to look out the window, coffee in hand, his eyes focused on something in the distance or maybe nothing at all. She traced the planes of his face, ending on the thick, almost black fan of lashes shielding his eyes. Was he worried she might back out of the trip? That she couldn't handle being close to him after what happened at the waterfall?

Can you?

She'd admit shared meals and traveling together in the confines and seclusion of the back of a limo might provide a few awkward moments, but it wouldn't be different from any other day. Like now. Just being close to him caused her body to tingle with awareness.

Memories of pressing against his chest, the feel of his lips, swamped her. It had been too easy to get lost in the feel and smell of him...

She cleared her throat, prepared to ask when they were leaving.

Shane spoke first. "Do you feel comfortable handling things while I'm away?"

Wait. What?

As if she'd asked the question aloud, he said, "I'm taking Murphy."

Crickitt frowned. "Peter Murphy?"

"Yes." He met her gaze. "Pete is a golfing buddy of one

of the owners. Plus, it would give you the opportunity to get caught up on Lori's requests."

Shane was taking Peter Murphy to Georgia and leaving her here to coddle the whims of his ex-girlfriend? Rather than do what she felt like doing, which was shoot laser beams from her pupils, she forced a smile.

"Sure," she said. "No problem."

"Great," Shane said. Then he blew past her, leaving the room without a backward glance.

CHAPTER TWENTY-TWO

*S*peedos? Seriously?"

Crickitt chuckled at Sadie's observation. Sadie sipped her margarita. The pool bar was crowded, giving them plenty of people watching to do today.

Crickitt, for one, was relieved for the distraction, even if it was Hairy Speedo Guy. Shane and Murphy were probably arriving in Atlanta right about now, a thought that only made her wonder what she'd missed out on staying in Ohio.

"I love Sundays," Sadie mused, leaning back in her lounger. "They're like free days."

Crickitt tilted her head at her friend. When Sadie called to ask her to go with her for a drink and a dip, Crickitt assumed it was because Sadie wanted to talk about Aiden. So far, she'd brought up everything but him.

"Are we pretending nothing is going on with you and Aiden?" Crickitt rolled to her side and studied Sadie's profile.

"That would be nice," she said flatly. Then Sadie turned, her eyes obscured by a giant pair of dark sunglasses. "What do you want to know?"

"What happened?"

She took a breath. "He's pretending he and Harmony are still married because he thinks keeping his mother worry-free gives her a better chance at beating the cancer."

Crickitt blinked as if she'd been slapped. That was a lot of information for one sentence.

"What's going on with you and Hot Boss?" Sadie asked, lifting her drink again.

"You're not going to elaborate?"

"Nope." Sadie's eyebrows rose over the rims of her shades. "So? Hot Boss? Details."

Crickitt thought for a moment. "He took a guy named Peter to Atlanta with him on a business trip instead of me and put me in charge of his ex-girlfriend while he is away."

"Yikes." Then she nodded sagely. "Told you all men were bastards."

Crickitt recapped Lori's conversation from last week. "What do you think she meant by 'he'd be worth it'?"

"That he's amazing in bed."

She was afraid of that.

"So, are you going to sleep with him?" Sadie asked.

"What? No! I mean, that's sort of...off the table."

"Oh, honey, that's never off the table." Sadie slid her glasses into her mane of sun-kissed blond hair and studied her through narrowed eyes. "You're falling for him, aren't you?"

Crickitt laughed, the sound born of nerves and the

need to stall while she thought of something reasonable to say. "Of course not. I might have a crush on him, but that's all." But it wasn't just a crush. And she knew it. "I never should've gone on a date with him."

"You went on a date with him?" Sadie sat up like someone threw a cold glass of water on her bare midriff. "Where did he take you?"

"John Adams Reserve. He packed a picnic. Baked me cookies. Kissed me within an inch of my life." She smiled weakly.

"Aww, that's kind of sweet," Sadie said.

"It was sweet." Until she'd overreacted to his suggestion of casual sex, which, she'd admit, was beginning to sound a lot better than *no sex*. In her defense, her date with Shane was the first date she'd been on in eleven years. It was also the first time in as long since she'd touched her lips to anyone's other than Ronald's. No wonder she'd pulled into her shell like a startled turtle.

"So what's the problem?" Sadie asked.

Me, Crickitt wanted to answer. "We work together. Sleeping together would be a bad idea." And he'd obviously agreed since then, an idea that made her chest ache. He hadn't been gone very long at all, and already she missed him.

"Yes, but it's not like you two can get fired over a fling," Sadie said. "He's in charge."

"Maybe that's what worries me," Crickitt muttered. Shane in charge of her heart, her feelings, her future... now that was worrisome.

"You are entitled to be nervous, you know," Sadie said, her tone softer. "You haven't been divorced all that long. I'm sure you were expecting to date a few jokers before running across some"—she waved a hand as if searching for the words—"billionaire hottie in a thousand-dollar suit."

"Right?" Crickitt wholeheartedly agreed. "It's a big adjustment."

"Huge." Sadie's lips kicked into an irreverent smile. "Well, let's hope it's huge. Otherwise, why bother?"

Crickitt couldn't help smiling.

Sadie dragged her sunglasses over her eyes and stretched out again. "Whatever you do, don't fall for him," she advised, her voice going guitar-string tight.

Crickitt started to ask about Aiden again, but Sadie pursed her lips and whistled long and low. "Geez-a-loo, look at the pecs on that lifeguard."

Crickitt let the topic drop, and soon her thoughts looped back around to the picnic by the waterfall and how, if she'd have said yes, Shane would have taken her on the trip instead of Peter Murphy. In between meetings and business dinners, she knew they would have shared more than cheesecake for dessert.

And regardless of her job or her convoluted feelings over her boss, Crickitt had a sneaking suspicion Lori LaRouche was right.

Shane would have been worth it.

CHAPTER TWENTY-THREE

Shane pinched the bridge of his nose as Peter Murphy launched into another story about a "smoking hot chick" he'd picked up at a bar. This time he blessedly glossed over the details. Details, after spending a week in the man's company, Shane decided were mostly fiction.

Peter was a twenty-eight-year-old manager who reminded Shane of a nineteen-year-old frat boy. Worse, Peter assumed his stories impressed Shane when, really, the overblown tales of testosterone did nothing but showcase the manager's idiocy.

They made it back a day early. As it turned out, Peter, while a blithering moron when he and Shane were one-on-one, was professional and friendly with the business owners, including the man he used to work for. His style was showy, but at least he knew when to rein it in.

They'd left the potential investors with enough information to make their decision. The board would talk to their shareholders at a meeting next month and get back to Shane with their answer then.

When the limo pulled to a stop in front of August Industries, Shane burst from the car like the hostage he'd been for the last eight hours and forty-seven minutes.

He should get on his knees in front of Crickitt and beg her forgiveness for not taking her. Of course he couldn't share the real reason he hadn't asked her to go—that his attraction for her was a snapping, snarling beast at the end of its tether. The last test either of them needed was an intimate out-of-town trip.

Still, she would have thrived in that environment. Peter's clumsy prose and self-focused conceit had nothing on Crickitt's confidence and pinpoint honesty.

Peter and Shane parted ways on the sidewalk, and Shane paused to glance up at his building. Crickitt was likely up there now, burning the six-thirty oil when she should have clocked out at five.

He dialed her desk phone. At the first ring, his heart buoyed to his throat. He hadn't spoken to her all week, choosing to e-mail instead. Partially because his traveling companion indulged in office gossip the way an alcoholic inhaled vodka tonics. Yes, Peter had plenty to say about his fellow employees. Once Murphy picked up on the casual manner in which Shane talked to Crickitt, the gloves would be off. It wouldn't take long for rumors to spread about the CEO and his assistant. In Peter's defense, it was getting harder and harder to believe Shane and Crickitt were "just friends."

He couldn't quite believe it himself.

Crickitt's smooth voice interrupted his thoughts. He

started to say hello, then felt his face fall as she continued speaking in a low monotone.

Voice mail.

Shane ended the call and frowned at his phone, weighed down by...something. Disappointment, maybe. He would have liked to update her on the meeting and have a good chuckle at Peter's persistent misuse of the word "literally." Hearing her throaty laugh would go a long way toward easing the tension in his shoulders.

"You're back."

Shane looked up to see Crickitt stepping out of August Industries, the glass doors swishing shut behind her. She strode toward him wearing a Caribbean blue blouse, which highlighted her eyes, and a short skirt over legs that stretched for miles. A smile slid across his face as he took in all of her bronzed skin. She returned it with one of her own, the sheer force socking him in the gut. Seeing her felt like coming home.

He wanted to touch her so badly, he had to stuff his hands in his pockets to keep from doing it.

"We wrapped early," he said. "How was your week?"

"Smooth sailing. I sent you a detailed e-mail this afternoon." She gestured with her head. "Are you going up?"

Not now that she was in front of him.

He was sorting through excuses to ask her to dinner or out for a cup of coffee when she spoke.

"I'd better go. I'm meeting a friend in a few minutes."

"Sadie?" he assumed.

"Um, no." Darting her eyes to one side, she said, "My ex-husband." She shrugged. "I know. I can't believe I agreed to meet with him, either."

She was right. He couldn't believe it. And he didn't

like it. He tried to read her expression but failed. Was it regret? Guilt?

Anticipation?

He hoped not.

"He wants to talk," she muttered.

Talk. Hadn't Aiden been "talking" to Harmony, too? And now look at him. Sacrificing himself for the good of the herd. Would Crickitt's ex wriggle his way back into her arms? And what would stop her from taking him back? Certainly not Shane. He'd inserted his foot into his mouth twice already, first recommending casual sex and then insisting their attraction for one another was temporary. Right about now he wanted to extract that foot and kick himself in the rear with it.

"Guess I'll go up." He took a step toward the building. "Thanks for holding down the fort."

"Have a good night."

Soon she'd be flashing that same tender smile to her ex-husband. A thought that made Shane's stomach sink like he'd swallowed a cinder block. He watched as she fished her keys from her bag, her hips swinging as she balanced the bag over one shoulder. One hand went to her head to arrange her curls, and Shane's gut twisted as he pictured her ex leaning in for a kiss hello, her hair brushing his cheek, smelling sweet and looking sweeter.

Even as panic rose within him, he knew he couldn't go to her. What would he say? *No, don't go back to a man who gave you over a decade of stability. Stay here with me, I can offer you a few hours of commitment at a time.*

Once she was out of sight, he stalked to the door and swiped his key card. He wondered if it was possible for her to look more beautiful than she did today, and then he wondered how angry on a scale of 1 to 10 she'd be if he followed her to her next destination and broke her date's nose.

In his darkened office he turned on the desk lamp, followed by his computer. As it hummed to life, he stood at the expanse of windows behind his desk and watched the cars below. Mothers headed home to make dinner for their families, fathers traveled to Little League games, and at least one woman was meeting with a former spouse who didn't deserve her.

Feeling uncharacteristically melancholy, Shane collapsed into his office chair and sorted through his e-mail. A message from Crickitt stood out, and he read it twice, hearing her voice and inflection as clearly as if she was standing there reading it to him. And wishing he'd had the guts to suggest dinner with him instead.

With more force than necessary, he clicked the mouse, shutting down his computer. He'd see her tomorrow morning and then he'd find out what happened during her "meeting."

Just as soon as he came up with a legitimate excuse to grill his PA about her personal life.

* * *

Eight o'clock came and went. So did eight fifteen, eight twenty-three, and eight thirty-two. Crickitt still wasn't in her office. Shane knew because he'd been standing there for several minutes, grimacing at her vacant desk chair.

He'd ended up working late last night. On the way home, he toyed with the idea of calling her under the guise of a work-related question. But when he palmed his cell phone, images of her with a faceless, nameless man popped into his head and he'd pocketed the phone. Shane didn't want to know what, if anything, they were doing.

Pivoting on his heel, he breezed through the waiting room, arriving at Keena's desk. "Crickitt?"

She answered his one-word query with a shrug.

He took out his phone. No missed calls, no text messages. No voice mails waiting.

Keena lifted the receiver and punched a button on her desk phone. "There is a new message."

He waited impatiently.

"She's ill, said she couldn't get out of bed."

Shane's fists clenched at his sides. An immediate and unwelcome image of her tangled in her mismatched bedding with her former husband flashed in his mind. By the time he marched back to his office, he'd envisioned the entire evening. The candlelight on the table highlighting her clear blue eyes, the bottle of champagne making her feel warm and loose and spontaneous. She and her ex had a history together, plenty of good-old-days memories to share. What else had they shared, he wondered, his gut giving a sickening twist.

He never should have let her go.

* * *

Shane slammed a file drawer closed on his finger and swallowed a string of swearwords. "Dammit," he growled, unsatisfied with the lame vulgarity. The day that started badly had continued to spiral.

Townsend called to give him the bad news. They'd since changed the company's name from MajicSweep to

Swept, but that wasn't the problem. The problem was the updated logo was virtually identical to the logo of a popular franchise in Florida. The establishment, named Sweets, boasted "Fifty Live Nude Girls a Night" on their marquee. Henry was not happy his flagship brand was, as he put it, "now associated with the dregs of society."

Shane sorted through Crickitt's desk drawer, locating the file for Swept, and lifted her desk phone. He spoke with Angel, arranging an emergency meeting in Tennessee. They'd work all weekend if needed, but this situation would be rectified by Monday. When she grew quiet, Shane realized he'd been on the verge of yelling, so he'd hung up before he took out his displaced anger on her.

He settled the phone onto the receiver and stared blindly at the file in front of him. There wasn't anything worse than revisiting past business. For August Industries to continue growing, he needed to spend his time on new business, new clients. Snafus like the one with Townsend cost the company valuable time, money, and manpower.

If the signs had gone up and the ads gone to print, the oversight could've ruined Townsend's chance at establishing a unique and remembered brand. Not to mention the risk of August Industries getting sued for stealing the strip club's trademark.

Shane slammed the desk drawer shut. He swore again, the harsher word making him feel marginally better.

"Shane?"

The small voice belonged to Crickitt, who stood in her doorway, dark circles under her eyes, a slight flush on her cheeks. He had the unexpected urge to pull her into his arms, ask if she was all right. Then he remembered what she spent the evening doing, and who she spent it with, and frowned at her instead.

"Feeling better, I see."

"We thought it might be food poisoning. He wasn't feeling well this morning, either."

She let him stay. So much for Shane hanging on to the thread of hope that he'd jumped to the wrong conclusion.

Shane stood stiffly and headed for her door. "Now that you're here, you can pack your things."

* * *

Crickitt's blood chilled. Pack her things? Was she fired? For calling in sick?

"Shane—" she started.

"I'd like to leave in the next hour."

Did he mean he'd like *her* to leave in the next hour?

"Angel and Richie are expecting us by nine tonight," he said. "You can sleep on the way if you need to."

When Crickitt responded, it was to his closed office door. Sighing, she turned to find Henry Townsend's file open on her desk. Her color drawings for Swept's logo had been crossed out with a bold black X. She lifted the paper, hands shaking. Crickitt spent several hours drawing it, the night she'd tentatively leaned in and kissed Shane for the first time. And he'd marked it through, effectively ruining the sketch, and in a way, nullifying a memory she treasured.

Swallowing down a gelatinous lump of sadness, she reached for the phone to call Angel and find out what she'd missed.

Crickitt had expected Shane to be grateful she'd shown

up today. She could have stayed home, wanted to after she'd barely held down a bowl of vegetable soup for lunch. Too late now. She was here, and soon she would be on her way to Tennessee.

During the limo ride to her apartment, Shane remained resolutely silent, his eyes focused on the newspaper open on his lap. At her apartment, she reached for the handle, not wanting to interrupt him but needing to know how many outfits to pack. "How many days are we staying?" she asked.

"As many as it takes," he said, spearing her with a look that made guilt swim in her stomach.

Fifteen minutes later, Thomas tossed her luggage into the trunk and she clambered into the backseat. Shane met her with an expectant glower.

"What's wrong?" she asked, tempted to tack on the word "now."

"You changed."

She smoothed her hands along the skirt of the light summer dress. Stylish and comfortable, it was the no-brainer choice for a six-hour car ride. Instead of asking why her changing chafed him, Crickitt simply folded her hands into her lap and looked out the window.

The car was quiet save for the classical music drifting from overhead speakers and the occasional pencil scratch as Shane jotted down notes. The monotony of wheels rolling on pavement soon lulled Crickitt to sleep.

She stirred from a dream starring Shane, but in it he wasn't cold and distant, he was holding her close, whispering promises into her ear. Before she could remember his pronouncements, the hazy, fringed edges dissipated, leaving her feeling empty and alone.

She tuned in to her surroundings gradually, becoming conscious of a pleasant weight on her arms, the smell of Shane teasing her senses. Crickitt opened her eyes. Her upper half was covered by Shane's suit jacket. Shrugging into a stretch, she pressed it against her nose and breathed in the smell of him.

Shane leaned back on the seat, arms crossed, his long body taking up the entire seat. His eyes were closed, but even in sleep a neat furrow dented the space between his brows. He wasn't menacing with his tie loose and three buttons open on his shirt, and she fought the very powerful urge to slip onto the seat and curl into him.

Crickitt eased up as quietly as she could, watching his chest rise and fall with each breath. Maybe she should have pressed him to talk to her instead of assuming his mood was caused by Townsend.

Maybe something had happened in Georgia. Maybe the deal fell through. Or maybe something happened last night when he'd returned to his office. Being greeted with a week's worth of messages and work would have been overwhelming enough without adding the bad Townsend news.

She finished her water bottle and dropped the empty container into the cup holder. At least she was feeling better. Whatever damage had been wrought by the fish dinner and her ex-husband, at least the former had worked its way through her system.

On some deep level she'd conveniently ignored, Crickitt knew she'd regret meeting with Ronald. He had a knack for needling her weak spot, and yesterday was no exception. Despondent, his voice wobbly, Ronald promised to be on his best behavior. His voice tight with emotion, he begged, *I need you. I miss you.*

While her gut cautioned her, her heart was far more magnanimous. "As friends, Crickitt," he'd pleaded. "Remember how we used to be friends?"

They were friends. For almost all of the nine years they were married, and the two years they dated before that. In the end, she couldn't justify refusing to see him. He was hurting. And if she was being honest she'd admit he wasn't the only one to blame for their ending marriage. She hadn't been a perfect spouse, either.

Dinner started innocently enough. Ronald gave her a polite peck on the cheek, and she'd struggled not to recoil. What used to be their favorite cabernet only tasted bitter as Crickitt found herself comparing it to the complex red wine Shane had introduced her to. She'd made painstaking strides to keep the conversation neutral, but Ronald grew suddenly serious.

"I love you," he'd blurted.

She'd nearly choked on her baked cod.

Resting her glass on the table, she patted the napkin to her lips, considering her response carefully. "No, you don't. According to you," she reminded him, "you haven't loved me for the last two years of our marriage."

"That's not true." He held up a finger as if it gave his argument more credence. "And you know it."

Casting a glance at the other diners, she'd leaned in and lowered her voice. "The last time we spoke, you said—"

"You found someone else."

She snapped back in her chair as if slapped. "What?"

He tossed down his napkin. "You've given up already. I can see it in your face."

She'd closed her eyes then, trying to make sense of how he could perceive that she'd given up when he'd been the one to turn his back on their marriage, and on her, in the first place.

Finishing off his wine, he stood from the table, raising his voice and attracting attention. "You know what? I take it back. You make it impossible for me to love you."

Impossible to love. After he'd professed he loved her.

"Hey."

She blinked and Shane's face came into focus. She must have zoned out staring at him. At least he wasn't scowling anymore. "Hi."

He straightened against the limo seat and stretched. She admired the muscled length of his body, unable to dredge up even the pithy irritation from earlier.

Folding Shane's jacket neatly, Crickitt leaned forward to hand it to him. "Thanks for the blanket."

"You looked cold," he said, accepting it. He took a breath before speaking again. "Earlier today, I didn't mean to be…" He shook his head as if unable to settle on a word.

She had a few. Rude, brash, short. Or was that just her taking out her anger toward Ronald on Shane?

"You're under a lot of pressure," she murmured.

He gave her a small smile. "You do give me the benefit of the doubt, don't you?"

One of her worst qualities, she thought, recalling last night's disastrous dinner.

They arrived at the design group building and Shane stepped out of the limo behind her, cuffing his sleeves as a light sheen of sweat glazed his forehead. Even with the sun setting, Tennessee was humid and ten degrees warmer than Ohio. Crickitt patted herself on the back for having the foresight to change into the light dress.

She paused under the sign over the door, a graffiti-style logo that read *Gusty's Design*.

"I have been meaning to ask you who came up with this name."

He paused, holding the door open, a memory flickering across his face. "Nickname when I was a kid," he answered, then he pressed his hand to her back gently.

Without asking him to clarify, she allowed him to guide her inside.

* * *

The meeting stretched into its third hour and Crickitt stifled another yawn. Richie and Angel hunched in the mod red chairs around the glass conference room table.

Shane was showing an impressive knack for dead-horse beating, having exhausted the topic a good hour and a half ago. Angel and Richie nodded their agreement whenever Shane circled the carcass, but Crickitt couldn't hold back any longer. "Maybe we could continue this tomorrow," she interrupted.

Shane tilted his head in her direction, and she suspected an argument. Instead, he said, "Yeah, we'd better get to the cabin."

Angel's eyebrows shot to her hairline. Crickitt felt hers do the same. She'd assumed they'd be staying in a hotel. A cabin sounded so . . . *tempting* . . . intimate.

"I have a vacation cabin about half an hour from here," he told her as they stepped outside. He gazed up at the midnight sky dotted with stars before angling a glance down at her. "It doesn't get much use, as you've probably guessed."

She rubbed her bare upper arms, gooseflesh popping up on her skin as she pictured sharing a bed with him.

"Sounds nice," she croaked, leaning her head back and tracing the Big Dipper with her eyes.

"If it makes you more comfortable, I can sleep in the limo." His tone was hesitant, as if asking for her permission.

"I'm—it's your house," she said with a shake of her head.

"The bedrooms are on opposite sides of the living room, each with its own en suite bathroom. You'll have plenty of space. Privacy," he added.

So much for sharing a bed.

He reached for her, tipping her chin and piercing her with an intense look. "If you're not okay staying there for any reason, I need you to tell me."

She pulled out of his grip and walked toward the limo. "I can handle it," she said, unable to explain away her disappointment. She should be relieved her boss wasn't trying to seduce her, that he was being respectful. Professional.

Irritatingly professional.

Thomas dropped them at the main cabin and then proceeded to the guesthouse down the lane. Shane lifted his duffel as well as Crickitt's small suitcase and followed her into the cabin.

Crickitt swallowed a gasp as the door swung aside. The cabin was the polar opposite of Shane's expressionless house. Tall, uncovered windows showcased the secluded forest and the mountain view beyond. Rounded logs made up the walls, stained a burning orange the color of the setting sun. A slate fireplace stood in front of a cushy couch, a flat-paneled television hanging over the mantel.

Who decorated this?

"I did," Shane said, and she realized she'd asked the question aloud. "It's not as suave as the house, I know. But this is the mountains. Rocks and logs double as décor," he said, his tone teasing.

"It's beautiful," she breathed, meaning it. Every square inch suited him. The *real* him. It struck her that she knew him well enough to say that.

Shane tossed his keys onto the table next to a fresh vase of wildflowers. He walked to the bedroom just beyond the kitchen. "Your room," he said, seeming to debate whether or not to enter. He dropped her suitcase in front of the doorway and tossed his bag onto the couch. He clapped his hands together and rubbed them in an adorably nervous gesture.

Here they were. And she'd bet his thoughts were gliding along the same rogue path as hers. She gauged the distance between them, wondering what he'd do if she took the twelve to fifteen steps separating them and covered his lips with hers. Then she regrouped, choking down on her self-respect with both hands.

"I had food delivered," he said. "The cabinets and fridge are fully stocked." He pointed at the television. "There's cable if you want to watch TV. If you want a drink, the bar is downstairs."

She shook her head. "No, thank you. I think I'll just go to bed."

"Yeah. Me, too."

They simply stared at one another, neither of them moving as the next thirty seconds stretched out between them, palpably tense.

Shane finally moved, angling across the living room as

Crickitt paced to her bedroom door and closed her hand over the knob. She stole a look across the room to find Shane watching her, hovering at the entrance of his own room.

"Um, good night," she said.

A ghost of a smile curved his mouth. "Sweet dreams."

And then he disappeared behind the door.

CHAPTER TWENTY-FOUR

Shane was attempting to suck up. Though he somehow doubted a bagel and cream cheese would make up for his behavior yesterday.

He didn't sleep well. He'd lain awake, thinking of Crickitt on the other side of the house and wondering if she hated him. He didn't make a habit of barking orders at his staff. And before yesterday, he'd never commanded anyone to go out of town with him. And he'd never, ever been callous to anyone for calling in sick.

He was embarrassed to admit his behavior mirrored that of a jealous high school boyfriend. Shane had no claim on her. If she wanted to go back to her husband, that was her business. It didn't alleviate his worries. He didn't want to see her get hurt, or make a mistake she'd later regret. But he wasn't exactly in a position to give her advice, was he? He was her employer, not her lover. And after last night, he could see she was more than okay with that arrangement.

By morning, it became apparent Crickitt had told the truth about the food poisoning. She strode into the kitchen, her cheeks pink instead of pasty, her eyes bright not glassy. Guilt, with a capital G, settled on his chest. He hadn't given her the least bit of sympathy yesterday, too wrapped up in his own feelings to even consider hers.

Now Crickitt sat at the kitchen table, picked a piece from her toasted bagel, put it into her mouth, and chewed. His palm found her knee beneath the table. Despite knowing how inappropriate it was to touch her, he was unable to stop himself.

"I owe you an apology for yesterday," he said. "I'm sorry I was such a bear."

She lifted her eyebrows. "Wow. Thanks."

"Wow, as in, wow, you can't believe I admitted it? Or wow, like you knew I was being a jerk and you can't believe I didn't realize it until now?"

She gave the ceiling a quizzical gaze before meeting his eye. "The second one," she said with a curt nod.

A laugh burst from his chest, surprising him. Crickitt's full, kissable mouth spread into an even more kissable grin. She looked pleased with herself. She should be. It'd been a laughless week. Man, she was nice to have around.

He dragged his hand from her bare knee and lifted his coffee mug, his thoughts reluctantly returning to the Townsend debacle and the long meetings ahead of them this weekend.

"There's no sense in worrying," she said, reading him like a headline in the Sunday paper. "We'll come up with a new logo he'll like. One that isn't being used by strippers."

Whether it was her dry tone or her choice of phrasing,

he didn't know, but Shane laughed. Hard. So hard he had to pull the mug away from his mouth before he spit coffee on himself. He coughed and she thumped him on the back. His coughing turned into wheezy laughter and she joined him, laughing until tears sprang to her eyes. After, his sides hurt and Crickitt had to sop her wet face with a napkin.

"I needed that," she said with a watery smile.

"Me, too."

Their smiles gradually faded, and they simply watched each other, longing hanging in the air between them. Each passing second tightened his chest, the tension increasing like an arrow drawn back in its bow. The emotions spiking his belly were frightening, unfamiliar, *welcome*. And suddenly, Shane found himself sympathizing with her ex-husband's attempt to win her heart. Because for the first time in his life, he was willing to draw his sword in a woman's honor.

Crickitt was worth fighting for.

* * *

As it turned out, handling the Townsend debacle was nothing four hours locked in a war room at Gusty's Design couldn't handle. Henry, via video conferencing, not only approved of the new design but preferred it to the old one.

Angel closed the laptop to end the chat, blowing out a relieved breath Shane could sympathize with entirely. "Thank God," she said. "We have a plan."

"Finally! I need to stretch my legs," Crickitt said, standing. She smiled down at Shane. "Join me?"

"Be right there," he answered, aware of Angel intently watching the scene play out from the other side of the glass table. She may acquiesce to his demands at work, but he knew she wouldn't miss an opportunity to butt into his personal life. Just like he was about to butt into hers.

"I'm going to get started on revamping the website," Richie said. He stood as well, reaching out to give Angel's shoulder a squeeze before he walked to the door.

Once their coworkers exited, Shane tilted his head at his cousin. "What was that?"

Angel's eyes widened innocently. "What?"

"Richie."

Rather than answer, one side of her mouth lifted into an impish smile. "How was the cabin last night?"

"None of your beeswax," Shane said, but found himself returning her teasing smile. He stood from his chair before she probed further. "If you'll excuse me."

"Of course," Angel said with an all-too-knowing shrug.

Shane found Crickitt sitting on a bench outside the building, head tilted back. Golden sunlight kissed her features as a soft breeze kicked her curls around her head, making her look like a displaced fairy.

"Didn't I tell you not to worry?" she crowed, her eyes shut.

He chuckled. She could tell him so all she wanted. He was relieved enough to dance a jig. And he wasn't a particularly good dancer. He sat next to her, his leg brushing against her bare one. She straightened from her lounge position, tugging down her filmy floral skirt in the process. Reluctantly, he dragged his gaze from her knees to her gorgeous face.

Shane watched her until she looked over at him.

"Thanks," he said.

Her eyebrows pinched. "For?"

"For all your help, for letting me drag you down here. For...being you."

She blinked twice in quick succession, her blue eyes filling with emotion. Hope, if he wasn't mistaken. So damn much of it, fear coiled in his gut. He looked down at her lips, considering a host of things he shouldn't.

Kiss her. Tell her you want her. You know you want to.

He did. Badly. The realization made him dizzy, like he was teetering dangerously close to a ledge he never should have ventured onto to begin with. Before he slipped off, he shifted his attention from her face to the tree-lined street in front of them and tried to gather his wits.

The Townsend issue was resolved. It'd be a good time to back off, let things between him and Crickitt return to normal.

"We should go out to dinner, celebrate," he said, evidently content to ignore his own advice.

"Oh. No, thanks."

At least one of them was thinking clearly.

But before he felt the sting of rejection, she added, "Restaurants are nice, but I need a home-cooked meal."

"I know just the place." It was a small battle, but he couldn't escape the idea that he'd won. "Great kitchen," he said, "but no cook."

"You cook," she teased, elbowing him.

"I bake," he corrected. "Unless you want cake or cookies"—he swallowed, remembering the afternoon by the waterfall, intense chocolate chip kisses, her lips pink and swollen from his whiskers. His next words sounded like they were coated in gravel—"then I'm afraid I'm not much help."

* * *

Shane underestimated his culinary abilities, in Crickitt's opinion. He helped pull together a perfectly respectable spaghetti dinner, knew what the term "al dente" meant, and she'd even found a fresh block of Parmigiano-Reggiano in the fridge.

She leaned back in her chair at the kitchen table and placed a hand on her stomach. "Not bad if I do say so myself."

"You're a regular Chef Boyardee," he said over the rim of his wineglass. Then he frowned and pulled it away without taking a drink. "Dishes."

"You're rich," she said, waving a hand. "Don't you have people who do that for you?"

"I don't have a house staff at home, let alone here."

"Is that really true?"

"Surprised?"

"Your house is so clean." The image of Shane on his hands and knees scrubbing a bathroom floor, a slightly damp T-shirt clinging to his hard back muscles, thrust itself into her imagination.

"One of my first clients when I started my company was Maid in Waiting," he said, pulling her out of the fantasy. "They come out twice a month to do the big stuff."

An image of her wearing a French maid costume popped into her brain.

"But"—he held up a finger to defend himself, probably thinking her smirk had to do with judgment rather than her ill-behaved hormones—"I do all my own laundry."

She tipped her head toward the mess on the stovetop. "And dishes?"

"And dishes."

Crickitt's domestic fantasy of Shane became a reality as she stood at his side at the sink. She watched through her lashes as he scrubbed a pot, elbow-deep in suds, his bare biceps contracting and rippling while he worked. Water dripping from his hands, he handed the pot to her, tugging the handle as she grasped it and dragging her a few inches closer to his face.

"I never asked you how dinner went," he said, relinquishing the pot. "Apart from the food poisoning, of course."

Concentrating too hard on drying the cookware, Crickitt debated her answer. She saw no reason not to be up front. "Terrible," she said.

"Really," Shane said, sounding intrigued.

She placed the pot in the cabinet over her head. "Yes. Really. Would you have expected a dinner with a former spouse to be anything other than terrible?"

He concentrated on washing a cutting board. "Maybe. You have a lot of history with…" He waited for her to fill in the blank.

She was reluctant to allow her ex-husband to intrude on their near-perfect moment, but because she didn't want to make it a big deal, she answered him. "Ronald."

"Ronald?" he said with mock alarm.

She swatted him with the dish towel. "Be nice."

"What went so terribly?"

"I don't know if I should tell you. You're far too giddy about my plight."

He cleared his throat and affected a stern expression. "Is this better?"

Crickitt smiled. Even scowling he was attractive. She may as well acknowledge the fact that they were getting closer. Close enough that she felt safe trusting him with the truth. More than that, she wanted to trust him.

"He told me he loved me." Crickitt spoke the words quickly, like ripping off a Band-Aid. She didn't have to look at Shane long to determine his frown was genuine. "I was stunned," she admitted. "We split up because he fell *out* of love with me. And after what he said the night he called me at work..." She trailed off. She hadn't meant to bring that up.

"The night you were crying."

The same night Shane held her, his arms shaking so much she'd worried for a moment she'd end up consoling him. But as soon as she leaned into him, they both calmed. As if he'd found as much comfort in her arms as she had in his. Then she swallowed, remembering every second of what happened after. "Yes."

"What did he say?" he asked.

She shook her head, not wanting to relive the hellish moments before the heavenly ones that followed.

Shane waited and said nothing.

"He just...he said his love for me was..." The words stuck in her throat like briars.

"Was what?" Shane pressed.

It was so embarrassing, so debasing. She didn't want to believe she'd cast her twenties into the wind. That she'd spent nearly a third of her life futilely, in a marriage where her husband was never more attracted to her than—

"Crickitt." Shane's voice dipped, gently scolding her. He pulled out of the soapy water and took the towel from her, drying his hands. "Was what?"

She steeled herself, then blew the words out in a huff. "He said he loved me like a sister."

Shane laughed.

She winced, the sound lancing her heart. She'd expected sympathy, a heartfelt apology.

"I'm sorry," he said, grinning.

Not the kind of apology I was looking for.

Crickitt pulled back her shoulders. Heated tears pricked the backs of her eyes and she blinked them back, refusing to make a bigger fool of herself than she already had.

His hands landed on her shoulders. She shook them off, unable to meet his eyes.

"It's not funny. I'm sorry," Shane insisted.

"Then why are you laughing?" She choked through the lump of raw humiliation. It hadn't been easy for her to leave her shell, to show her barely healed underbelly.

"Because...because..."

She blew out an exasperated growl and started to step away from him.

Shane bent, meeting her eyes. "Because I'm relieved, okay? I thought you slept with him the night you had dinner."

She blinked. Then laughed. He was wrong. It *was* funny. "You thought I slept with Ronald that night?" she said. Shane looked chagrined. She was more amused. That explained his bad mood yesterday. "I was wondering why you were so angry—" She stopped, her jaw dropping slowly as she comprehended exactly why he was angry. She moved to meet his shifting gaze. "Shane, why *were* you angry?"

He turned back to the sink instead of answering. But he didn't need to. She remembered Lori LaRouche and Shane laughing together and the feelings of jealousy that pricked her like a thousand tiny needles.

He was *jealous*.

Her world flipped on its axis, taking her stomach with it. Had Shane been pacing the floors that night, worried she was being lured into another man's arms? Had he been worried he'd lost her, regretful that he hadn't stopped her?

Did Shane want her for himself?

He turned toward her, propping a hip against the sink. She sought his eyes for the truth.

"Remember when I said it would pass?" he asked.

She nodded as she crossed her arms over her stomach, a literal attempt to hold herself together if he said what she hoped to hear.

He gave her a sheepish half grin. "I was wrong."

Fingers tightening around her arms, she tried to contain her heart as it beat relentlessly against her rib cage. "Yeah, me, too," she whispered.

Shane stood. "Really?"

A thin laugh escaped her lips. Was he kidding? How could he not see how much she desired him, how much she cared for him? How much she needed him? Even now, when she should be guarding her heart, all she could think about was leaping into his arms and telling him to go for it. But she'd done that already. What she needed to see was that Shane was as desperate for her as she was him.

"So," she croaked, her throat Sahara dry. "What do we do?"

Shane raked a hand through his hair, shaking his head as if he didn't know.

She saw only two options. Retreat to neutral corners, or... "We could try."

He reached her in two steps, his eyes locked on hers like a pair of heat-seeking missiles. Crickitt lifted her hands, catching his face as he speared his fingers into her curls and dove into her mouth. His brief, rough kiss brimmed with promise and tasted like raw desire. He pulled back so suddenly, a tiny whimper escaped her throat.

He pulled her hands into his, searching her face. Doubt clouded over the passion in his eyes. "I can't give you what you want, Crickitt."

Afraid of losing this moment the way they'd lost so many others, she put a finger over his mouth and shook her head. She didn't want to talk about the future, commitment, or promises. Those were things stretching into the beyond in a big gray blur. Once upon a time she wanted the fairy tale romance and, arrogantly, assumed she'd found it with Ronald. Now she saw that the path between now and forever had several forks, each veering off into unknown directions. The only way to find out where she'd end up was to commit to a course.

And right now, she wanted Shane. She needed him. No matter how short-lived. Regardless of the consequences.

Sliding her finger away from his lips, she whispered, "Then give me what you can."

Shane took her mouth captive, his lips firm and urgent. Crickitt echoed his response, opening her mouth to his exploring tongue, pawing at his clothes with greedy hands. A chair scraped the floor as Shane backed her across the room, his mouth sealed with hers. Her hip collided with the edge of the kitchen table.

"Sorry," he said against her lips.

"It's okay," she answered around his kisses.

He navigated her through the living room, either not willing or able to come apart for the seconds it would take to cross the room safely. The back of her knee hit the recliner and she lost her balance, clutching Shane's collar and tugging him with her. He caught them both, bracing an arm on the chair and locking his other arm around her waist to keep her from falling.

He helped her to her feet, his breaths shaky, and pierced her with a desperate look. "I don't think I can make it to the bedroom."

"Then don't," she said.

His mouth hit hers hard as he bypassed the couch and tumbled them to the floor. She lost sight of him briefly when he yanked her shirt over her head and tossed it aside. Then he was staring down at her, dark hunger in his eyes.

"I was hoping you'd wear this one," he said, cupping her black lace bra in both hands.

She gave him a curious smile before recalling the day she'd lost a button, the day she bent over him and massaged his assumedly aching head. "You faker," she breathed.

Shane mumbled something, but since it was between her breasts, she opted to let it go.

He let her roll him onto his back where she stripped him of his shirt. She paid equal attention to his chest, exploring his tight abdomen and tapered waist. Straddling him, she fingered the cool metal button on his jeans. Purposefully slowing her movements, she flicked the stud from its denim enclosure and drew the zipper down, hearing only her shallow breaths and the raspy *snick-snick* of metal tines. She parted the material, her own personal peep show as she revealed inch by delicious inch the man beneath her. Dark hair peppered his belly button, his lower abdomen, his...

She drew in a sharp breath, mouth agape as she stared.

Shane August was not wearing underwear.

Mesmerized by her newfound discovery, she reached for him.

Shane made a strangled noise, moving her hand and rolling her onto her back.

"You're killing me," he said, gently pinning her wrists above her head.

Desire trickled molasses slow into her belly as a smile spread across her mouth. She'd weakened Shane's knees, and that made her feel downright...powerful.

He must have noticed the bold look on her face because next, he cocked an eyebrow and released her hands. "I'll be right back." He lifted off of her, making quick work of shucking his jeans and relieving her of her skirt and her panties.

He returned a millisecond later. "I'm back," he said, swallowing her laughter in a blistering kiss. He pulled away, his eyes roving over her like twin heat lamps, making her feel hot everywhere they touched. "I promise to take my time with you later, but, Crickitt..."

She clamped on to his arms, hauling him toward her, giving her permission. He came willingly, positioning himself atop her, kissing her slower, deeper, than before. When he pulled away, their gazes locked. Once she'd looked into his amber eyes and found distant warmth, but now she saw familiarity, friendship.

Love.

Her throat constricted, choking the words that threatened to rise. So she swept a shock of damp hair from his forehead, cradled his face in her hands, and silenced them with his mouth.

He sank into her, consuming her in the fire that had been burning between them since the moment they met. She clung to him as he moved inside her, crossing her ankles over the rough hair on his thighs. She grasped his rounded, muscular shoulders, savoring all of his male hardness, before sweeping down to mold her palms over his perfectly taut butt.

Shane worshipped her body as well, his talented fingers dancing over her skin, leaving sparks in their wake. And she let him do his worst, writhing beneath him while he lavished attention to her most sensitive spots.

"You're gorgeous." He brushed the tip of his nose over hers. "Absolutely gorgeous."

She reached up and weakly clapped a hand over his mouth.

He shook it off. "And sexy." He dodged her incoming hand this time. "Don't muzzle me while you're having the best sex of your life."

She let her hand fall away. After all, he was right.

Everything was right. The way their bodies lined up and fit together, how easily she met and matched his rhythm. He glided over her, winding her tighter and tighter *and tighter* until she all but burst, unfurling like a cresting wave, Shane's name on her lips as she bucked against him.

Palms tensing around her hips, Shane followed her over, his sounds of completion primal, guttural. He collapsed in a heap, pressing Crickitt into the carpeted floor. She welcomed his weight, feathering his hair with her fingers as his breathing grew heavier.

She didn't know how long they lay there, their bodies cooling, heartbeats slowing. But finally, Shane pressed a kiss to her neck.

Crickitt flattened her palms and pressed against his shoulders. Shane pushed himself up but didn't move away, hovering over her, a curious smile on his face. "Going somewhere?"

She had to think about that. Her body had sort of moved of its own accord. Then it hit her. She was about to gather her clothes and get dressed. Ronald never liked lying skin to skin, and for the past decade, she'd dutifully complied.

Old habits die hard.

"I was...um, I thought you might need a minute." She gestured to the protection Shane had the foresight to put on.

He assessed her for a moment before rolling to his side and tromping to the kitchen. Crickitt watched his bare backside flex in the subdued light coming from the range hood. He extended one arm to point a finger at her, the muscles in his shoulder bunching. "Don't move," he instructed.

After the briefest moment over the trash can he returned, catching her reaching for her shirt.

He snatched it away and tossed it behind the couch. "No," he said, pulling her flush against him.

Her breasts brushed against the hair on his chest, and she decided skin to skin with Shane was nice. Very nice.

Shane loosened his grasp on her to run a hand down her rib cage, over the swell of her hip and back up again. "We should have done this a long time ago." He lightened his touch, dragging the tips of his fingers down her side again. Gooseflesh popped up on her skin and she shivered. "Cold?"

"Yes. Someone wouldn't let me have my shirt."

He crushed her against him. "No shirt," he mumbled into her throat, flicking his tongue out to taste her neck. She angled it toward him, giving him room to stray. Soon a surge of heat headed south.

Shane maneuvered himself between her thighs and braced himself on his arms when Crickitt pushed against his chest.

"What's wrong?" he asked.

"Nothing," she said truthfully. "I just—don't you need a minute before … ?"

He lowered himself, his arousal brushing against her belly. Breathing in through flared nostrils, he brushed the curls away from her forehead with both hands. "No," he murmured. "Do you?"

She darted her eyes to one side, unable to meet his heated gaze. Shane was a caliber of lover she wasn't used to, and now they both knew it. The remark only fueled his confidence. He kissed her, his roaming hands precise and perfect.

After making love again, Shane cradled her against him. She wound her fingers into the hair at the back of his neck before lifting up on one elbow to taste his perfect lips. The taste went from sweet to fiery in the span of a few seconds.

He untangled their limbs, stood, and extended his hand. "Come on." Helping her to her feet, he led her to her room and crawled under the comforter next to her.

And she didn't give putting on a shirt a second thought.

CHAPTER TWENTY-FIVE

Crickitt didn't want to open her eyes. If she did, it would mark the end of the most amazing night of her life. And she didn't want it to end. Ignoring the sun streaming through the window over her bed, she squeezed her eyes shut and snuggled into the sheets, letting the memories of Shane's hands on her skin wash over her.

Light seeped in, interrupting her daydream. She flung out an arm in search of a pillow when her hand encountered nothing but cool, empty sheets on the other side.

She sat up. And frowned. Even though she'd prepared herself to wake up alone, to not feel slighted if Shane wandered off sometime in the middle of the night, she couldn't help feeling a pang of loss.

Then again, why should she feel slighted? It wasn't as if he was *gone* gone. She could hear him clattering around in the kitchen on the other side of the wall. And he was...*humming*?

A satisfied smile curved her lips. She couldn't blame him. She felt a little like humming herself. She tossed the blankets aside and climbed out of bed. She suspected spending the night with him would be nothing less than mind-blowing. Shane didn't disappoint. Muscles she hadn't used in a long while flinched as she tiptoed across the room, sore in all the right places.

You had sex with your boss.

"Yes, I did," she murmured to herself. Her ridiculously hot, kind, funny, more-money-than-God *boss*. She refused to feel even an ounce of regret. She hadn't made any promises or proclamations. She had no reason to feel upset just because she didn't wake up next to him. Probably better to avoid that whole morning-breath thing anyway.

Crickitt hustled into the bathroom to shower. She scrunched her hair with a towel, leaving her curls to air-dry, and dressed in a pair of shorts and a tank top. She bypassed her shoes, padding into the kitchen with an extra zip in her step.

But when she encountered Shane's broad back, she froze, her self-confidence falling away like autumn leaves. He stood at the counter buttering a stack of toast, the soft scratch of the knife bringing goose bumps to her skin. Just seeing him there, so real and solid, reminded her of every pulse-skittering thing she'd done with him last night. *Sans clothing.*

Her arms ached to encircle his waist, and her fingers curled recalling knotting them into his thick, dark hair as he peppered her belly with kisses. She didn't have any casual sex history to draw on, but she was pretty sure mornings after didn't include cuddling. Cuddling seemed so...*personal*.

More personal than what you did last night?

No, but that wasn't the point, was it? Last night was last night and this morning was...confusing.

"Good morning," Shane greeted her. "I let you sleep."

"Thanks." She drew a curl behind her ear and reminded herself this didn't have to be awkward. Even if all she could do was picture what was beneath his cargo shorts.

He brushed by without touching her, resting the plate of warm toast on the table next to an open jelly jar. "Help yourself."

"Thanks." Was his smile genuine or practiced? It irked her that she couldn't tell. Shaking off the thought, she sat and reached for a slice of toast, nibbling on one corner.

Unanswered questions gnawed at her. Questions like, Would they talk about last night? Or pretend it never happened? Would he want to do it again? Three times last night suggested he wasn't dissatisfied with her...didn't it?

Insecure and edgy, Crickitt rose to pour herself a cup of coffee she didn't need. At least it would keep her hands busy. "So, what's the plan for today?" The question was supposed to sound bright and cheery, but it came out a little loud and desperate.

"Stop by Gusty's, check on Angel and Richie's progress. I want to make sure they don't need anything more from me," Shane answered as he took a seat at the kitchen table.

Crickitt stirred soy milk into her mug, wondering if Shane requested it with her in mind or if it was part of his usual delivered foodstuffs. The idea that he bought it for her made her smile.

Moved by a container of non-dairy milk, really?

"We'll head back tonight, then?" She returned the container to the fridge and spotted a can of whipped cream in the door. Frowning at it, she closed the door without adding it to her coffee.

"Or sooner. There's no reason to stay."

No reason to stay.

The inoffensive comment shouldn't have stung, but it did. Soon they'd be on their way back to Osborn, back to work, back to whatever they were before they were lovers. Crickitt felt her shoulders curl forward, her stomach knot. She didn't want to go back. She wanted to stay here, cocooned within the walls of his cabin, where clothing was optional and Shane made bone-melting love to her.

A clap of thunder shook the house and she jumped, slopping coffee onto the countertop. The sky split open, sheets of heavy rain spilling from the rip in the clouds. She mopped at the puddle of coffee, alternating her attention from the lightning-silhouetted trees against the black daytime sky to the incandescent lights overhead dimming and then brightening.

"Don't worry," Shane said. "There's a generator."

A phone on the wall rang and he rose to get it. She listened as his tone went from casual to tight.

Cordless phone to his ear, he walked a few steps closer to Crickitt and stared down at her, his eyebrows pinching.

She recognized the voice on the phone as Thomas's and made out two words that had her pressing a palm to her chest. "Flash flood."

Crickitt turned back to the window, the darkened sky looking more ominous than before.

Shane hung up the phone as he crossed into the living room, dropped onto the sofa, and flicked on the television. A weather map dotted with angry red and orange blotches filled the screen.

"Where are we on that map?" She still held the cloth she'd used to wipe up her coffee as he studied the screen. She wrung it between her hands.

"The middle." In the center of the map, a small circle of magenta highlighted the worst of the weather. Crickitt felt the blood drain from her cheeks as she sank onto the couch next to him.

Shane reached over and took one of her hands to reassure her, the gesture so genuine it made her heart squeeze. "Guess we're staying."

He stood, flicking off the television, and walked to the kitchen. She couldn't read his body language. Was he disappointed?

Shane rinsed his mug in the sink and tipped it upside down in the dish drainer. "The road to the cabin is flooded," he said in the same indistinguishable tone.

"Is Thomas okay?"

"He's fine." Shane leaned on the counter, facing her. "The guesthouse is well stocked and runs on the same generator as the cabin."

"Oh," she said vacantly, striding over to the front windows. Being stuck in a cabin with Shane should be akin to a lottery win. But he'd been distant this morning, hard to read. Doubt riddled her like buckshot. Hugging herself with her arms, she watched the rain beat the ground outside, unsure how to react to him.

Shane surprised her by coming up behind her and wrapping his arms around her waist. "You okay?" he breathed into her ear, nearly buckling her knees. "Tell me you're not regretting last night."

She rested her head on his solid chest, eyes on their reflections in the pane. They looked good together, him bent around her, nuzzling her neck. She brought her hands over his at her waist, tempted to offer a half-truth.

"I don't know how to act," she confessed. "But no, I don't regret it."

Shane turned her in his arms until she was facing him. "What do you mean, you don't know how to act?"

Not wanting to unload the pile of questions that had busily stacked themselves into one corner of her mind, she summarized. "I wasn't sure what kind of...arrangement you had in mind."

"Arrangement...I see." He stared down at her, considering. "I guess we didn't go into details before we"—he gestured between them—"you know."

Crickitt blushed. She'd bet even the tips of her toes glowed pink.

"And you'd like to establish some ground rules?" he asked.

She resisted squirming and stared at her feet.

"I'll take that as a yes. We could write it up if that would make you feel better. Like a contract? One we could both sign after agreeing on the particulars. Let's start with frequency..."

Crickitt snapped her head up. Shane was grinning. She dropped her shoulders. "You're teasing me."

"Yes," he said, "and frankly, I'm insulted you didn't pick up on that sooner."

She groaned, pressed her hands to her face. Stepping past him into the living room, she said, "I promised myself I'd be cool." She dropped her hands, tucked them into her pockets. "Unaffected. Like you."

Shane winced. "You think I'm unaffected?"

"Maybe that's not the right word. But you probably know how to handle this." She shrugged. "Since you've done it before."

He moved to her, his face serious now. "I've never spent the night with you before." His fingers wrapped around hers. "You *are* new to me, Crickitt."

Tears of relief, or maybe joy, heated behind her eyes, and she blinked furiously, testing the weight of his hand in hers. Dangerous emotions, ones she refused to name and shouldn't be having so soon for this man, tore at her chest. She repressed them.

She'd deal with them later.

"Since we're rained in," Shane said, "what would you like to do today?"

She knew what she wanted to do today. Mustering the courage to say it aloud proved impossible, so instead she said, "I—uh, what do you want?"

"I'm not sure if I'm lucky enough to get what I want," he said with a self-effacing grin. He tipped her chin and kissed her as thunder rumbled long and low in the distance. His breath tickling her lips, he whispered, "Tell me, Crickitt. What do you want?"

* * *

Shane watched the emotions play across Crickitt's face for several seconds. He held his casual smile and her hand in his, but inside, his mind raced to piece together the last twelve hours.

He wasn't exaggerating when he said she was new to him. She was so far outside of what he knew how to handle he didn't quite know how to behave. When he was with her, his professional barriers disintegrated into a blurry, hazy fog that left him exposed. Now, *that* was scary. And when he'd climbed out from under the covers it wasn't to return to his own room. He'd been awake, but reluctant to leave, staying until just before the sun lit the sky.

He made himself a cup of coffee and sat on the front porch watching the clouds descend and a light drizzle blow in from the distant mountaintops. It wasn't like he was a stranger to "the morning after." Though, admittedly, he never stayed somewhere he couldn't make a quick exit from before sunrise. With Crickitt, he'd made an exception. Where she was concerned, he'd made *lots* of exceptions. Around her he felt like a kite in the wind, helplessly tethered to her, following wherever she led.

The moment he laid eyes on her this morning, his three-part plan to act normal, focus on business, and keep his distance went the way of the dodo bird. Rather than go about his routine, which is what he *should* have done, he recited the numerable reasons why he shouldn't ask her about last night. And then what had he done?

Tell me you don't regret last night.

Could he be more insecure? And now, here he stood, unable to unsay the neediest words he'd ever spoken as he waited for her answer, his breath caught in his lungs. He cared about what she wanted. And, worse, he knew he'd give it to her, whatever it was.

Breakfast, a game of Scrabble, a foot rub…But no

matter what happened between them, he wasn't a man who could offer more than a little fun. Okay, *a lot* of fun.

This morning, she'd ducked into the shower without so much as poking her head out to say good morning. He told himself he should be relieved. Not so long ago, a past version of himself would have been relieved. Would have encouraged her in the general direction of "cool and un-affected."

But he wasn't relieved.

Ever since he spotted her rounded butt in those short shorts this morning, he'd been hit with a blast of longing like none he'd ever felt. And yes, part of it was physical. He wanted her again, wanted the promise her body held, the searing heat of her mouth on his. But he also wanted to make sure she knew that he, for one, was far from un-affected. Because she mattered, and not just in a general sense. She mattered *to him*. And last night, he'd watched her eyes soften as they'd bored into his, feeling the power of her emotions in the pit of his stomach. And he couldn't have been more helpless than if she'd shot him with a stun gun.

The terrifying truth was he'd found solace in her. And found himself wishing he had more to offer.

Which was why he stood, palm dampening in hers, his throat constricting and cutting off his air supply. Had she seen the truth written across his face? Was she about to call him on it?

"Okay," Crickitt said, yanking him out of his thoughts. "But only because you asked."

Shane licked his suddenly parched lips, involuntarily squeezing her fingers as her blue, blue eyes rose to meet his.

"I'd like to do what we did last night," she said, her voice low. "All of it. Right now."

A laugh burst from Shane's lips. "Oh, honey"—he blew out a breath of relief—"so would I."

* * *

Crickitt sat up in Shane's bed and ran a hand through her unruly curls. She grumbled about how rolling around on her damp hair made it a tangled mess, but Shane thought she looked ravishing. And since he'd ravished her, he supposed it was an accurate description.

They'd made love twice today already, stopping for sandwiches he insisted on eating in bed. The term "made love" made him twitchy, but he couldn't label what happened between them as mere sex. It was more than that. An idea that should have him running screaming into the hills. Instead, he stayed at her side and forced himself to relax. Just because Crickitt was different didn't mean they were slip-sliding into relationship territory.

He could enjoy spending time with her without crossing the line into neediness. And how could he not respond to her when she was so transparent? So genuinely open. He touched her and her eyes grew dark and wide, he kissed her and she kissed him back, he complimented her many glorious assets and she swatted him playfully.

Then again, who was he kidding? He'd have to be superhuman to keep from reacting to this woman. And he'd been happy to return the favor. *Over and over.* Remembering the cry he'd wrung from her moments ago, his chest puffed with pride.

"You're looking awfully smug." Crickitt clutched the

sheets to her body and scrambled for her shirt. Shane wrenched a hand around it.

"It's not every day a beautiful woman appreciates my smooth moves."

"Only every other?" she asked drily.

"What is with you and getting dressed?" he asked, ignoring her comment.

She tugged on the shirt, but he held tight. Realizing the standoff could last a while, she let go and moved the sheet to cover herself again. "Ronald didn't like us to be naked, after."

Shane frowned. He'd already relegated Ronald to the role of village idiot. This new information slid him down the scale several notches. What sane man wouldn't want Crickitt's supple, nude body pressed into his?

That thought had him frowning deeper. He didn't want to think about Crickitt with anyone other than him. Yet she'd hinted she was mentally calculating his past lovers, hadn't she? Maybe it wouldn't hurt to save a little face. "There haven't been as many women in my life as you might think," he told her.

Crickitt held up a hand like a stop sign. "I don't want to know."

"I wasn't going to tell you"—he shrugged—"unless you asked."

Keeping the sheet over her breasts, she put her fingers in her ears and hummed. When she stopped, he said, "It's not like I do this all the time. The last time I had a girlfriend was—"

She hummed louder. Shane pulled her hands away. "You are doing a striking imitation of your Hear No Evil monkey." She smirked at him. Now that he had her attention, he said, "For the record, I don't care how many sexual partners you've had."

"Ha! Now there's a short subject."

He waited.

"No, no," she said. "I don't think so."

"Come on." He wasn't sure why he wanted to know. He'd never asked anyone that question before. But it was too late. His curiosity was piqued. Especially since she didn't want to tell him. "Come on."

"You think that two-word command gets you whatever you want, don't you?" She was trying to reprimand him, but her mouth broadened into a smile of defeat.

Yeah, she was going to tell him.

"Ronald."

Shane rolled his eyes. "Duh. You were married for nine years, I figured. And?"

"You," she said.

"Again, duh." He gestured to his naked body.

She looked at him.

"Just tell me," he said.

"I just did."

Shane lifted his eyebrows. "You mean until last night the only person you ever slept with was your husband?" Primal, and maybe even downright prehistoric, possessiveness made him want to beat his chest. *Mine.*

Crickitt made a face, mistaking his pride for surprise. Before she could hide under the sheets and stay there, he laid her flat on her back beneath him. A startled yelp followed by a throaty laugh escaped her beautiful mouth.

"I'm a lucky guy."

She rolled her eyes.

He meant to claim her with a deep kiss but found

himself pressing his lips softly against hers. Heat burned between them all the same. "Now would be a good time for you to massage my ego. Tell me how I stack up to your former lover."

Crickitt squirmed, but he kept her caged between his arms.

"Right," she said, stilling. "Like your ego needs massaging!"

He narrowed one eye. "Uh-oh. Does that mean I wasn't any good? Because I'd be glad to make it up to you. I'm a quick learner. A hard worker."

To prove his point, he kissed a trail from her collarbone to the freckle on her neck, which had become his fifth favorite part of her body. He flicked out his tongue and she giggled. He found the unique ticklish spot this morning. "Told you I was a quick learner," he said, doing it again.

He assaulted her until she shrieked, "Fine! I give!"

Her face grew serious, her voice quiet. "You make me forget"—she trailed a finger along the stubble on his face—"what it's like to be with anyone else."

Damn. Shane gulped. *That was honest.* He didn't think he could say something like that to himself, let alone out loud. Even though, he realized as sweat beaded his temple, it would have been true for him, too.

Crickittt's eyes were moist from laughing, her cheeks flushed. Sifting her fingers into his hair, she looked past him. "What about me?"

Hesitation laced her voice. She had no idea how amazing she was. No clue. He leaned in and kissed her, slowly this time, until she made a needy sound in the back of her throat. When he lifted his head, he could make out the doubt in her eyes, but now passion competed for space.

"You," he said, "are the only woman I've ever spent the day in bed with."

He didn't know if it was enough, but it was as much as he could give. He waited for her to push him away. Instead, she tugged his head to her mouth and nipped his earlobe.

"Get comfortable," she purred. "I'm keeping you here all night, too."

Then his brain quit functioning altogether.

CHAPTER TWENTY-SIX

Crickitt passed her suitcase to Thomas and climbed into the rear of the limo while he loaded the trunk. Shane followed, unfolding his long body next to her as he reached for her hand. He didn't speak, only brushed her knuckles with his thumb, his head down.

"Thanks for breakfast," she said, doing her best to keep from grinning. He'd been scrambling eggs for two this morning when she'd joined him at the stove. He'd moved the pan from stove to sink, lingering over her lips instead.

He pressed a fingertip into the corner of her mouth. "I see that," he murmured. "We can stop if you're hungry." He grasped one of her curls, winding it around his finger.

"I'm good," she said, her grin emerging.

"I'll say." He put a smacking kiss on the center of her mouth.

Thomas angled down the mountainside to take them home.

After the third hour of repeating tree-and-hill landscape outside her window, Crickitt was nearly mad with boredom.

"Do you only travel by ground?" she asked Shane, who had since relocated to the bench opposite her.

He looked up from a newspaper he'd been flipping through. "Hmm?"

"Why don't you fly? If you had your own plane, you could be to Tennessee in, like, an hour instead of sitting through a six-hour car ride."

"I like the ride. Gives me time to think."

"Have you heard the phrase *time is money*?"

"Have *you* heard the phrase *stop and smell the roses*?"

"Yes," she said, "but I don't think it applies here."

He returned to his article. "I don't fly."

Well. That was unexpected.

"I don't like it and I have the means to avoid it, so I do," he said.

"Oh."

"I have a passport."

"Okay."

"It's not like I've been in a plane crash or have a phobia," he continued defensively. "I just don't like it."

"I didn't say anything."

"You were thinking it."

He was adorable when lacking confidence. She moved to sit next to him, even though facing backward made her woozy. She curled her legs beneath her and plucked the paper from his hands. In what she hoped was a seductive move, she flicked her wrist and tossed it in a pile at his feet.

"You"—she poked a finger into his chest, batting her eyelashes—"don't have a clue what I'm thinking."

The corner of his mouth curved. "Guilty."

She plucked one button from its buttonhole, followed by another. He pulled her onto his lap and she straddled him, taking the opportunity to muss his thick hair with her fingers.

"You're becoming a habit," he murmured.

Oh, she liked the sound of that. Shane was a routine guy. Every day sounded like a habit she could get into. His hands closed around hers, stroking her fingers and sending the blood zinging through her veins like a laser light show.

"Kiss me."

She obeyed.

As she moved her lips on his, she considered it was Shane who was becoming the habit. It was hard to imagine not being this close to him, not touching him, not kissing him.

His hands slid down to cup her bottom, where it rested on his lap. He deepened the kiss, sending her pulse racing. Closing her eyes, she kissed him back and returned to the task of opening his shirt. The future would happen whether she worried about it or not.

And for now, she chose *not*.

* * *

A bowl of half-eaten popcorn and two wineglasses rested on Shane's coffee table. Crickitt sat, knees tucked to her chin on the stylish black leather couch. Her heels began to slide and she pushed herself up for the twelfth time. And, for the twelfth time, slid right back down. "I hate this couch!"

Shane chuckled.

She faced him. "I can't enjoy my movie if I'm constantly slipping onto the floor."

He turned his attention to the television, where an enormous alligator chomped on a hapless fisherman's remaining limbs. Shane screwed his mouth to one side. "I'm not sure how you can enjoy it as it is."

She couldn't help laughing. He'd pandered to her fondness for horror movies, letting her pick what to snuggle up and watch after each of their weekday dates. Though, in her defense, they did more making out than watching the screen. Still, he could probably use a break.

She pointed the remote and the television winked off. "Let's do what you want to do tonight." Wasting no time, he reached for her. She pushed against him. "I'm serious. I have been eating up your evenings every night since we got back from Tennessee." So far, the most amazing nights of her life.

He frowned. "You make it sound like you're keeping me from something."

"Aren't I?"

Shane patted his flat stomach. "My workouts. If I miss too many more, I'll lose my figure."

"Okay, well, let's be active."

Shane's grin was predatory. "Yes. Let's."

He smothered her attempt to shove him away by nuzzling her neck. Moving her shirt aside, he kissed her bare shoulder and slipped his tongue under her bra strap.

"I meant a real workout," she managed weakly.

"Oh, it will be."

The clock on the wall chimed and his shoulders went

rigid, his mouth hovering over her neck. As the last chime echoed across the room, his arms tightened around her and he returned his lips to her skin.

It was a subtle reaction, the briefest response. But she noticed.

She grasped Shane's face between her palms. "What was that?" She smoothed the crease between his brows with her thumb.

He pushed a hand through his hair, swiping her hands from his face in the process. "What was what?"

"Your reaction. To the clock." She wasn't sure that's what it was until he shot her a look, confirming it.

He recovered quickly. "Just noticed it was late, that's all."

"Late," she said flatly. It wasn't, not for them. Each of their dates lasted until they were both yawning, their eyes heavy.

Shane clenched his jaw. A piece of his hair stood out from the side of his head. She reached for it, but he dipped his head to one side, avoiding her.

He stood, gesturing toward her half-full wineglass. "Done?"

"Uh...I guess so."

He carried their glasses to the sink and washed them at the island, his face drawn. Had the room cooled several degrees, or was it her? She shrugged her shirt back over her shoulder as Shane came to stand between the kitchen and the front door.

"Should I go?" she asked. *Surely not.*

"Yeah, it's pretty late." He palmed the back of his neck and avoided looking at her.

Crickitt slipped on her shoes and stood, straightening

her shirt. He spared her a glance. She took the opportunity of eye contact to ask, "What just happened?"

"Nothing." His voice raised a note. Calmer, he added, "I've been up late all week. Makes me grouchy." He offered a stiff smile. "I'll rest up this weekend, be back to normal by Monday."

Monday? They spent every day together and now he wanted to go all weekend without seeing her? She felt the pull of an argument, the words jumbling in her head. She thought they'd shared a deep connection and had since dismissed the day by the waterfall. The day he'd suggested something casual.

Had she been fooling herself this whole time? Maybe nothing had changed. Maybe he still wanted to keep things casual. And if that was the case, she was in no position to argue with him.

The thought stung like a fresh paper cut.

Crickitt paced to the door, talking herself down along the way. Shane was a bachelor. He wasn't used to having someone soak up his every free minute. Maybe he really did need to rest, to be alone.

She shouldered her purse, putting on a smile that wasn't full of doubt and resentment before she faced him. "See you Monday." And then out of nowhere, she added, "Sorry for asking about the clock."

At the same time she grasped the doorknob, Shane's palm wrapped around her arm. His expression was a mix of pain, uncertainty, and hesitation. Like he wanted to talk to her but couldn't. Or maybe he wasn't ready.

When he didn't say anything, she tipped her head and kissed him, half hoping he'd grab her up and tell her not to go. He didn't. "Monday," she said, giving him her best unaffected smile.

He nodded.

Then, forcing her doubts to the pit of her stomach, she left.

CHAPTER TWENTY-SEVEN

Crickitt unloaded the contents of her canvas bag on Monday morning, her movements jerky. She flitted another glance at Shane's closed office door across the hall. He wasn't in there. She'd arrived at work an hour early, hoping she could talk to him before the rest of the staff hustled in. True to his word, he hadn't called her over the weekend. Twice, she'd dialed his number before clearing the screen instead of hitting Call.

She'd tried to convince herself she was overreacting, but her intuition popped like water in hot oil.

Were they through? Had their brief affair met its expiration date? Was she more foolish for sleeping with him in the first place, or for wanting to continue to sleep with him now?

She shook her head to dislodge the erratic thoughts. It was possible she was being overly sensitive. And after the last twelve months of dealing with Ronald, who could blame her? Who wouldn't look for early warning signs of The End after missing so many in her marriage?

She'd never been good at holding back. When she got involved with someone, she was as see-through as cellophane. But with Shane, she'd tried. She never asked or expected him to stay overnight. She didn't pack a bag when he invited her to his house, didn't linger in his office or call him or text him unless it was work-related. She'd done her best to be what Shane needed. And for what? So he could usher her out of his house, out of his life?

Crickitt slumped in her chair. She felt horrible. She felt used. She felt unwanted. What started out as magical had morphed into a dirty one-week stand. And she hated it.

But before the burrowing insects of doubt made their way into her heart, Crickitt squared her shoulders and straightened in her chair. She refused to do this. To allow their affair, no matter how short-lived, to annihilate her. She wasn't about to curl up and let another man kick her around like a soccer ball. She'd dismantled a marriage, her home, her former persona. Surely she was strong enough to handle this.

Snatching her empty mug, she headed for the coffeepot. Shane may be capable of compartmentalizing relationships, but she wasn't as shallow. And that was okay. Better than okay, it was admirable.

Lengthening her legs as she walked, she strengthened her gait, stiffened her spine. Every experience in her life had brought with it a lesson. This one was no different. And if the lesson was that she was unable to seal off her emotions, that she couldn't separate her heart from her head, well, then, she had nothing to be ashamed of. And in the future she wouldn't pretend to be someone she's not.

Her inner cheerleader dropped her pom-poms the moment she entered the break room and nearly collided with Shane's wide shoulders. Because no matter how inspired her speech was, no matter how carefully crafted her wall of protection, when she saw him, she couldn't deny the truth.

She didn't want to lose him. Not now, maybe not ever.

For a split second, he looked surprised to see her, then masked the expression beneath one more neutral.

Watching him rein in his emotions threatened to crumble Crickitt to her knees.

It's over.

"Sorry, I can come back." Her voice wobbled, her throat filled with words she couldn't say. She turned to leave.

"Crickitt, wait."

"Oh! Excuse me." Keena stopped short of the doorway, flicking a look from Crickitt to Shane. "Am I interrupting something?"

"No," Crickitt said.

At the same time Shane said, "Yes."

She flashed him a warning look before sliding past Keena and marching toward her office. They weren't doing this. Not here. Gathering speed, she angled down the hallway. He caught her easily.

"Crickitt," he called behind her. "We need to talk."

She didn't slow down; as if she could outrun the truth she'd seen in his eyes.

"Please?"

She reached her office and clutched the door frame.

Running would only delay the inevitable. He was going to break up with her. She nodded without turning.

He disappeared inside his office.

She stood, staring down at her desk, attempting to gather her strength. Every appendage from the tips of her fingers to the tops of her toes had gone numb.

Carrying a pen and a legal pad she didn't need—she obviously hadn't been summoned for business reasons—Crickitt walked the short distance from her office to Shane's and settled into the chair across from his desk.

She heard the *snick* of the door as he pulled it shut. He rounded his desk and sat. Crickitt wrote the day's date at the top of the paper and refused to look at him.

Here it comes. Like the cresting wave of a tsunami and just as unstoppable.

Crickitt's throat constricted as she attempted to swallow around the unwanted lump of emotion. The breath meant to steady her stuttered from her lips, and the dam blocking her tear ducts burst, salt water splashing onto the notepad on her lap.

Shane moved to stand but she held up a hand. "Ignore me." She swiped her eyes, drying her fingertips on her pant leg. "This is—I'm not doing this on purpose." She added the afterthought, "I wish I weren't doing it at all." She cleared her throat, and despite feeling crepe paper thin forced herself to meet Shane's gaze. "Just say it."

But the sympathy etched on his features said it all. She would give anything to fast-forward through the next five minutes, get it over with as soon as possible. She'd cry later, when she was alone and when Shane wasn't watching her like a fragile valuable teetering on a high shelf.

"Do you think you can continue to work here?" he asked.

She almost laughed. But it wasn't funny, it was annoyingly pragmatic. He was dumping her yet clarifying she was a swell assistant. Well, wasn't that lovely?

Current situation aside, she liked her job. And she was good at it; she and Shane were good partners at work. She swallowed down a wave of hot tears as she realized the truth. That she'd been hoping to be partners outside of work, too.

Still, with both of them willing, maybe they could get back to the way things were before—before—

She couldn't even think it.

"Yes," she answered with a certainty she didn't feel.

"Good. I don't want to lose you."

What she would give to hear those words in a different context. Questions swirled around her, blowing up debris better left at rest. What went wrong? What wasn't he telling her? Wasn't she worth an explanation? How could he be so composed when she was seconds away from dropping to her knees and begging him back?

A sharp rap sounded at the door. Even muffled through the panel, Crickitt recognized the cocktail of overexcited female mixed with earthy male baritone.

Oh, no.

The door swung inward. "Mr. August," Keena said. "I'm sorry to interrupt."

Crickitt stood, mouth dropping open as she watched her mother and father file in behind Keena. They'd barged in on her before, but never had their surprise visits been this unwelcome, or their timing this poor.

"Sweetheart!" The woman behind Keena burst in and

clasped on to Crickitt, squeezing the air from her lungs. The man followed, pumping his arms and giving her a rosy-cheek grin.

"Mom. Dad," Crickitt managed, aware of Shane standing directly behind her. "What are you doing here?"

CHAPTER TWENTY-EIGHT

Shane's office turned into a three-ring circus in the span of a few seconds. He tried to keep tabs on the melee in front of him, but it happened too fast. Keena apologizing for interrupting, Crickitt's mother shushing her. Crickitt's father's hearty laughter as he grasped Crickitt's arm and shook her.

"Gerald and I demanded to see our beautiful daughter," Crickitt's mother said to Shane. "It's not Keena's fault."

Shane was still working to formulate a response when Gerald rushed forward. The short wall of a man grasped Shane's hand and gave it a solid pump. "Shane August," he said, "I read about you in *Forbes*."

"Nice to meet you," Shane said, pulling his hand back and testing it to see if Gerald had broken any of his fingers.

"My wife, Chandra."

Crickitt's mother stopped fussing over her daughter's

shirt collar to extend a hand. "How do you do?" She turned back to Crickitt. "We're in town early, dear."

"Yes, I see that," Crickitt said, voice flat, giving Shane a glimpse at what she must have looked like as a surly fourteen-year-old.

The thought made him chuckle, earning smiles from her parents and a glare that could melt ice from Crickitt.

"Oh! You're warm. Are you all right?" Chandra swept Crickitt's forehead with the back of her hand.

His smile fell as he considered what her well-assuming parents interrupted. He'd been about to reestablish the perimeters of his and Crickitt's relationship. He didn't want to stop seeing her. Look at her: beautiful, smart, funny...but Friday night sent an alarm bell clanging in his head. She'd tipped into deep, dark family territory asking about his father's clock, and for the first time, well...ever, he wanted to explain. Felt the words press against the walls of his chest and scream to get out.

He'd talked about that day exactly twice, many, many years ago, and would rather never speak of it again. Yet there he'd been, standing in the foyer of his own house, about to tell Crickitt how he'd sneaked out to toilet-paper a friend's house, how his mother had to drive to pick him up, how the slick winter road caused the accident...He'd swallowed the words down like a spoonful of glass and kept them there until Crickitt left his house.

Despite whatever uncharacteristic "feelings" over-came him that night, Shane had no desire to time travel back to his childhood where guilt, pain, and anger met at an apex.

"Shane August." Chandra Day turned her sunny

smile on him. There was such bald appraisal in her voice, he nearly toed the carpet. "I was so excited to learn my daughter worked for you. I read your *Forbes* article." She batted her eyes. "I loved it." Placing a hand on her husband's back she said, "You know, Gerald has a business."

"I'm a brewer," Gerald beamed. "Beer."

"Dad."

Shane started to give Crickitt a reassuring smile, but she was trying so hard to maintain control of her reaction for her parents' sakes, he couldn't muster more than a twitch of his lips.

He recognized that look from Friday. While he waged an internal battle, she'd pasted on a smile and kissed him good night. She hadn't liked it, but she didn't push. It occurred to him for the first time she'd done that *for* him.

"There are several local pubs in St. Louis," Gerald was saying. "I'd like to peddle my ale at some of 'em, but I'm not sure where to start. Do you know anything about beer, Mr. August?"

"I—"

"Dad," Crickitt said, forcefully this time. "Shane is a very busy man. You can't expect him to drop—"

"I have several afternoon appointments, but my evening is free," Shane interrupted. "I've been meaning to treat Crickitt to dinner, given how she practically single-handedly landed our most prestigious account."

Crickitt frowned.

"Would you join us?" he asked.

Crickitt's nostrils flared. Chandra reacted as if Shane called out the winning Powerball number.

"If that's okay with you." Shane met Crickitt's gaze. Her eyes were so full of doubt, he wanted to drop to his knees and apologize right there.

"Of course it is!" Chandra insisted.

"Yes, we would all be delighted," Gerald said. "Thank you, Mr. August."

"Please, call me Shane."

* * *

Call me Shane?

What was he up to? Moments ago, he was dumping her, now he was treating her and her family to dinner?

She closed her parents into her office as they meandered around lifting whatever wasn't nailed down. A cup full of ballpoint pens, a framed picture of the new Swept logo, a small potted cactus.

"This needs water," Chandra said before returning the plant to the top of the file cabinet. "What a lovely setup, and you're doing so well. This is much better than peddling someone else's wares, don't you agree?"

Only her mother could reduce being one of the top national earners of a reputable direct sales company to the visual of selling trinkets out of a wheelbarrow.

"What are you two doing here?" Crickitt asked, forcing herself to be pleasant.

"We wanted to see where you work," Chandra said with overt innocence. "What's wrong with that?"

"We are very proud of you, sweetheart," her dad said, reaching to pinch her cheek. Years of practice had taught her well. She easily dodged the incoming pincers.

"Nothing is wrong with it, Mom, but you really should

have called. I was in the middle of a meeting with my boss."

"He's such a generous man," Chandra said. "Offering to include us in your congratulatory dinner."

"Very generous," her father parroted, making himself at home in a chair.

Crickitt rolled her eyes.

CHAPTER TWENTY-NINE

...so generous," Crickitt's mother repeated for the umpteenth time, now from the backseat of the town car Shane arranged for them.

The driver took them downtown to the Palisades, a ritzy restaurant fifty floors into the night sky, and impossible to get into if one was less elite.

Her parents pressed their noses to the windows, doing their best impression of country mice in a not-so-big city. She was glad to see them, but their early arrival by several days hadn't been the best timing.

Whatever words Shane hadn't said, thanks to her parents' interruption, continued to rattle around Crickitt's head. And since he'd given her the remainder of the day off to spend with them, she hadn't had the chance to confront him. She had a feeling the conversation was far from finished.

A maître d' with pointy features and a pained smile led

them through the plush dining room humming with quiet chatter and the ringing of crystal stemware.

"Mr. August reserved the Parisian Room for the four of you," the man commented, ushering them through a wide, curtained doorway. Chandra entered first, gasping her approval.

The room mirrored Shane's house. Black and cream in color, and no more homey than a private suite in a hotel. A plush seating area with a couch and two chairs rested in a corner next to a fireplace. Across from it, a mahogany bar with gleaming bottles lined the wall. And their table, set to impress with white bone china and more forks than Chandra and Gerald Day had in their cutlery drawer, was capped by two leather C-shaped benches.

"Gorgeous," Chandra said beside her.

Crickitt agreed, but the décor was long forgotten the moment she met Shane's eyes across the room. He abandoned the bar to greet them, dressed in charcoal slacks and a pale blue shirt.

"Mr. and Mrs. Day, please, come in."

"Gerald, make me a hot toddy!" Chandra cooed, dragging him to the bar.

Shane watched them, his relaxed smile fading as he turned back to Crickitt. "Thank you for coming."

Like she had a choice. "It's nice of you to entertain them while they're in town."

"My pleasure."

"Look, Shane—"

"I owe you an explanation," he interrupted. "The truth is—"

"Gerald! Leave it alone!"

They turned in the direction of her mother's voice.

Gerald stood in the corner of the room rubbing the leaves on a tall, potted tree. "It's real!"

Shane's gentle laughter rolled through her. Placing a hand on her elbow, he led her to the table. "Maybe we should eat first."

The moment the waiter left to fetch their drinks, Gerald started in about his "beer business," which Crickitt knew was more of a retirement hobby than any viable means of income. He told the story of how he got his start brewing ale, a story Crickitt had heard a hundred times, involving a guy named Polly, a bathtub, and a hefty fine.

Shane genuinely listened, commenting on occasion, asking frequent questions, joining in on her father's contagious laughter. Like she had before, she marveled at how well Shane blended in with everyone. Her father never meshed with Ronald. Their interactions were forced, tense. Dull. Whereas anyone who watched these two carry on would assume they were old fishing buddies.

Business talk was behind them by dessert. Shane had requested coffees for everyone, a separate set of condiments for Crickitt. The waiter returned, announcing, "Soy milk and whipped cream," as he settled the extra dishes next to her mug.

"How thoughtful," Chandra said with an approving smile.

Crickitt stirred her coffee.

"Are you married, Shane?"

"Mom!" Crickitt jerked, mortified, clanking her spoon onto the edge of the mug and sending coffee onto the white tablecloth.

"What? It's a fair question." Chandra batted her eyes at Shane. "I'm sorry, I don't mean to pry."

Yes, she does.

"I'm not married, never have been," Shane answered.

Chandra dipped her chin toward Crickitt. "You probably know my daughter is single."

"Of no fault of her own," her dad interjected.

Maybe no one would notice if she crawled under the table for the remainder of this conversation.

"That's true. She'll see that one day," her mother continued as if Crickitt wasn't there. "When some wonderful man snaps her up and doesn't let her go."

"Unlike that idiot she was married to for a decade," Gerald grumbled.

Crickitt lifted a hand to massage her temple, but Shane stopped her, pulling her hand into his and gently stroking her fingers. She flicked a look at her mother who watched their interaction with bald interest.

"You appreciate her," Chandra said.

"I do. I'm not the best at showing it, but I do."

Crickitt tugged her hand out of his. She wasn't sure what was going on here, but she'd had about enough. "You guys are probably ready to go, aren't you?" She aimed the question at her parents.

Gerald paused, his coffee cup hovering in front of his lips. Chandra frowned.

"You had a long car ride today." Crickitt gave her mother a meaningful nod.

"Oh, oh! Yes, that's true," Chandra said, nodding in return. She faked a yawn. "The drive was tiring, wasn't it, Gerald? We should get going."

Dutifully, Gerald put his coffee down and stood.

"Thanks for dinner, Shane. And thanks for the business tips."

"I'd like to try your ale sometime," Shane said.

"I'd like that."

"Okay, then," Crickitt blurted, eyes on the exit. She wanted to get out of here before the three of them planned a family vacation. "See you tomorrow, Shane."

"No, no." Chandra waved her napkin frantically as she stood. "You stay. Don't let us old folks curtail your evening."

Shane was out of his seat before she could argue. "We did have a few things to go over."

Her blood ran cold. This morning's conversation wasn't forgotten. Only postponed.

"You keep Mr. August, er—Shane," Chandra said with a plump smile in his direction, "company. We'll see you at home." She elbowed Gerald and he reached for his wallet.

"I'll give you some cab money."

"Dad, I have money."

"I'll see her home, Gerald," Shane said, corralling them to the door. "I won't keep her too late."

Chandra waved a hand. "Just because we're staying at her apartment does not mean she has a curfew."

"I think I will take that cab." Crickitt snatched the out-stretched bills from her father.

Her mother pulled her to one side. "You stay as long as he needs you, you hear?"

Pimped out by my own parents. "Yes, Mother."

They vanished behind the curtain and Crickitt turned to find Shane stepping up to the bar. "Drink?"

"I'm fine," she said, anything but.

In the seating area, Shane settled onto the couch.

Crickitt plopped into an adjacent chair rather than sit at his side. One arduous minute passed as she searched the room for something to focus on. Her eyes returned to Shane, who said nothing, his elbows on his knees as he studied his intertwined fingers.

A lead vest of dread weighed down her shoulders. Someone needed to start this conversation.

"I know you probably feel guilty because I cried this morning," she blurted. "But dragging it out is making it worse. If you want to break up with me—even though I'm not sure we were officially seeing each other—then you should do it. And get it over with." She could hardly believe she'd just said that.

"Is that what you want?"

It was the last thing on earth she wanted. "What I don't want is to be blindsided again."

Say you won't. Promise you won't.

But Shane didn't say anything; only fell silent, his lips pressing into a thin line.

"This morning—" she started.

"Can we forget this morning?" Shane gave her a beseeching look.

She'd love to, but… "Not until you tell me what you were about to say."

He licked his lips. "It was a mistake."

Crickitt was tempted to search her chest for a knife. No matter what happened in the future with them, she'd never think of making love to Shane as "a mistake."

Shane met her eyes, his growing wide as he took in her pained expression. "Not that, Crickitt." He shook his head. "I mean this morning. What happened in my office. It was a mistake."

Relief swamped her. She closed her eyes and blew out the breath she'd been holding.

"I freaked out." He lifted his eyes. "It was stupid. I'm sorry."

Her heart went from hammering to melting. Had Mr. Forbes really just admitted he was stupid? And sorry?

"Forgive me?"

She searched his amber eyes. Oh, she wanted to say yes. Just say yes and ignore the last seventy-two hours.

So do it.

But if he kicked her out of his house over a clock, how could she be sure he wouldn't do it again, and over something equally unimportant?

You're afraid.

She was. Terrified.

He slid to his knees in front of her, his eyes never leaving hers. "I can't...Crickitt, please?"

She brought a palm to his face and he leaned into it. The shuttered distance in his eyes replaced by so much regret, it made her heart ache. By the time she'd moved her fingers to his hair, she already knew what she'd say.

"Okay," she whispered.

His eyes sank closed and he pulled her into his arms. She went, hating and loving how perfect they fit together.

"Come home with me," he murmured into her hair.

She closed her eyes against his shoulder, feeling the steady *thump-thump* of his heart against her chest. There were several good reasons to say no. But she couldn't.

So she didn't.

* * *

"Thread count?" Shane's eyebrows hit his hairline. "That's what you're going with?"

She'd admit, asking about his Egyptian cotton sheets wasn't the best conversation starter. Especially after the electrifying roll around on top of them.

"I can't help it," she said. "I like your bed."

He cupped her hip with his palm, a certain seriousness in his small smile. "I like you being in my bed."

This is the way it'd been all evening. He was gentler, his touch more sincere. As if every caress held something…more.

Dangerous thinking.

He met her eyes, watching her intently. "Stay."

Keep it light. *Casual*, she warned herself. She tossed out the first excuse she could think of. "My parents."

"What are you, sixteen? Like they haven't figured out what we've been doing for the last three hours?"

There was a thought. She made a face.

Just when she thought the weighty moment had vanished, Shane moved a curl away from her eye and there it was again. The intense look on his face highlighting the spark behind his eyes. That spark excited her…and made her nervous.

She forced a casual smile. "Yes, but we can all pretend you and I spent the evening playing board games if I go home now."

He sighed, and she hoped he wouldn't press the issue further. "Board games, huh?" His hand slid from her hip to her stomach and up to her breast. He leaned in. "Who's winning?" he whispered against her lips.

You. Definitely you. "I am," she breathed.

He kissed her briefly, brushed his thumb over her sensitized flesh. "But I have one more turn."

He kissed her again, his teasing lips mimicking the movements of his fingers.

"One more," she whispered, her resolve crumbling. Before he could kiss the sense right out of her, she caught his face with her hand. "Then home."

She thought he might argue for a second, and Lord help her if he did because she was about to agree to stay, consequences be damned. But he only grinned, pushing past her hand, a feeble attempt to keep his lips from hers, and said, "Deal." Then he closed his mouth over hers.

An hour later, Shane stood on Crickitt's front porch, lingering over her lips for an unhurried kiss good night. "Not too late to change your mind and come back home with me."

"Or *you* could go home and I could go inside," she said, but made no effort to unhook her hands from around his neck.

"If you can live with yourself for sending me away, then I'll go."

"Okay, I'll see you Wednesday," she said brightly.

"Ouch," he said, tipping his lips. "Why not tomorrow?"

She shook her head, winding a finger around in his hair. "Sorry, I'm going to take tomorrow off. I promised Mom I'd take her shopping and to dinner at the Hard Rock Café."

She waited for him to argue, but instead he said, "I love the Hard Rock Café."

"Are you fishing for an invitation?" As if he needed to. She was halfway to inviting him already.

"Yes." He muttered an expletive. "No. I just remembered I have a meeting at five thirty." He clasped his hands behind her waist. "After?"

"Sorry," she answered entirely out of self-preservation. She needed some distance to be able to think clearly. Whenever he was near, looking at her the way he was now, she was far too likely to agree with everything he said. "I'll see you all day on Wednesday."

"And all night?" he asked, sealing his lips with hers.

The kiss was short-lived, but it still managed to evaporate her good sense. "And all night."

CHAPTER THIRTY

Shane got home in time to hear his father's clock strike twelve. He hung his keys on the hook by the coatrack and considered how close he'd come to losing Crickitt over the stupid thing. And while he wasn't sure, exactly, what the definition of their relationship was, he was willing to admit he wasn't anywhere near ready to let go of her.

He flipped his security box closed after keying in the code and turned on his floodlights outside. In his bedroom he stripped down to his boxers and fell onto the mattress, his thoughts on the woman who'd been on it beneath him. And on top of him. A goofy smile stretched across his face as he closed his eyes and watched flashes of what they'd done together this evening on his eyelids. He wished she had stayed, but he couldn't blame her. She had family in town. Even though he was pretty sure he'd already won over Gerald and Chandra Day. He waited for panic to tighten his chest, but it didn't come. He felt lighter than he had in...ever.

And he'd see her Wednesday, he reminded himself, exhaling, anticipation draining from his muscles as he sank lower into bed. And if he could somehow get out of his ill-timed meeting tomorrow night, maybe he'd find a way to see her then, too.

It was his last thought before he drifted off to sleep.

Shane woke up with a jolt, blinked at the darkened room, and tried to orient himself. He was in his bed. Light filtered through the spaces in the blinds and striped the sheets. Sheets he was strangling with balled-up fists. He opened his hands, untangling the blankets and kicking them from his legs. He was sweating, his heart racing.

What the hell?

It was like he'd been having a nightmare, but not so much as a wisp of it clung to his memory. He sat up, breathed in and out, and tried to recall even a flash of it. He couldn't.

Heading for the attached master bath, he splashed a few jittery palms full of cold water on his face and neck before facing his mirror. His grainy, dripping reflection looked back at him. "What the hell?" they said to one another.

He headed back to his bedroom and stood over his bed, his unfocused gaze on the rumpled sheets. If Crickitt had taken his suggestion and stayed, she'd be there now. He could imagine her lying on her side, blinking sleepy eyes at him, asking what was wrong. The temptation to crawl into bed beside her and bury whatever was wrong beneath her silken skin jolted him like an electric fence. That would have been a far better prospect than having a panic attack wearing only his skivvies.

He was half tempted to jump in the car and go and get

her. A thought that sent a shiver reverberating through his body. Because if Shane was one thing, it was independent...or so he thought. His palms shook and he balled up his hands. Right now, he felt pretty damn needy.

Four chimes interrupted his thoughts, their echoes hanging in the air long after the clock fell silent.

He'd been alone a lot in his life. His father moving in with him was the first time he'd lived with someone since...well, since he lived at home.

And if anything immunized him from wanting another person close by, it had been Sean August. "Your mother loved that stupid clock," he'd grumble day after day, insisting to Shane it was "his duty" to hang it. "Piece of junk if you ask me," he'd say after demanding it be wound. And each time it clanged the hour, Sean reminded Shane that he was responsible for his mother's death. When Sean died, Shane kept the clock. Kept it out of some misguided sense of loyalty. Or maybe it was guilt.

Well, no more. He stomped into the living room, arranging a patterned armchair he'd never sat on over to the wall. Climbing on top of it, he lifted the clock in both hands, yanking it from the wall. Heavier than he remembered.

Yeah, it's packed with twenty years of baggage.

Hefting it in his arms, he marched out to the curb. The trash cans sat in the darkened morning, awaiting the pickup. Shane tossed a lid aside and dumped the clock, face-first, into one of the cans.

Hands on his hips, he stared at it for a moment, waiting for peace to cover him. When it didn't come, and he realized his neighbors were probably wondering why he was standing in his boxers regarding his garbage, he turned and went back inside.

Shane padded to the kitchen, determined to shake off the sense of dread consuming him. But his hands still rattled, his breaths still came out in uneven pants.

Relax, idiot, nothing's the matter.

Silence greeted him from the direction of the living room, where a naked nail marked the wall. No ticking. No chiming. No echoes of his father's voice prodding him.

He filled a glass with water from the sink and downed it, pausing to take a few deep breaths. Then he crossed to the fridge and held the door open long enough that, if his mother was alive, she'd have scolded him. In the bluish light from the appliance, his body cooled, his heart rate gradually returned to normal.

See? You're fine.

Shutting the door, he turned to the coffeemaker, then thought better of it and opened the fridge and poured himself a glass of orange juice. He drank it down, replaying his curious physical reaction, searching for its source.

He thought of Crickitt's face as she sat across from him and waited for him to put an end to the most incredible week of his life. At the time, he'd been sure it was the right thing to do. They were getting too close. *He* was getting too close. He needed to establish some healthy distance between them before...before something happened.

Something he couldn't name.

Or something you're afraid to name.

For whatever reason, he'd been unable to end it, to say the words that would allow him to get his footing. When he saw her with her parents, the interaction between a real family that, while not perfect, had its own special rhythm, he ached to be included. And then he had been. Chandra and Gerald had ushered him into conversation, praised his accomplishments. Made it clear he had their approval to be with their daughter. For the first time in his adult life, Shane felt needed, and like he needed someone.

Shane rested the empty glass on the countertop, staring blankly at the granite surface. Their relationship had advanced without his permission, without his knowledge. Crickitt had utterly invaded his life. But that wasn't the problem, was it? The problem, the real one, was Shane *liked* having her there, coiled around his heart and squeezing. He liked how, when she was around, he thought of the future rather than the past, or sometimes didn't think at all, just got lost in the smell of her skin.

If he could lose himself in her, if simply being in her arms made him forget everything else, then he was in bigger trouble than he thought. Spending time with someone, passing the hours, was different from *needing* someone.

Needing Crickitt meant when she left—and she would leave, either by her own doing or by God's undiscerning hand—Shane would get hurt. He missed her *already*, and it would be a fraction of how much he'd miss her if they continued to be together. His heart splintered as he considered the very real possibility of her telling him she didn't want to be with him any longer. How much more could he take? Losing his mother, then his father, had hurt him enough for two lifetimes. Maybe three.

If he gave in to the intense feelings for Crickitt, then lost her, it'd kill him.

Or worse. He'd shut down like his father had. Become as fragile and paperlike as the cicada shells he used to pluck off the trees in his backyard when he was a kid. If he allowed that to happen…

So don't.

A shiver shook his arms, rattling the glass in his palm. If he continued down this rocky path of thought, he'd be crushed under the pressure, do something stupid. Like tell Crickitt everything he was thinking.

I can't be with you anymore because I…because I…

What? What did he feel for her? He shoved the thought away. It didn't matter. Because he wouldn't tell her. He couldn't.

Just imagining the pained expression on her face wrenched his heart. He needed to get out of here. Away from everything for a while. The house, work, Crickitt…just until he could think rationally. Just for a few days.

He should say good-bye to her, but he packed an overnight bag knowing he wouldn't call. If he did, and she started to cry, he'd crumble at her feet. What he needed was a good two or three days absent from his own life. He'd locate his pragmatic side, separate his haphazard emotions, and plan the best course of action.

Before he left, he put in a call to Keena and another to Angel, letting them know he'd be unreachable for a few days. Then he climbed behind the wheel of his Porsche and pointed south. When guilt began to nag him, he cranked the radio. If he gave in now, he'd make an emotional decision. And that was a bad idea, considering a certain someone had taken over his emotions.

CHAPTER THIRTY-ONE

Crickitt balanced the to-go cup holder on one hand and rang Shane's doorbell with the other. She'd called the office this morning and Keena let her know Shane was "unreachable" for a few days, which she assumed meant Shane was planning on spending some extra time with her. An assumption she began doubting as she pressed his doorbell for the third time.

They had agreed to wait and see each other tomorrow at her insistence, but she woke up missing him and couldn't resist the urge to drive over to see him. Last night he'd asked her to stay, and she told him no. Not until this morning did she recall the flash of hurt in his eyes at her refusal. Remembering the tender way he kissed her good night at her doorstep caused tears to burn her throat.

Their relationship was shifting, moving them closer to one another. But it wasn't a tectonic plate shift happening gradually and quietly over many millennia. This was more of a seven-point-oh-on-the-Richter-scale earthquake forcing them together. And she, for one, had been knocked on her butt.

She clapped the brass knocker on the door, but still no answer. Until now, she thought Shane had been knocked on his butt, too.

"Hello, Ms. Day," came Thomas's friendly greeting. He was dressed in his driver's finery, cap in hand.

"Good morning. Have you seen Shane?"

He shook his head. "No, but he called a few minutes ago. Asked me to check on the place, then gave me the week off." He glanced at the tray in her hand holding two coffees and a bag of Danishes. "Didn't he tell you?"

The tray shook in her hands. He hadn't told her. But that's not what bothered her. What bothered her was *why* he hadn't told her.

"I'm sure he left me a voice mail," she said dismissively. "Darn phones, they never work when you need them to." Shane had called everyone. Everyone but her. Her premonition tingled, but she refused to give it her attention. Especially with Thomas looking on.

"Guess he won't need this, then." She lifted a Styrofoam cup out of the tray. "Coffee?"

Thomas grinned. "Thank you, Ms. Day."

She handed off the Danishes, too, her stomach suddenly unfit for food. Wherever Shane went he hadn't bothered to tell her. After all they'd shared . . . or rather, all she *thought* they'd shared.

* * *

As promised, Crickitt returned to work on Wednesday. Shane did not.

Throughout the day, she left a few voice mails on his cell. She tried to sound casual, relaying messages and ending with a cheerful "Give me a call when you can." Where was he? And why did he take off? He seemed fine the last time she saw him. He'd kissed her, pressed her against the door, and promised to see her today.

But by the end of the day, he hadn't returned her calls or her e-mails. Drained, she entered her apartment and mumbled hello to her mother, who stood over a pot of homemade chili and quizzed her conversationally. How was work, how was Shane, what did you have for lunch? Crickitt dutifully answered her questions before heading to bed early with a headache she didn't have to feign.

In the morning, Crickitt poured herself a cup of coffee from the pot her mother had brewed. She glanced into the hallway at her parents' luggage lining the wall. It was just as well they were leaving. She could expect an equally long day today and tomorrow if Shane didn't show up. And she didn't expect him to, probably because she was afraid to hope he would.

Crickitt bottomed out the coffee mug and rinsed it in the sink. She reached for a banana on the countertop as her mother strolled into the kitchen, a well-worn book open against her pink bathrobe.

With her free hand she straightened Crickitt's shirt collar. "Are you going to tell me what's going on?"

She gave her an overexaggerated shrug. "Nothing's going on, Mom."

Chandra Day tilted her head to the side in an age-old gesture of disbelief.

"Shane's out of town," *I guess*, "so it's really busy at

work." She shrugged again, as if that would really sell it.

Chandra watched her daughter for a few seconds before sighing. "He's a good man, Crickitt. I have a sense for these things. I could tell that about your father, too. Remember when we first met Ronald? He treated us to that fancy Japanese dinner where they cooked the food right in front of you."

Crickitt smiled. "I remember. The chef tossed a shrimp into Dad's pocket, and he jumped out of his chair like he'd been doused with fire ants."

They shared a laugh.

"He won't eat a shrimp to this day." Chandra considered her. "Ronald took us there because he wanted to convince us he was good enough for you. All that forced conversation and his bragging about how well loved he was at work."

She remembered. Ronald acted more like a smooth salesman than her date.

"Shane didn't do that," Chandra continued. "He didn't try to buy our affections. He took us out not because he was *trying* to be generous, but because he is."

Crickitt thought of the waitress from the diner and smiled. "You're right, Mom. He is. With his money, with his time." *Just not with his heart or emotions*, she added silently.

"All men have their problems," her mother said, making Crickitt wonder if she'd spoken aloud. "He may be afraid of expressing his feelings, dear, but it's obvious how much he cares about you."

Crickitt let out a disbelieving sniff. "Yeah? Then why did he ask me to stay the night with him only to leave first thing in the morning without telling me?"

Chandra's forehead bunched. Palming Crickitt's arm, she gave her a squeeze. "Oh, sweetheart."

"I have to go, Mom." She pecked her mother's cheek. "You and Dad drive safe."

"It'll work out," Chandra said, walking Crickitt to the door. "I have a sense for these things."

$\mathcal{C}$HAPTER THIRTY-TWO

$\mathcal{O}$n Friday Crickitt was huddled over a pile of papers, fingers nested in her hair. Distracted by her scattered thoughts, she didn't notice the woman in her office until she cleared her throat.

"Ms. LaRouche."

Lori helped herself to a chair.

"Won't you come in?" she said flatly.

"You're spunky. I like that."

Crickitt's patience was wonton-wrapper thin, but she forced a smile. "What can I do for you?"

Lori slid a look over Crickitt's wrinkled wardrobe before meeting her eyes. "You need a facial, darling."

She couldn't be offended since it was the truth. She left the office around ten last night, and considering how poorly she'd slept, may as well have stayed at her desk.

"I came to see Shane," Lori said, "but I see he's out. Will he be back soon?"

"I don't know."

Lori's perceptive eyes narrowed. "You don't know? But you're his PA."

"I know." Crickitt sagged in her chair.

"When's the last time you talked to him?"

She swallowed, remembering the moment under her porch light and winding his silken hair between her fingertips. "Monday."

Lori shook her head, then stood, motioning to Crickitt. "Come on, kitten. I'm buying you a drink."

Crickitt had never set foot in the swanky martini bar across the street until today. Lori was right at home, ordering "the usual" for herself and a glass of red wine for Crickitt.

"Iced tea," Crickitt corrected, explaining to the waitress, "I have to get back to work."

"Bring the wine," Lori said, shooing the woman away and pinning Crickitt with a look. "Trust me, doll face. You're gonna need it."

Drinks in hand, they sipped in uncomfortable silence. Lori extracted a cigarette from her purse before scowling at it, muttering something about the no smoking laws, and setting it aside.

"I met Shane when he was twenty-one," Lori said. "I was newly divorced and he was a hotshot hunk with a cocky attitude and a great ass."

Crickitt reached for her wineglass. Lori wasn't kidding. She was going to need it.

"I couldn't have cared less if he had any talent at all, but turns out, he did. We imported these luscious silk scarves from Thailand, and he hooked me up with local retailers. He was grassroots all the way, baby. Working out of his apartment, driving a tin can on wheels."

Her smile turned nostalgic. "I was terminally single, but I didn't mind a little fun. Without boring you with details"—she waggled her eyebrows—"we'd been together a few months when he disappeared."

Lori ate an olive from the glass skewer in her martini, chewing slowly and regarding Crickitt, her eyelids tight. "Probably wondering why I'm telling you this. It's not like a new girlfriend ever wants to hang out with an old one." She frowned. "Former girlfriend. Not old." She waved the tiny ice pick. "Never old."

Crickitt's stomach clenched. "Okay, I'll bite. Why are you telling me this?"

"Because he needs you."

She wanted to believe that. Badly. All evidence suggested the opposite.

"He's got a funny way of showing it."

"Yes. He does." Lori watched her for a second. "In an effort to help him in his budding business, I'd been introducing him around to some of my wealthier friends. It was going great until he stood up my good friend Norman Weaver."

Crickitt's eyebrows jumped. "Weaver's Ice Cream Stands?"

"Yep. At the time Norman had five. I thought it was a great opportunity for Shane to venture into the world of franchising. Norman and I waited at his office for an hour, and Shane didn't show. I was so angry, I drove to the ratty hovel he called home and pounded on the door until he opened it. He looked awful. Sleep-deprived, pale, distant. I demanded he tell me what was going on. He wouldn't. Until I threatened to call all of my friends and tell them to pull their business." She crooked an eyebrow. "I'd have done it, too."

Crickitt believed her.

"Has Shane ever talked to you about his parents?" Lori asked.

"Other than he owns his father's clock and they've both passed?"

Lori let out a sound between a grunt and a laugh. Then her face grew serious. "He's been through hell. Without telling you everything, just know that Shane blames himself for his mother's death. He was being a bratty teenager the night she drove to pick him up before the cops did. The roads were icy. It was dark. She didn't see the tree."

Crickitt set her wineglass aside, feeling sick. "I had no idea."

"She didn't die at the scene. Lived the rest of her short life in a wheelchair. Shane's father slipped into depression, and Shane took care of her since his father was never home. About a year later, Shane and his mother had an argument." She shrugged. "Typical parent-kid stuff. He stormed out of the house but when he returned..." Lori shook her head.

Crickitt's eyes beaded with tears. "What happened?"

"They think it was a seizure."

She couldn't imagine the guilt...Crickitt closed her eyes, swiping at the tears on her face.

"His father never missed an opportunity to lay blame squarely on Shane's shoulders, I'll tell you that. By the time he was dying and Shane took him in—"

"Took him in?" Crickitt asked.

Lori nodded. "Until he passed. Told you. Shane's the best."

Crickitt stared through her wineglass. As a teen, she was busy with her friends, discovering makeup, suffering through braces. Shane was mourning his mother, blaming himself for her death, and shouldering his father's bitterness.

"I'd have left the bastard to die alone." Lori finished the last olive and dropped the skewer into her empty glass. "He needs you. He doesn't know it, won't admit it, but I see it." She spread her hands. "I see all."

She thought back to her mother's conversation, to what Lori told her now. Was it possible she wasn't seeing the situation clearly? Did Shane need her? As much as she needed him?

"I don't know where he is," Crickitt said. Even if she did, would she go to him?

Yes. I would.

"He only goes to work and home. Where else could he be?"

"I checked his house. I called his home office. I—" Then it hit her. "Tennessee." The cabin. Of course. "He's in Tennessee."

CHAPTER THIRTY-THREE

$\mathcal{S}$hane stared into the thick forest behind the cabin, breathing in the air and trying not to think. He planned on staying for a day or two. That was three days ago. Or maybe four, he'd lost track.

He'd come here to take a levelheaded, sensible look at his and Crickitt's relationship and come to a levelheaded, sensible decision. But he missed her so much he couldn't think straight. Since desire was his reigning emotion, he refused to call her. He might blurt out he missed her. Or something much, much worse.

So he completed a jumbo crossword puzzle book and started a second, watched all four seasons of *The Tudors* on Netflix, and grew a beard.

Every time he started to open his e-mail or turn on his phone, he felt the same surge of panic as the day he left to come down here. Meaning the shallow breathing, shaking, and night sweats he'd experienced at home were caused by something other than a collection of cogs and gears hanging on his living room wall. It was almost funny. Except it wasn't. So he'd transferred the blame for his physical reactions to other inanimate objects and left his phone turned off, his laptop in its case, and did his best to pretend neither had been invented yet.

It didn't keep Crickitt from invading his thoughts, though. Just thinking of her made his chest hurt, his eyes burn. And he'd thought about her often. Too often.

He'd had girlfriends in the past. There was Lori, for starters. She was the one who got him thinking about family and marriage. Not because he wanted those things with her, but because *he didn't*. When thoughts of family and kids led to memories of his mother, his complex feelings surrounding her death, he felt the palpable tug on the thin thread holding him together.

After he and Lori called it quits, Shane wrote a set of life rules. Number one was *Don't get married.* He'd witnessed Fate's ugly sense of humor firsthand when his mother passed. Thanks, but no thanks. Number two was *Rely on yourself* followed by *Earn enough money so you never need more.* And as far as he could tell, they'd all worked out well for him.

Until Crickitt came along. Then he'd taken his rules, bound and gagged them, and shoved them into a dark corner. Each time she'd pulled away from him, he pursued her. She wasn't the one trying to snuggle into his life and get cozy, more like the other way around. He'd been the one to insist on an "official" date. He'd been the one to invite her parents out to dinner. And he was the one who cuddled closer to her in his bed and asked her to stay.

He thought if he gave himself some time away the fog

would clear from his brain, but he may as well have been in the center of London Bridge during the rainy season for all the clarity he had.

A crunch of leaves called his attention and he turned, expecting to see a deer or squirrel or other curious woodland creature at the edge of the forest. She was a curious creature all right, but far from woodland, in a bright purple blouse and short white shorts.

"Crickitt." His voice was tight, gravelly. And his heart gave a dangerous squeeze. Like before, his palms grew sweaty, his hands shaky.

Can you be glad and terrified to see someone at the same time?

"Hi," she said carefully, stepping onto the stone patio.

Her expression said it all. She knew. And he'd bet dollars to dot-coms Lori had been the one to tell her.

"What are you doing here?" He couldn't stop the edge from entering his voice.

"I called." There was that doe-eyed look again, soaking in pity, dripping with compassion. "Lori told me," she said.

He clenched his jaw.

"Shane, I—"

"Don't," he warned, holding out a hand. At least it wasn't shaking. But the blood beneath his skin was racing, hot. "Don't say you understand. Don't say you're sorry." That was the worst. And he'd heard it plenty from friends and relatives over the years.

"I wasn't going to say that." She took another step, kneading her hands together.

His face started tingling, eyes blurring. Was he...*crying*? He ducked his head and backed to the sliding glass door before traitorous tears broke through his flimsy facade of composure.

"Leave, Crickitt," he grated over his shoulder, holding
it together with both hands. "I don't want you here."

* * *

That didn't go well.

The door slammed, leaving Crickitt alone on the patio.
Rather than follow him in, she took the seat he was in
when she first saw him. He looked tired, haggard, and,
because she missed him so very much, wonderful and
handsome at the same time. She wanted to rush over and
kiss his scruffy face. But the pain was so present in his
eyes, eating away at him, it'd scared her a little. So she'd
kept her distance.

She made the decision to come here and take care of
him, regardless of his reaction. Lori said he needed her,
and Crickitt chose to believe her. On the plane ride over
Crickitt admitted to herself it was so much more than
that.

This was about more than taking care of him, more
than making love to him, even more than saving him.
Crickitt wanted to be with him because he'd taken half
her heart and held it hostage. Even as she sat here, part of
her was in the house with him.

No going back now.

She stood from the chair and crossed to the back door,
hoping Shane hadn't flipped the lock behind him. She
pulled on the handle, her hopes lifting as the door slid
easily in the track. If only everything went as smoothly.
The downstairs was dark, quiet, but she could hear the

shower knobs turn and boards creak underfoot over her head.

Padding up the stairs, she set out to find her new temporary office. If this was the new home base for August Industries, so be it.

She wasn't going anywhere.

* * *

Crickitt stretched her back and twisted in the hard oak chair. Her butt was numb from sitting, her bare legs sticking to the seat. She peeled them free, rubbing the backs of her thighs as she stood.

She'd found Shane's laptop gathering dust in a corner. After hacking his simplistic password, she checked his incoming mail. Since then she'd weeded through some two hundred–odd e-mails. Even after throwing out the correspondence from herself, there had been several requiring immediate attention and a few requiring a bit of corporate butt-kissing.

Her stomach rumbled and she glanced at the clock, surprised it was after nine. She'd been at the kitchen table for hours. Pacing to the fridge, she pulled out the fixings for a sandwich, at the same time wondering if Shane had eaten yet. She hadn't seen him since he vanished into his bedroom, where he still hid.

Crickitt made three sandwiches, unable to ignore Shane or his possible hunger, and piled them onto a plate. Grabbing a bag of unopened chips, she headed for his bedroom door and knocked. The television went quiet, but he didn't answer. She tried the knob. Locked.

"Shane? Would you open the door?"

Nothing.

She'd lifted her fist to pound but the door swung aside. Shane was cleanly shaven, wearing a T-shirt and worn jeans that led down to tanned, bare feet. Dark circles decorated his eyes, and she wondered if between the two of them they'd managed one full night's sleep all week.

"I made us sandwiches."

His eyes went to the plate.

"You can eat yours in your room if you don't—"

"Why are you here?" he asked.

"Because..." *I love you.* "I thought you'd be hungry."

He gave her an impatient look. "Why are you in Tennessee?"

Same reason.

But he wasn't ready to hear a profession, and she wasn't stupid enough to give one. As much as she wanted to believe he'd pull her into his arms and repeat the sentiment, she knew he wouldn't. And she'd been there before, not all that long ago. Sometimes love didn't conquer all. Sometimes love wasn't enough. Especially when it was one-sided.

He shoved his hands into his front pockets. "Sorry about earlier. I'm— You surprised me."

She clenched the potato chips and heard the bag crinkle. If only this were a movie. Then she could drop their dinner and fling her arms around him, tell him she loved him while he kissed and held her and assured her everything would be all right.

"What's going on?" He stepped past her and strode into the kitchen where his laptop sat open.

Crickitt deposited their food onto the table. "You haven't checked your e-mail all week."

He frowned at her, hand on the mouse. "And you thought you'd take it upon yourself?"

She could bring up the fact he'd all but abandoned his business for a week and a half. Or she could bring up the profits lost on two clients who fired them because they hadn't heard back from Shane. "Did you know Henry's having a launch party for Swept?" she said instead.

"When?" Shane asked, scanning the screen.

"Tomorrow afternoon. I received the e-mail on Wednesday. Investors, employers...everyone will be there."

"Were you planning on telling me about this?" He growled.

She hated seeing him like this. Hated more that she was grieving the playful, smiling man who turned her heart inside out with a single brush of his talented lips. Would she ever see him like that again?

Don't go there.

"You mean, like, call you?" she asked.

He looked away, chagrined. He should be. About something.

"Anyway, we'd have to fly," she said.

Shane's eyebrows slammed down. "No, we don't."

She used to think money meant freedom, but Shane had tons of it and had used it to build a padded room to hide in. And if he couldn't risk something as simple as a two-hour flight, how could she hope he'd step outside of his comfort zone to be with her?

She shook her head, disappointed. "You're afraid."

His jaw clenched.

"But I'm not," she said before he could argue. "I already booked a flight on a private jet for tomorrow afternoon. I'm going, but I refuse to spend the night riding down there."

And have to see him sitting across from her, distant, untouchable after all they'd shared, after how much he meant to her. The ride would be unbearable.

"I have to go to Gusty's to see Angel in the morning about my new accounts," she said. "Then, I'm off."

He stood. "Well, reschedule with her—you closed new accounts?"

"Three of them."

"Wow."

The pride in his eyes had her pulling back her shoulders. Couldn't he see he could depend on her? Trust her?

"I can't cancel, Shane." Because that would be giving up. And she wasn't going to give up. On her new accounts, on August Industries.

Or on the man who built it.

CHAPTER THIRTY-FOUR

The next morning, Shane came along when Crickitt went to see Angel. Once he focused on work, he relaxed, an easy smile replacing the frown lines around his mouth. He was acting so normal it was hard for her to believe the circumstances that brought her down here in the first place.

After their meeting concluded, Shane put his arm around his cousin. "Thanks for helping Crickitt with things while I was out. I appreciate it."

Angel patted him on the back, understanding in her eyes. "Sure. You know, you're like family to me."

Shane smiled, giving Angel a brief squeeze and kissing her forehead.

When he pulled away, Angel cocked her head. "You seem...okay, Shane." She flicked a look at Crickitt, one filled with gratitude if Crickitt wasn't mistaken. "I'm glad you came," she said.

Crickitt nodded, speechless. "I'd um, better get going. I'm due in Miami soon."

"Yes." Shane straightened and walked over to her, pinning her with a meaningful gaze. "We have a flight to catch."

"We?" she asked.

"Yeah," he said, Adam's apple bobbing in his throat as he swallowed thickly. "We."

* * *

"Would you stop staring at me?" Shane barked from his plush leather chair in the private jet. The pilot announced takeoff in five minutes, and since then Shane had been clutching the seat's arms like they held the plane together.

The engines whined and he mumbled something incoherent, the color draining from his face.

"Shane—"

"Don't talk." He scrunched his eyes closed. A sheen of sweat slicked his brow.

The wheels rolled beneath them, his breathing speeding alongside them. Crickitt worried he might hyperventilate if she didn't do something to distract him. Thinking fast, she lifted her phone and pretended to study the display. "Did you happen to see Angel's e-mail?"

Shane sent her a pasty look. "Don't use your phone during takeoff." He gripped the seat tightly. "Man, it's hot in here."

"Aren't you concerned about replacing her?"

"Replacing her?"

"She sent it an hour ago. I guess she was uncomfortable telling you in person."

"Telling me what?"

"She put in her notice. She's leaving us next month."

"The hell she is." Shane reached into his pocket. Halfway through dialing, he tucked the phone away again. "Remind me to call her when we land." Under his breath he muttered, "If we land."

The plane angled into the air, and the captain's voice crackled to life over the speaker. Shane returned his death grip to the armrests, pressing his head against the back of his seat. Eyes closed, he slid the panel over the small window next to him.

"She won't let you talk her into staying," Crickitt called over the scream of the engine. "She's too excited about being a stay-at-home mom."

Shane snapped his eyes open but only stared at his lap as the plane's speed increased. "She's pregnant? I didn't even know she was seeing someone."

"You didn't?" she asked as the wheels left the ground.

"No," he said, frowning at her. "I didn't."

The plane leveled out.

"It's Richie's. The new assistant designer?"

"What?"

Crickitt smiled at him, sliding the screen away from her window. A calm blue sky filled each corner and fluffy white clouds sailed by.

Shane reached over and lifted his screen, staring out the window for a few seconds before turning back to Crickitt.

"You were teasing me," he said.

"Yes. And frankly, I'm insulted you didn't figure it out sooner."

$\mathcal{C}$HAPTER THIRTY-FIVE

$\mathcal{S}$hane took a gulp of his drink, watching as Crickitt moved across Henry Townsend's patio like a pro. She charmed everyone equally, be it Henry, his wife, or a member of the catering staff.

"She's incredible."

Shane turned toward the gruff voice reading his mind. Henry stood behind him, his usual scowl replaced by a neutral expression. Crickitt stood next to a man on Townsend's payroll, a glass of champagne in her hand, a wide smile on her lips.

"Hope she doesn't give Rogers a heart attack." Henry added in a low tone of appreciation, "That dress."

He didn't have to tell Shane twice. Crickitt was wearing the same dress she wore for her second interview, the night he asked her to Triangle. It was hard to keep his thoughts clean and hands to himself then, let alone now that he knew what treasures she kept hidden beneath the swinging material. His hands choked his glass. He'd wanted to touch her all day, but how could he after what he'd put her through? What he was still putting her through.

She's better off without me.

That hurt, as truth was wont to do.

"You're good together," Henry said.

Shane snapped his head around to protest.

Henry didn't let him. "Oh, please," he said. "My wife used to be my assistant, too." He clapped Shane's shoulder. "Married thirty years." With that said, Henry excused himself.

Shane finished his wine, shaking his head at the man. Boy, did ole Henry have it wrong. He and Crickitt may have had a chance before Shane left without a word as to where he was going. They may even be able to work together amiably in the future, but he doubted they'd get back to the way they once were.

After the first restful night's sleep in over a week, he awoke this morning certain of one thing. He didn't have any right to expect more from her. Amicable working relationship, maybe. Her in his arms, in his bed? Absolutely not. Even if she knew how much he loved her—

Shane's steps slowed as if he were slogging through wet cement, every muscle in his body growing as heavy as lead.

I love her.

The glass started to slip from his hand, and he tightened his fist before he dropped it and it shattered into a thousand pieces at his feet.

Like his heart.

No, no. No, no, no.

He wasn't good for her. He'd only cause her pain. And…and…there was probably another reason. Probably a hundred of them why he was bad for her. But he was having trouble arranging his thoughts, which jumbled in his brain in a confused mess.

"Having fun?" Crickitt asked.

Shane jumped. He didn't notice she'd sidled up next to him until she spoke.

"Randall Rogers is interesting. Not." She rolled her eyes. "Sparkling wine, please," she said to the bartender.

Tell her.

But he couldn't. His mouth was as dry as if he'd eaten a handful of saltines and then washed them down with a glass of sand. One thought had solidified in his brain, rendering him speechless.

He loved her with everything he had. And it still wasn't enough.

Crickitt accepted her fresh wine, watching him warily.

"Sir?" the bartender prompted.

Shane released his stranglehold on his empty stemware. "Water," he croaked.

"You okay?" Crickitt reached out and touched his bare arm, causing Shane's stomach to flip.

No, I just realized I'm in love with you. God help me.

Shane twisted the cap off the water bottle and guzzled down half its contents. Taking a few breaths, he swallowed one final gulp before giving her an exaggerated nod. "Fine."

Crickitt lifted an eyebrow at him before scanning the crowd. "How much longer would you like to stay?"

Until I get a hold of myself.

He massaged his temple. "I, um, don't want to be rude and leave too soon."

"Okay." He worried Crickitt might say more, but she didn't, thankfully.

His heart squeezed. Good God, he loved her. What was he supposed to do with *that*?

Henry's wife approached, looping an arm into Crickitt's. "I promised you a tour," she said into her ear. "Let's get away from these stiffs." She smiled over at Shane. "Present party excluded, of course."

Then she towed the woman he loved toward the house.

* * *

Hildy Townsend pointed out fine works of art including a van Gogh original and a vase from the Ming dynasty. Crickitt oohed and ahhed where appropriate, but inside, she was far too depressed to care about the twelve thousand square feet of luxury the Townsends called home.

She was worried about Shane, despite the fact he was a grown man and she had no claim to him. She'd kept an eye on him from afar today, watching him prowl the sidelines of the party, mostly keeping to himself.

When her champagne glass ran empty, she'd taken the excuse to check on him. He'd stepped off his first flight hours ago, and the takeoff and landing had both been a bit rocky. He didn't seem to be over it, his movements jerky as he tugged his collar and flitted his eyes around the patio.

Hildy stepped out onto the balcony and scanned the patio, surveying her queendom. Strings of lights covered with white paper lanterns reflected in the lagoon-style pool beneath them, its surface as still as glass. The partygoers had dwindled from a hundred and fifty to about twenty-five, Hildy proclaimed. Shane crossed through the crowd, his gray shirt and dark slacks showcasing the strong line of his body.

"He's quite handsome." Hildy elbowed her.

"Yes. Painfully so."

"Where are the two of you staying this evening?"

Not together, that was for sure. Shane had scheduled separate return flights. One to take him to the cabin, and one taking her straight back to Ohio. Fine by her. Crickitt couldn't bear the idea of spending another lonesome, tense night one room away. Last night had been agonizing. She'd lain awake in the guest room and listened to the television in the living room. The last time she was there with him, they'd barely been able to tear themselves from one another to watch television. Or eat. Or sleep.

"We're flying back tonight." Crickitt told herself she was glad, but her voice betrayed her. She sounded beaten. She felt it, too.

"Poppycock!" Hildy said, not picking up on her tone. "You'll stay here. We have too many bedrooms to count. You've brought your things, I presume."

"I couldn't impose." *So* not the real reason.

"But you have your luggage," Hildy reminded her.

"Yes."

Hildy shrugged, her mind made up. "You're staying."

CHAPTER THIRTY-SIX

Crickitt found Shane in front of a metal fire bowl staring into the flames, a bottle of water hanging loosely between his fingers. She settled onto the chaise longue next to his. "We're spending the night," she said.

"Yeah, I heard." He tilted his head toward Henry on the opposite side of the expansive courtyard.

"I didn't know how to say no to Hildy." And she couldn't think of a plausible excuse other than the truth.

"She's persuasive, I hear."

She studied Shane's profile. The firelight touched the curve of his bottom lip, the arch of his brows, highlighted the gold in his eyes. She hadn't stood a chance with a man like him. He was the fire, volatile, unpredictable. She was more like the wood, willingly being ravaged to her ultimate demise.

And she'd fallen in love with him. Loved him so much, the unspoken words burned her throat. She refused to say them. She could imagine the look of apology, his refusal to accept it. If that happened, she'd fall apart. And crumbling under the weight of this man's unreturned affections was not an option.

All you have to do is get through this weekend.

Once they returned to work on Monday, Crickitt would bury herself in her to-do list and not come up for air until she was over Shane.

Which sucked, but what choice had he left her?

Despite her hectic thoughts, Crickitt muffled a yawn. She leaned forward to check Shane's watch and he bent his wrist to accommodate her. His aftershave tormented her, reminding her of kisses and caresses it would take her a lifetime to forget.

"You didn't have to do everything you did this week, you know," he told her.

"Just doing my job."

"Saving my ass again." He faced her, so close. Too close. "Like you did with Townsend." He rested his chin on his left shoulder and watched her. She traced the line of his jaw, the shape of his mouth with her eyes, then watched, stone still as he glanced down at her mouth.

Not so long ago, he would have sent her a flirty smile, dared her to kiss him. And she would have accepted his challenge, regardless of the attention it drew from the Townsends' party guests. But she felt as if she were imprisoned behind an invisible glass wall.

Look, but don't touch.

He sucked in a breath, and she held hers as she waited for him to speak.

When he did, he turned his head and addressed the flames. "I should've told you I was leaving."

"Why did you leave?"

He shrugged.

She thought of everything Lori told her. Crickitt wanted to say she was sorry about his mother. That it wasn't his fault, that his father had been cruel and unfair. That Shane had been admirable and strong in an impossible situation. That she'd be here for him, always, whenever he needed her.

His elbows resting on his knees, he crunched the empty water bottle in his hands.

But he didn't need her. She blinked, taking in his demeanor. He was as cool and calm as the pool behind them.

But, oh, she'd been busy making herself feel needed, hadn't she? Busy being important and organized. Busy closing new accounts and mending broken ones.

What Shane hadn't said was, *Thank you, Crickitt! August Industries would have been a pile of rubble if you hadn't stepped in this week while I went all Howard Hughes.*

What he said was she "didn't have to do" what she did. And he was right. She didn't. Sure, she'd landed new customers. But it was no less than Keena or Angel would have done in her absence. In fact, now that she thought about it—

Her stomach tossed as the simple truth behind why she'd done all those things assaulted her. She'd been trying to prove herself. Prove she was worth loving. Prove she was worth keeping. Had her marriage to Ronald taught her nothing? Was it an exercise in futility? All those years of trying to make him see she was worthy of his love, that she was a good wife, a nurturing future mother of his children . . . and none of it mattered.

It didn't matter if she had dinner on the table before she left for work. It didn't matter if she picked up his dry cleaning, or bought his favorite kind of toothpaste. It didn't matter when she lost ten pounds or gained back five. Ronald didn't love her regardless.

Foolishly, she'd vied for Shane's love in the same way. She was no more capable of making Shane love her than she was Ronald. She saw that now. A quote sprang to mind, the one about repeating the same action and expecting different results. The very definition of—

"Insanity," she whispered.

"There you are!" Henry Townsend's brusque voice cut into her thoughts. "A bottle of hundred-year-old Scotch waits."

"But for us girls," Hildy said, taking Crickitt's hand, "champagne." She lifted Shane's arm and placed Crickitt's hand in his. "Escort this beautiful young lady." She gestured to a hutlike tiki bar on the far side of the pool before grasping Henry's arm and joining their guests.

Shane stood, keeping hold of Crickitt's hand. She was wishing for this earlier, but not now, not with the look of compliance on his face. She didn't want to be who Shane settled for. She wanted to be wanted. She *needed* to be wanted.

Shane started in the direction of the bar, his fingers loose around hers.

"Chilly out here," she said, using the excuse to pull her hand away, breaking his grip easily. She rubbed her arms with her palms for effect.

Shane didn't move to warm her, to hold her. He didn't so much as look at her. The closer they got to the bar, the wider the distance grew between them. And when they sat, the seats were several feet apart with strangers in between.

* * *

A man halfway down the bar flirted with Crickitt, tipping his Scotch glass in her direction as he cajoled her into taking a sip. She accepted his challenge, wrinkling her nose in a final show of apprehension before emptying the contents down her throat. She slammed the glass on the bar, earning a round of applause. Shane could see she was fighting the whiskey burning a trail down her throat, but she kept smiling. He loved her for it.

Damn.

It almost made him laugh.

He'd purposely avoided relationships so he wouldn't fall in love and get hurt. And even though he and Crickitt made no proclamations about their future, here he sat. In love and hurt.

And the thing that stopped him from jumping up, dragging her away from Johnny Big Neck over there and kissing her senseless *was* how much he loved her.

He hadn't been fair. Not to her. He'd been looking out for himself for so long, it didn't occur to him Crickitt may not appreciate the crumbs he offered. Not that he'd classify what happened between them as crumbs. Thinking back to the last time he made love to her, he was hyper-aware of how he'd done everything to show her how he felt about her. Everything but say it.

But how could he? He'd been in denial, wasn't sure if the truth had even registered in his waking consciousness. Until he'd nearly lost it. Boy, he could see the truth now, so clearly. How hard he'd fallen, and how hard he'd fought to keep from admitting it.

Idiot.

He glared at the man at the end of the bar, the ugly green-eyed monster twitching to life inside of him.

Shane wondered what would have happened if instead of trying to control his and Crickitt's relationship, he'd let it take its course. Would they have built a future together? A family? Would he walk through the front door and announce, "Honey, I'm home!" like a 50s-era sitcom, Crickitt at the stove, stirring a vat of fragrant pasta sauce?

Promptly the picture morphed into his dilapidated childhood home, Crickitt wearing his mother's worn apron, Shane carrying a battered red and white Igloo cooler. He watched their lives fast-forward from wedding to baby. Shane returning home half drunk from the bar after work, Crickitt exhausted but working tirelessly as a mother and a teacher.

The baby grew into a toddler who burned his arm on Dad's cigarette, then to a ten-year-old who busted up both knees falling out of the bent tree in the backyard. And, finally, into a misbehaving teenager who sneaked out of the house to cause mischief with his best friend.

By the time he pictured Crickitt climbing into the family station wagon to pick up their son, bone-chilling fear gripped his heart with icy fists.

The ambulance. The hospital. The wheelchair. The deep sadness permeating the house the weeks before she'd died. The argument between mother and son, Shane leaving in a huff. Coming home to find the swirling lights of the paramedics in his driveway. His father's accusatory glare. His mother's cold, still body.

Loving Crickitt was one thing. But building a life with her, seeing her day in, day out, coming to rely on her, need her. Becoming *entrenched* in her.

He couldn't do it.

Even knowing he'd never ever, *ever* treat his child the way his father had treated him, he still couldn't do it. If he lost Crickitt, if their son lost his mother, how could Shane be sure her death wouldn't rock the kid's foundation? Scar him for life?

He couldn't.

Life held no guarantees. Crickitt could die tomorrow. His mother died when she was his age now, his aunt fought for her life this very minute. His father died at fifty-five.

If he expected the same fate, that gave Shane, what? Twenty-some years, tops?

He'd known since his mother died he was alone. Terminal bachelorhood wasn't the most appealing prospect on the planet, but it was a hell of a lot safer than the alternative.

Henry must have caught Shane grousing down at his glass because a moment later, he offered a refill. At his insistence, the bartender poured another nip and Shane lifted his drink. He didn't want it, but the shake in his hand suggested he might need it.

Crickitt's rich, velvet laughter sliced into the air, and he looked over to see Big Neck stroke meaty fingertips over her bare shoulder.

Shane started to lift from his chair to intercede, but Crickitt shrugged off the man's hand as smoothly as she'd unlinked hers from Shane's earlier.

"Mr. and Mrs. Townsend, thank you for a lovely evening." She directed her gratitude toward their hosts behind the bar. "I'm afraid I'll have to call it a night."

"Absolutely, dear," Hildy said. "Jean is inside. She'll show you to your room." Hildy made a shooing motion to Shane. "Walk her in. It's the gentlemanly thing to do."

Shane didn't miss the scowl the man sent him from the other side of the bar. He rose, sending a smug smile in the man's direction and joined Crickitt, pressing a palm to her back as they headed for the mansion. "Sharks are in the water," he murmured into her hair.

She laughed, and the sound tore at his heart. Despite his reassuring speech earlier, he was already questioning his logic. Was loving her from afar really any better?

"I think Hildy sent you to protect me. That guy probably would have followed me inside." Crickitt emulated a shudder.

He opened the door and she stepped inside, pulling away from his palm. He missed the feel of her but stuffed his hand in his pocket anyway.

Jean led them to the second floor. Fate, or Hildy's hapless matchmaking, he wasn't sure which, placed them in side-by-side rooms.

"Your luggage has been delivered," Jean instructed. "Toiletries and fresh towels are in your rooms. The bathroom is at the end of the hall."

Jean left and Crickitt hovered in her doorway, admiring the lush furnishings within. "Beautiful. Every inch of this place." She waved a hand. "I suppose this highly catered-to lifestyle is all very blasé to you," she said, the hint of a smile teasing her lips.

"You know me, born with a silver spoon."

Crickitt shook her head, her smile slipping. "That's not true." She slipped her hand into his and squeezed. "You're the least spoiled person I know, Shane."

It was enough to make him go back on everything he'd decided moments ago. No one got him like this woman did. No one knew him the way she did. But when he opened his mouth, he changed the subject. "You, uh, really impressed everyone tonight. Thank you, by the way."

She dipped her chin in a tight nod, pulling her hand from his. "Just doing my job."

They watched one another for a long moment. Neither of them moved. Neither of them *breathed*. He finally took a deliberate step away from her. "Feel free to take the bathroom first," he said, turning for his room.

"Shane?"

"Yeah?"

For a moment he thought she might come to him, but then she backed into her room. "Sweet dreams."

"You, too," he said. Because he couldn't say it back.

He just couldn't.

CHAPTER THIRTY-SEVEN

It'd been two long weeks since the Townsend party.

Crickitt gave an award-worthy performance at work. Unaffected, easy-breezy, happy-go-lucky. Until she got home and nearly collapsed under the weight of the lies she had to tell herself to make it through a day.

She left work a few minutes before five o'clock each day to avoid running into Shane in the halls. She couldn't risk being alone with him, but not because she was in danger of being seduced. Oh, no, quite the opposite. Shane borrowed a page out of Henry Townsend's playbook. Rigid and professional, he rarely smiled or cracked an off-color joke. Nor did he lean casually on her door frame in the morning or sit on the corner of her desk and steal candy out of the crystal dish she filled for just that reason.

Instead, he debriefed her with the efficiency of an army general. Like this morning, when he'd popped his head through the door and said, "I'm going on vacation.

E-mail the proposal for Mayfield Furniture over to Stephanie." And when he wasn't busy *not* giving her an ETA, he ignored her completely. Yesterday, she'd found herself alone with him in the break room, and Shane pulled his phone out of his pocket and stared at the screen as he walked by.

And here she thought he couldn't hurt her worse than he already had.

She found herself wishing her parents hadn't interrupted what she'd come to think of as "The Breakup Speech." If Shane had dumped her that morning, maybe she would be on the road to recovery. Or on the road *leading to* the road to recovery. Anything would have been better than his pretending she was never anything more than the assistant across the hall.

Crickitt took off work Friday. She was particularly tender, as if the bruise on her heart had spread to her entire body. She'd uncorked a bottle of white wine and was arranging crackers on a plate when Sadie burst through her front door.

"I'm here!" she announced. "You call, I come. Oh, good, I'm starving."

Sadie dove into the bowl of fresh strawberries, taking a juicy bite. "I've had such a rotten week," she said, chewing. "Mickey Dodd completely stole an account out from underneath me. I worked with that customer for almost a whole month—"

Sadie stopped mid-sentence, and Crickitt met her eyes expectantly.

"You look awful." Sadie dropped the green stem into the trash can.

"Thanks," Crickitt grumbled, tipping the wine bottle

over her glass. She splashed in an inch of liquid and drank it down in one swallow.

"I don't mean awful. I mean you look like something's wrong." Sadie moved to the counter to stand in front of her. "I should probably know what it is since I'm your best friend. But I don't. 'Cause I'm a selfish, shitty person." She touched Crickitt's arm. "What happened?"

Crickitt opened her mouth to explain, but a sob came out instead.

Sadie snatched the bottle from the counter and filled Crickitt's glass to the top. Then she grabbed a second glass and corralled her into the living room.

An hour and a half later, two empty wine bottles sat on Crickitt's coffee table. Sadie was at one corner of the sofa, knees to her chest, Crickitt at the other, legs folded beneath her. Crickitt had finished speaking at least thirty seconds ago.

Sadie had yet to comment, her mouth hanging open in stunned silence. Finally, she said, "That's horrible."

"I know."

"How could his father blame him for an accident?"

"I know." She'd felt the same disbelief when Lori told her.

"And to take the man in when he was dying?" Sadie shook her head. "Shane's a better person than I am. He's incredible."

Tears burned Crickitt's throat, but she managed a nod. The truth was the truth. Shane was incredible.

"Oh, honey," Sadie said. "I didn't mean that. He's not incredible. If he was, he would have held on to you with both hands."

She appreciated the support, but couldn't agree. It may have been easier to be angry with Shane, but how could she fault him? He'd been transparent from the start. Crickitt told him to give her what he could, and that was exactly what he'd done. She was the one who became disappointed when it wasn't more.

"We agreed to keep it casual," Crickitt explained. "I was the one who changed the rules."

"Yeah," Sadie said, "I know what you mean. I did the same thing with Aiden." She quirked her lips. "I was so sure I wouldn't fall…" She shook her head, unable to finish her sentence. Resting her chin on one knee, she stared at the sofa cushion between them. "The night I met him, we spent the entire night talking."

"Talking? Is that what you kids call it now?"

"Ha-ha." Sadie gave her a good-natured eye roll. "I told him things I never tell anyone. We talked about my crazy family, about Trey marrying Celeste."

Crickitt raised a brow. Sadie never talked about her ex-fiancé. Never.

"I know, right?" Sadie said, noticing Crickitt's silent reaction. "Aiden's mother is dying and here I sit, unable to feel anything but jealousy because he's pretending to be married to his scumbag, cheating ex-wife."

Crickitt's stomach clenched. "And he believes lying to his mother is better than telling her the truth?"

Sadie shrugged.

Crickitt considered the blessing of having both her parents alive. Sadie didn't have her father. Shane didn't have his father or his mother. And Aiden's mother was terminally ill. "It must not be easy for him. To balance obligation, duty, and grief." Realizing she was on the verge of defending the man who broke Sadie's heart, Crickitt added, "Oh, my gosh. Sadie, I'm sorry."

Sadie shot her a remorseful smile. "No, you're right. I'm being selfish. Which is nothing new. He's going through this horrific family turmoil, and all I can think about is how he didn't even give me a chance to step up." She pinned Crickitt with a look. "I would've."

"Of course you would've," Crickitt said, meaning it.

Tears ran down Sadie's face for the second time tonight. "I don't understand how I got in so deep so fast."

"Oh, honey." Crickitt moved to hug her best friend, but Sadie held up a hand. "Right." Crickitt resettled against the back of the sofa. "I forgot."

An earlier hug, when Crickitt 'fessed up about Shane, reduced them into a puddle of wailing sobs. They agreed not to touch each other for the rest of the night.

"If it makes you feel better, I don't know how to stop loving Shane, either. I've tried hating him, I've tried ignoring him. Nothing works," Crickitt said. "Maybe I can ask Ronald for some pointers."

Sadie laughed, pressing her fingers to her lips as if surprised by the sound. "You are so strong, Crickitt."

"No, I'm really not."

"I play strong on TV, but you, you're the warrior of the two of us."

Crickitt was going to argue, but the truth was, she felt strong. "Thanks, Sadie."

"I love you, you know."

She couldn't help smiling at Sadie's rare display of affection. "I love you, too."

Sadie smiled wistfully for a moment before hopping off the couch and reaching for the empty wine bottles.

"Enough of this Mush Fest," she said, heading for the kitchen, bottles clanking against one another. She turned in the doorway. "I assume you'd like more wine."

Crickitt grinned.

"That's my girl."

* * *

Shane couldn't believe he was in Mexico, and not just because he had to board a plane to get here. When he found out Angel was dating her co-designer, Richie, he couldn't have been more surprised. Then they announced their nuptials, and suddenly, he was.

As instructed, Shane wore an all-white linen suit and stood in the sand at Aiden's side to witness Angel's whirl-wind romance advance to the next level. Shane glanced at Angel's flat stomach, recalling Crickitt's made-up story about Angel wanting to be a stay-at-home mom and wondered how close that dart came to hitting its target. Then he pushed the thought away, preferring not to think of Crickitt at all.

Aiden watched his sister say her vows, his smile wide and genuine. How did he do it?

Harmony had returned along with Kathy's cancer di-agnosis, but she didn't stick around. Aiden opted not to tell his mother, allowing her to assume Harmony was at work, or make up some other plausible excuse, whenever the topic came up.

Aiden had every right to be angry, but nothing in his relaxed posture or easy expression suggested he was any-thing but happy for his sister.

Shane couldn't say what he'd do in his position. He

glanced over at Aunt Kathy, as frail and pale as the white folding chair she sat in. She watched her daughter with unshielded pride, her eyes filling with tears. And suddenly, Shane understood why Angel and Richie rushed to the altar. If he were in Angel's position, he may have done the same.

After the wedding on the beach, they went back to the couple's cabana for a reception that was more of a cookout. Pulled pork, an array of salads, and plates filled with colorful fruits decorated a long table on the deck. The expanse of white sand and a sparkling ocean made for a gorgeous backdrop.

Shane's aunt had been ushered back to her room to rest. Uncle Mike approached him as Shane reached into the ice for another Corona. He offered the bottle, ice sliding down its label. "Beer, Uncle Mike?"

"You know it." A salty breeze sent his gray hair flying. Burly, tanned, and with a jagged scar running the length of one cheek, Mike had been Shane's hero for as long as he could remember. He reminded him of some world explorer: adventurous, daring, and brave. But ever since Aunt Kathy got sick, he'd lost some of the fire that burned like a green torch in his eyes.

"How is she?" Shane didn't need to qualify who he was talking about.

Mike shook his head. "She's exhausted but won't admit it. Wild wolves couldn't have kept her from this wedding." He gestured to the scar on his cheek. "Trust me, I know."

Shane chuckled. Mike had a thousand different stories about how he'd gotten that scar. He never tired of hearing his newest tall tale.

"How's your love life, Studly?" Mike grinned.

Shane took a pull from his beer bottle.

"That good, huh?"

The two men stared at the ocean for a moment before Shane turned to his uncle. "You make it look easy, you know that?" At Mike's questioning glance he added, "You and Aunt Kathy have been married, what? Thirty-some years? And you make being together look as easy as breathing in and out."

Mike's mouth twisted into a comical grimace. "She'd laugh you off this deck if she heard you say that. But you're right. Being with her is as easy as breathing in and out. It's the big life-altering stuff that knocks you for a loop. Having babies. Working your butt off to make sure they have everything you didn't. Watching them grow up, break bones, get married. That stuff is the test that, ironically enough, you wouldn't pass without one another."

Mike squinted at the sunset, an orange ball descending into the clear blue water. "The cancer should have made it harder, our lives," he said quietly. "And it has, but it also made her easier to love. Easier to appreciate. Easier to be with. Every second is a blessing. I wouldn't change a single bit of it."

They moved on to shallower topics after that: football, food, Mike's last hunting trip. A few hours later, Shane excused himself to wish Angel and Richie well.

Afterward, he found Aiden at a bonfire on the beach and strode out to say good-bye. Shane didn't leave right away, settling in for a few beers. Eventually, the beach emptied and just the two of them sat in front of the embers.

"I wish you'd reconsider staying. We have a whole block of rooms reserved," Aiden said.

Shane understood what he meant. It didn't make much sense to leave in the wee hours of the morning. But, with any luck, Shane would sleep through the flight home. "Thanks, but I've got a ton of work to do," he said. It was an exaggeration, but it was the truth.

"All right, but I hate to see you go." Shane could see he meant it, but Aiden didn't press him further. "Have a safe flight."

It was those last four words he'd later recall, and laugh at. Because, really, how much control did Shane have when it came to having a safe flight?

As it turned out, none. None at all.

CHAPTER THIRTY-EIGHT

Shane set aside his empty glass, glad he'd decided on having a drink after all. The plane hit another bump, and he clasped the arms of his seat, wondering if he'd ever get over the idea of shooting across the sky at six hundred miles an hour.

"Done, sir?"

He nodded at the attendant, a service he didn't think twice about adding on to his private flight. While it was a little embarrassing to need a chaperone, he still felt better having someone on board who knew what to expect.

The young man took Shane's empty glass and straightened his own pristine business attire before hustling out of the cabin again. Shane had even insisted on the poor kid going over safety precautions even though it wasn't protocol for a personal jet. He wasn't sure if the tutorial had made him feel better or worse about his travel accommodations.

He leaned his head back and sank into the seat. The alcohol flowed into his limbs, relaxing him. His thoughts bounced from Angel's and Richie's genuine joy at their wedding to Aiden's steadfast outlook and sheer determination to be happy regardless of what life threw at him. He thought again of Uncle Mike's stoicism as he spoke of his wife. Shane hoped against hope a miracle would occur, allowing Aunt Kathy to live a long life after all.

He was blessed to have the Downeys. With his parents gone and no siblings, Shane had become accustomed to being alone. Being around his aunt, uncle, and cousins reminded him he wasn't.

His seat gave a violent jerk, and it took Shane a few seconds to realize it wasn't only his seat but the entire plane that was vibrating. Then came another, more forceful drop, followed by the attendant swooping in like some waifish superhero.

His voice studiously calm, he said, "Buckle your seat belt, Mr. August." No sooner had Shane snapped the clasp on his belt than the oxygen masks dropped from the ceiling. Shane fumbled, hands shaking as he slid the mask on.

The attendant—Charlie, Shane remembered in a rush—strapped into the seat across the aisle. "Air pocket!" Charlie shouted through his plastic mask.

But before Shane could respond, the plane tipped, angling in a decidedly less favorable direction.

This was it. He was going to die.

A thousand thoughts lined up and paraded through his head, maybe the most amusing of which being his relief at having changed out of his cardboard beachwear before boarding the plane. If he was going to go down in a ball of flames over the ocean, he'd rather not be dressed like an islander. It was somehow disingenuous.

The screeching of the plane in full dive took over his thoughts as fear carved a serpentine path in his gut. The horizon slanted at an awkward angle outside his window, and Shane forced himself to breathe, sucking in oxygen in greedy gulps and musing how he wished it was nitrous oxide instead.

The seat belt ate into his waist as the plane nose-dived, anchoring Shane to a seat that would more likely double as a diaper than a floatation device. Despite that terrifying and slightly humorous reality, Shane's next thought came as certain and as strong as his heart slamming into his breastbone.

If he was in love with Crickitt, why were they apart?

Without warning, the plane stopped its earthbound descent, leveling with all the abruptness of a tilt-a-whirl coming to a halt. Panting, Shane took in the view outside his window at the now level horizon, as if the last several seconds had been nothing more than an imagined scenario.

He turned his head to find Charlie giving him a shaky smile from his seat. After a few moments, he tentatively lifted his mask from his face. "We seem to have lost altitude," he said, Adam's apple bobbing in his skinny neck. "I'll just check in with the captain."

Shane nodded, yanking the mask from his face and wondering if Charlie was about to run to the adjoining cabin and puke his guts out. It's what Shane would have done if he was in the kid's shoes.

By the time it'd become apparent that Shane, Charlie, and the captain were no longer in danger of becoming grease spots on the plane's little black box, Shane's heart rate had regulated. Charlie returned to give an impressively calm synopsis, explaining what had happened with a pile of technical jargon as Shane nodded numbly.

Now left alone to nurse his second Scotch and soda— he didn't recall needing a drink more badly in his life— he replayed his near-death experience in his head. With it came his last lucid thought.

If I love Crickitt, why are we apart?

It hadn't been his life flashing before his eyes on the way down, not memories of his childhood, his parents, or even the business that had become an extension of himself over the last decade. No, what flashed before him like the reel of a never-before-seen movie was a future. A future that would never happen if he died.

Opening his eyes in the morning to find Crickitt next to him in his bed. Her laughter, rolling through him like thunder coming from miles away. Crickitt at the end of a long white aisle in a simple, clean dress. Crickitt pressing his hand against her round stomach. Crickitt asking what names he liked for their child.

Grief choked out his next breath as the glass rattled in his hand. He set it aside, covering his face with a shaky hand. He cleared his throat, sucking in a stuttering breath. Loss unlike any other radiated through his limbs, stronger than when he'd lost either of his parents. Pain sliced him open, left him feeling raw. Empty.

How could he mourn a life that never was?

He thought of Uncle Mike's words, how he said the hard stuff brought him and Aunt Kathy closer together, made them stronger. Shane had worked hard to avoid that kind of closeness, to avoid the pain of loss should something tragic happen. If Crickitt was taken from him, the way he and his father lost his mother, how would he survive?

But now, he considered another option. Maybe she'd live to be well into her eighties like his grandparents. Maybe they'd grow old and gray and hard of hearing together. They could retire to the cabin in Tennessee, be surrounded each holiday by a dozen grandkids. And their children didn't have to be scarred and distant. Maybe they'd be impressive adults, with his mind for success and Crickitt's unshakable character.

What if a long, abundant life stretched out ahead of them? Another fifty-plus years filled with amazing memories…How many days was that? How many hours? How many minutes?

Minutes like the ones when he'd last lain across from Crickitt in his bed. Minutes that lingered, endured, stretched out seemingly endlessly before him.

It was a future that could've gone down in a ball of flames. He dropped his hand, felt an unsteady smile spread across his face. But it didn't. Because he was still alive. Still breathing.

And he was going to put every next breath to good use.

CHAPTER THIRTY-NINE

Shane slid the divider in the limo to the side and addressed Thomas with an impatient, "Well?"

Thomas, weaving in and out of traffic on the highway, the needle hovering fifteen miles per hour over the speed limit, addressed him with a quick glance to the rearview mirror. "No answer on Crickitt's office line, sir."

Shane knew it was a long shot to try the office on a Sunday, but when he didn't get an answer on her cell phone, he had to try.

"What now?" Thomas asked.

Find her, that's what. Find her and tell her everything.

An idea that scared him so much, his voice came out as taut as piano wire. "Do you remember how to get to her apartment?"

Thomas's eyes crinkled as he smiled back at him in a gesture that was almost fatherly pride, or what Shane imagined fatherly pride might look like. "Yes, sir," he said.

Half an hour later, Thomas pulled into Crickitt's apartment complex, and Shane pressed a button to slide the tinted window down. Like that would make her car magically appear in the empty parking space.

Shane scrubbed his face, swore into his hand. He'd pictured a big Hollywood finish, him telling her how he felt, her throwing herself into his arms.

Where is she?

With any luck, she'd run a quick errand and would be back any minute. Another call to her phone went to voice mail without ringing, which meant her phone was off or the battery was dead.

It also means she's not avoiding you.

Was it completely pathetic that made him feel better?

"Sir?" Thomas interrupted, apology in his dark eyes.

"Home," Shane said. "I'll get the car and come back." And then he'd wait for her.

He pulled a small wrapped box from his pocket and turned it over between his fingers.

He'd wait as long as it took.

* * *

After a day of shopping, dinner, and an evening movie, Crickitt dropped Sadie at her apartment, watching as Sadie wrestled her multitude of purchases through her front door. Crickitt stayed long enough to wave good-bye before heading for her own apartment.

Crickitt glanced to the backseat at her own pile of shopping bags. She'd purchased four new pairs of pajamas today since, by her calculations, she'd be spending every nonworking moment in them. Sadie tried to convince her that a date would fix her, but Crickitt assured her she was done dating. Maybe not for forever, but for a good long while.

"You should quit," Sadie had said on the drive home. "Go back to Celebration, rebuild your team."

It was a thought Crickitt had recently entertained. Particularly during the extended, uncomfortable hours spent across the hall from the man she loved.

"That would take a lot of committed effort," Crickitt mumbled.

"And seeing Shane doesn't?"

Touché.

But her excuse for not going back to Celebration was just that, an excuse. Crickitt wasn't afraid of hard work, of concerted effort. But she was afraid of moving backward. The pages of the previous chapter of her life were bookmarked by her direct sales career and dog-eared by an unsuccessful marriage to Ronald Wachowski.

"I'm finished with that part of my life," she'd told Sadie.

"Well, you can't continue to see him at work every day."

But that was just it, she *could*. As much as it hurt to be near him, she couldn't imagine walking away. Even if Shane continued to ignore her, or went from harboring ambivalence to contempt, she still wanted him. She realized that made her one sick puppy, afflicted with a warped version of Stockholm syndrome, but she couldn't help it.

She'd come to welcome the sharp pain in the region of her heart. Pain reminding her that she hadn't imagined the Shane August who was warm and open, regardless of how disengaged he'd become. Crickitt knew what she felt for him and what she'd had with him was as real as it got. Every heart-wrenching, beautiful, soul-stealing minute of it.

And if she stayed broken for months, years, then she'd accept it. At least until she found someone to fill in the break left there by Shane.

She turned into her apartment complex, trying fruitlessly to picture another man at her side. But they all had Shane's amber eyes, dark tumble of hair, and corded, strong arms. Tears threatened again and she swallowed them down. Someone would have to fill the role someday...eventually. That's what people did when relationships ended. Dusted themselves off, got out there, and tried again. At one point in her life she couldn't imagine being with anyone other than Ronald, and now look at her.

"Yeah, look at me," she said, misery evident in her toneless voice. "Oh, my gosh." The car jerked beneath her as she stepped on the brakes with too much force.

There, in her numbered spot, was a gleaming black Porsche.

Shane.

Hands shaking uncontrollably, Crickitt maneuvered her car into the guest spot next to it, her mind whirring. What was he doing here? He couldn't see her like this, desperate, pining for him. Did she even still have makeup on? She reached for her visor to check her reflection, then froze in place as she spotted him.

His long frame filled her doorway as he stood sentinel in a pair of casual cargo shorts and a loose-fitting T-shirt. A pair of dark sunglasses covered his eyes, keeping her from seeing the love for her that wasn't there.

On unsteady feet, she stepped from the car, forcing herself to stand straight. She couldn't have him here. This was her house, her sanctuary, the only place she went that wasn't marinating in Shane-themed memories.

"I've been waiting for you," he said as she made her way to her apartment.

"I didn't realize I was on the clock," she snapped at her reflection, irritated she couldn't see his eyes.

"I needed you today."

I needed you, too.

"I'll be at work tomorrow," she said, making a show of finding her house key on the chain in her hand. "I can help you then."

She tried to step up to the door, but one tanned, sinewy arm launched out in front of her, successfully blocking the way. "I didn't mean at work."

She meant to pretend not to hear him. Instead, she faced him and found his sunglasses perched on top of his head, his golden eyes expressive instead of flat. And, oh, what she saw there made her unable to look away. The pain, so prevalent the last time she saw him, had vanished. His eyes were bright, clear, and there was something else, too. Something she refused to acknowledge.

"Brought you a gift from Mexico," he said. A small wrapped box appeared in his palm.

"Mexico?" Crickitt asked, focusing on his words rather than the box in front of her face. "You flew?"

"Yeah." He chuckled, making a face at the same time. "Here, open it."

It was a simple gold foil box with a bow, but it may well have been cloaked in barbed wire and poisoned dart tips. Whatever was in there wouldn't fix anything. It couldn't. Could it?

"What is it?" she asked, stalling.

"Something to complete..."

Don't say me.

"...your collection."

She should hand it back. Thrust it into his chest and state, unequivocally, that she was moving on. If she had any hope at all of getting their relationship back on a professional plane, then he couldn't show up at her apartment...

She watched as she took the box from his hand, seemingly powerless to stop herself.

What had she been saying? Oh, right, apartment. He couldn't show up at her apartment...

Her fingers tugged the cream-colored ribbon tying the box closed.

...looking all tanned and sexy, and...

She wiggled the lid and started to lift it.

...smelling amazing...

She lifted the lid.

A porcelain monkey stared up at her with wide eyes, both hands covering his mouth.

Words failed her as her brain stalled. She plucked the tiny primate from the box, rolling him between her fingers and trying to tamp down the hope that bloomed against her breastbone. Dangerous, terrifying hope.

Shane stepped closer, absolutely choking out the air around her that she desperately needed. She sucked in a breath on a gasp. "Crickitt?"

"I love..." *you.* "It." She refused to take her eyes off the figurine in her hand. And she couldn't look up at

Shane. She couldn't let him see the emotions racking her. What if his being here was nothing more than a platonic gesture? Or worse. What if he'd stopped by to drop off a few files before work tomorrow? Or just happened to pick up Speak No Evil while away on business?

She rolled the monkey between her fingers. But it had to mean more than that.

Maybe he wanted to go back to being friends. Friends would be better than losing him altogether... wouldn't it?

"I'm curious to see if he matches his mates," Shane said. She tipped her head up to look at him. His casual smile all but crushed her.

Friends, then.

Sometimes a monkey is just a monkey.

He stepped aside so she could unlock the door, which, to her credit, she did in one clean motion. He caught her purse as she pulled it from her shoulder and hung it on the antique hall tree that used to be her mother's. Refusing to look at him, she led him to the living room, and he followed, too close behind her, smelling beachy and soapy and manly.

She placed Speak No Evil next to his counterparts, where he sat a full inch taller than the other two, his painted fur black instead of brown.

"Not perfect, I guess," Shane muttered just over her ear. She jumped, having no idea he was standing so close. He reached out and turned the collectible so that he lined up with the others. "I was thinking about what you said about how even though the set wasn't perfect"—he paused to face her, assaulting her with his closeness—"it was still worth keeping. And I was hoping..."

Oh, my gosh.

"That might apply to me as well."

The very air around them shifted as she tried to respond, and failed. Shane linked his hand with hers, licked his lips. A truncated sound came from his throat. He blew out a sharp laugh, giving her a bemused smile.

"I've said it a hundred times in my head over the last two weeks, and I can't speak a single syllable now that I've got you here." He dropped her hand to drag his palms over his face, swearing into his hands.

Please say what I think you're going to, she begged with her eyes.

Hands folded into prayer pose, he watched her over his fingers for a second before dropping his arms and speaking. "The plane that brought me home almost crashed."

"What?" She clutched at her heart, which came to a full stop before mule-kicking her rib cage. Almost crashed? He could have *died*. All of her earlier excuses about them working together, and her getting over him, and the petty, pithy thoughts about how he'd been neutral and businesslike slipped away in an instant.

"It wasn't a big deal."

She raked him with a glance, swept grateful eyes over his four intact limbs, the fact that he wasn't bruised or scarred or bloody. *Not a big deal?* Was that a joke? She could have returned home from shopping for useless, meaningless stuff and received a phone call saying Shane's plane had crashed. And if that had happened...she couldn't even...

"I was a coward," he said.

Mind still playing out her worst nightmare, she reached out and stroked his arm, unable to stop herself. "It must have been terrifying...awful." She was crossing the line consoling him, but she couldn't seem to stop touching him. She swept her hand into his. "I'm just glad you're okay."

"I'm not talking about the plane."

She lifted her chin.

His face softened as he smiled down at her. "I meant with you, I've been a coward."

She couldn't have looked away from his face if a plane crashed into her kitchen.

Shane squeezed her hand. "I love you, Crickitt."

She couldn't speak. Couldn't think. Couldn't *move*.

"And I don't want to lose you."

She stood statue still, fingers curled over her lips even though she couldn't remember lifting her hand to her mouth. He didn't come here because of work. Her eyes filled with tears. He'd come *for her*. Because he loved her.

I've said it a hundred times in my head over the last two weeks.

"Say something," he said.

Thoughts ricocheted off the interior of her skull. Say something? Like what? She was halfway between screaming at him for keeping this from her for so long, and kissing him senseless. She pulled her hand away, tears streaming down her face.

"I'm so glad you didn't die," she choked out.

Shane chuckled softly, reaching up to wipe the tears from her cheeks. "So am I."

She cried harder, and he pulled her against his chest and shushed her, his hand rubbing circles on her back as her arms came around his waist. The moment reminded her of the night he sat on her desk, arms shaking as he held her. And she realized now how afraid he must have been, fearing he wouldn't be enough for her, worried he'd come up short.

She released him, backing away only enough to spread her palms over his chest. His heart beat strong and steady. She gazed up at him, tears drying on her cheeks. "You weren't a coward, Shane," she said, meaning it. He'd risked everything to get close to her, reopening a wound twenty years old to love her. "You're the bravest man I know."

He swept her curls from her face and lowered his lips to hers.

"Wait."

He halted over her lips, his eyebrows pinching ever so slightly, lips poised to kiss her.

"I love you, too," she whispered.

"Thank God," he growled, tucking her close and searing her lips with his.

PILOGUE

*C*rickitt dusted her hands on her jeans and surveyed her new office. The desk and shelves were still in cardboard flat packs leaning against the walls of the room. But once they were assembled, she knew she was going to love working from home.

Well, technically, Shane's home. No. Technically, *their* home.

Shane came up behind her then, linking his arms around her waist. "Hi," Shane murmured into her ear, kissing her lobe. He pulled her against him, all hard, warm, male muscle. Her knees turned to jelly but he held her solidly against him.

"Who's gonna put all this stuff together?" he asked.

She brought her hands up, lacing her fingers between his. "The movers?"

He nuzzled her neck, put an openmouthed kiss over her now-racing pulse. "Hmm-mm. They're gone."

"I guess that leaves you," she breathed.

He backed away from her neck and kissed her hair. "Bummer."

She turned in his arms, missing his mouth already. Linking her arms around his neck, she kissed him, humbled and nearly overpowered by how much she loved him.

Shane wasted no time asking her to move in. She'd suspected that step was coming. They were always together, whether it was her coming here to stretch out on his ginormous bed, or it was him taking up most of her queen-size lace duvet.

And things had been good. Better than good, great. Shane was healing a little more every day. He talked about his past, his parents, without much prompting on her part, and without bitterness on his. And he'd gotten really good at telling her how he felt. And how much he loved her, which she never tired of hearing.

"There's a box in the living room," he said, pulling away from her lips. "I need you to tell me where it goes."

She sighed. She'd no idea how much stuff she had until she'd packed it all into boxes. Even after a generous donation to her neighborhood Goodwill, she'd still filled a moving truck. Shane assured her there was plenty of room for all of it, but she'd insisted on paring down. Even so, it hadn't made the task of unpacking any less dreadful.

"One more box," she said. "Then I'm taking a nap."

Arms still around her waist, he slid his hands beneath her shirt as he tagged behind her down the hall. "Me, too."

She pressed his hot palms against her rib cage, stopping what was sure to be a slow, distracting exploration she'd be helpless to stop. "Your idea of a nap and mine are two entirely different concepts," she teased.

He laughed lightly in agreement and slipped his hands away. In the living room, boxes lined each wall, stacked two or three high.

"Which one?" she asked, her shoulders sagging.

"This one," Shane said from behind her.

She turned to find him on the floor. Knee bent, a black velvet box in his hand.

"Oh, my gosh," she breathed through her fingers.

"I thought you might say that." He grinned. "It's not a monkey this time."

She opened her mouth to speak but couldn't. Tears streaked her face as she blinked them away and focused on the man she loved. The man who loved her.

"From partners in business," he said, opening the lid, "to partners in life." He pulled the ring from the box, but she didn't take her eyes off his. "Have I won you back yet, Crickitt?"

She saw the slightest hint of doubt flicker in his eyes.

Still battling his fears.

For her.

"If I have more work to do," he continued, licking his lips in a nervous gesture, "I'm willing to—"

She flung herself at him, knocking his breath from his lungs and nearly toppling him onto the carpet in the process, mashing her lips against his. Then she covered every inch of his face with kisses...wet ones, since her eyes were leaking uncontrollably.

Shane caught her against him and lay on the floor beneath her. He reached up and wiped the tears and damp curls from her cheeks, the engagement ring, *her* engagement ring, resting on the tip of his index finger.

He cradled her face in his hands, and her body pressed against his. "Is that a yes?"

She nodded, blinking back another barrage of emotion.

He leaned up and kissed her softly. "I love you, Crickitt," he said, eyes shining with unshed tears. "I'll never let you down again."

"Shh." She pressed fingers to his lips and smiled down at him. "Speak no evil."

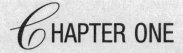

CHAPTER ONE

Aiden spun the beer bottle by its neck, the now warm contents sloshing against the sides of the bottle. He'd been watching Sadie from his chair at the back of the reception tent for the better part of thirty minutes, unable to shake the guilt swamping him.

Shane and Crickitt, God bless them, had been so careful when they asked Aiden and Sadie to be the only two members of the wedding party. But if there was one thing he and Sadie could agree on, it was to do right by their friends. They'd put aside their differences for the big day and had managed to be cordial, though not sociable, until the start of the reception.

That's when Aiden had bumbled his way through a long overdue apology. While he'd never apologize for prioritizing his mother during her fight with cancer, he realized too late it was a mistake to allow his ex-wife back into his life. He meant well when he decided to keep the divorce quiet, but Aiden should have told his mother before she died. Now, she'd never know the truth. And that was something he'd have to live with.

Sadie's buoyant giggle, a fake one if Aiden had to guess, lifted onto the air. He turned to see her toss her blond head back, curls cascading down her bare back, as she gripped Crickitt's younger brother's arm. Garrett, who'd been Krazy-glued to Sadie's side the entire reception, grinned down at her, clearly smitten. Aiden dragged his gaze from her mane of soft waves to her dress, a pink confection hugging her every amazing, petite curve, and couldn't blame the kid. Sadie was beautiful.

"Rough," he heard Shane say as he pulled out the chair next to him and sat, beer bottle in hand.

His cousin looked relaxed with his white shirt unbuttoned and sleeves cuffed at the elbows. He'd taken off the tie he'd worn earlier, a sight that almost made Aiden laugh. Before Shane met Crickitt, Aiden would've bet he slept wearing one. Crickitt may have shaken Shane's inner workaholic from his tree, but Aiden couldn't give her all the credit. Shane had stepped up to become the man she needed.

Aiden had a similar opportunity with Sadie. It was a test he'd failed spectacularly. "She has a right to be mad," he said, tilting his beer bottle again.

"You were in a difficult situation," Shane said magnanimously.

Maybe so, but after his mother succumbed to the cancer riddling her body, after he'd grieved and helped his father plan the funeral, Aiden had seen things more clearly.

"If I could go back, I'd tell Mom the truth." He swallowed thickly. "She deserved the truth."

"Don't do that, man." Shane clapped him on the shoulder. "You did what you believed was best. It was never going to be an easy situation."

True, but he'd taken an already hard situation and complicated the hell out of it. At her diagnosis, Aiden went into Responsibility Mode. With his sister in Tennessee, a brother in Chicago, and his other brother in Columbus, it'd all fallen on him. Later, his siblings would argue with him about how they would have helped if they'd known about any of it. But Aiden knew in his gut there wasn't enough time to pull everyone together for a powwow. When his mother said she wanted to move to Oregon to seek alternative treatments, Aiden rearranged his entire life and did just that.

"I appreciate you being here," Shane said.

Aiden snapped out of his reverie. "Oh, man, I'm sorry. I'm being a jerk on your big day." He straightened in his chair, ashamed to have let melancholy overshadow his happiness for Shane and Crickitt.

Speaking of, here she came, poured into a slim, white wedding dress, fabric flowers sewn into the flowing train. She grinned at Shane, her face full of love, her blue eyes shining. When she flicked a look over to Aiden, he promptly slapped a smile onto his face.

"You look amazing, C," he told her.

Crickitt's grin widened. "Thank you."

"And this reception." He blew out a breath for effect. "The lights"—he gestured to the hundreds of strands draped inside the tent—"the flowers, the band." The three-piece band included a formerly famous singer a decade past his heyday, but the guy still had it.

Crickitt rested a hand on her husband's shoulder. "Shane insisted on all this. I wanted something simple.

When he suggested getting married in a tent in Tennessee...I didn't expect *this*." She waved a hand around the interior of the tent: the shining wooden dance floor, the thick swaths of mosquito netting covering every entrance, the tall, narrow air conditioners positioned at each corner to keep the guests cool and comfortable during the warm June evening.

She smiled down at Shane. "But it is pretty great."

"You're pretty great," Shane said, tugging her into his lap and kissing her bare shoulder. The wedding photographer swooped in, capturing a picture for all of posterity, a good one by the looks of it.

Aiden picked the moment to excuse himself for a refill.

Or maybe two.

* * *

Sadie caught movement out of the corner of her eye and swept her attention away from Crickitt's attentive brother to see Aiden tracking his way across the tent in that easygoing lope of his.

She'd never seen him in a suit until today. He didn't wear the tie he wore earlier, pale pink with an intricate design, picked to match her dress. She knew the design by heart. It was the only safe place to rest her eyes when he'd come to her earlier and tried to apologize for last summer. Hearing the regret in his voice, feeling the emotions well up inside of her again, had almost been too much. She'd cut the conversation short, recalling the promise she'd made not to show her vulnerability to this man ever again, and stalked away from him as fast as her sparkly pink heels would carry her.

Garrett had since turned his attention to someone else standing in their little circle, and Sadie took the opportunity to watch Aiden. His tailored black pants hugged his impressive thighs and led up to a tucked white shirt open at the collar and showing enough of his tanned neck to be distracting.

I made a mistake last summer, Sadie. One I'll regret always.

Sadie felt the pang of guilt stab her. She'd planned to tell him she was sorry he lost his mother. And she was. Losing a parent was one of the worst things in the world, she knew. What she hadn't expected was the flood of emotion that crashed into her when she saw him for the first time in nearly a year. From the moment she'd rested her hand on his forearm and smiled as they walked down the aisle, she'd been tamping down one emotion after the other. Thank goodness girls were supposed to cry at weddings.

Then when he'd approached her at the reception, she'd been angry. Since then, she hadn't been able to feel much else. Which is why she'd been avoiding him. Aiden had a knack for seeing right through her.

And being called out by Aiden Downey was at the tippy top of her to-don't list.

Aiden pulled a hand through his coarse hair, the length of it landing between his shoulder blades. Sadie recalled the texture of it as if she'd run her fingers through it yesterday. She hated that.

Damn muscle memory.

Crickitt's mother, Chandra, approached him at the bar, sidling up to him and giving him a plump hug. Aiden smiled down at her but Sadie saw the sadness behind it, and for a split second, it made her heart hurt.

She kept up with Aiden's mother's illness via updates from Crickitt. The decision not to go to the funeral went without saying, but Sadie hadn't been able to stop herself from sending an anonymous bouquet to the funeral home.

As hurt as she was over Aiden, she'd empathized with the pain he must have gone through. Kathy Downey had refused chemo this time around, insisting on alternative treatment instead. Aiden and his father moved her across the country to the best alternative medicine facility in the United States. She died anyway.

Whether it was the cord of awareness strung between them or coincidence, Sadie wasn't sure, but Aiden chose that moment to look in her direction. His smile faltered, the dimple on his left cheek fading before he flicked his eyes away.

Sadie used to love the way he shook her up. From across a room. With a look. But now her heart raced for a far different reason. One she refused to name. She frowned down at her empty champagne flute. She was going to need more alcohol if she hoped to toughen her hide. This exposed, vulnerable feeling simply wouldn't cut it.

"Refill?" Garrett asked, gesturing to her empty glass.

"Yes," she said, grateful for his doting. She handed it over. "Keep 'em coming."

ABOUT THE AUTHOR

Jessica Lemmon has always been a dreamer. At some point, she decided head-in-the-clouds thinking was childish, went out, and got herself a job…and then she got another one because that one was lousy. And when that one stopped being fulfilling, she went out and got another…and another. Soon it became apparent she'd be truly happy doing only what she loved. And since eating potato chips isn't a viable career, she opted to become a writer. With fire in her heart, she dusted off a book she'd started years prior, finished it, and submitted it. It may have been the worst book ever, but it didn't stop her from writing another one. Now she has several books finished, several more started, and even more marinating in her brain (which currently resides in the clouds, thank you very much), and she couldn't be happier. She firmly believes God gifts us with talents for a purpose, and with His help, you can create the life you want. (While eating potato chips.)

Jessica is an ex–meat-eater, writer, artist, dreamer, wife, and den mother to two dogs.

You can learn more at:

JessicaLemmon.com

Twitter @lemmony

THE DISH

Where Authors Give You the Inside Scoop

♥ ♥ ♥ ♥ ♥ ♥ ♥ ♥ ♥ ♥ ♥ ♥ ♥ ♥ ♥ ♥

From the desk of Jennifer Haymore

Dear Reader,

When Mrs. Emma Curtis, the heroine of THE ROGUE'S PROPOSAL, came to see me, I'd just finished writing *The Duchess Hunt*, the story of the Duke of Trent and his new wife, Sarah, who'd crossed the deep chasm from maid to duchess, and I was feeling very satisfied in their happily ever after.

Mrs. Curtis, however, had no interest in romance.

"I need you to write my story," she told me. "It's urgent."

I encouraged her to sit down and tell me more.

"I'm on a mission of vengeance," she began. "You see, I need to find my husband's murderer—"

I lifted my hand right away to stop her. "Mrs. Curtis, I don't think this is going to work out. You see, I don't write thrillers or mysteries. I am a romance writer."

"I know, but I think you can help me. I really do."

"How's that?"

"You've met the Duke of Trent, haven't you? And his brother, Lord Lukas?" She leaned forward, dark eyes serious and intent. "You see, I'm searching for the same man they are."

My brows rose. "Really? You're looking for Roger Morton?"

"Yes! Roger Morton is the man who murdered my husband. Please—Lord Lukas is here in Bristol. If you could only arrange an introduction...I know his lordship could help me to find him."

She was right—I did know Lord Lukas. In fact...

I looked over the dark-haired woman sitting in front of me. Mrs. Curtis was a young, beautiful widow. She seemed intelligent and focused.

My mind started working furiously.

Mrs. Curtis and Lord Luke? Could it work?

Maybe...

Luke would require a *lot* of effort. He was a rake of the first order, brash, undisciplined, prone to all manner of excess. But something told me that maybe, just maybe, Mrs. Curtis would be a good influence on him... If I could join them on the mission to find Roger Morton, it just might work out.

(I am a *romance* writer, after all.)

"Are you *sure* you want to meet Lord Lukas?" I asked her. "Have you heard the rumors about him?"

Her lips firmed. "I have heard he is a rake." Her eyes met mine, steady and serious. "I can manage rakes."

There was a steel behind her voice. A steel I approved of.

Yes. This could work.

My lips curved into a smile. "All right, Mrs. Curtis. I might be able to manage an introduction..."

And that was how I arranged the first meeting between Emma Curtis and Lord Lukas Hawkins, the second brother of the House of Trent. Their relationship proved to be a rocky one—I wasn't joking when I said Luke was a rake, and in fact, "rake" might be too mild a term. But Emma proved to be a worthy adversary for him, and they ended up traveling a dangerous and emotional but

ultimately sweetly satisfying path in THE ROGUE'S
PROPOSAL.

Come visit me at my website, www.jenniferhaymore
.com, where you can share your thoughts about my books,
sign up for some fun freebies and contests, and read
more about THE ROGUE'S PROPOSAL and the House
of Trent Series. I'd also love to see you on Twitter (@
jenniferhaymore) or on Facebook (www.facebook.com/
jenniferhaymore-author).

Sincerely,

Jennif Haymore

♥ ♥ ♥ ♥ ♥ ♥ ♥ ♥ ♥ ♥ ♥ ♥ ♥ ♥ ♥ ♥

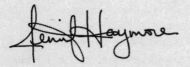

From the desk of Hope Ramsay

Dear Reader,

My mother was a prodigious knitter. If she was watching
TV or traveling in the car or just relaxing, she would
always have a pair of knitting needles in her hand. So, of
course, she needed a steady supply of yarn.

We lived in a medium-sized town on Long Island. It
had a downtown area not too far from the train station,
and tucked in between an interior design place and a
quick lunch stand was a yarn shop.

I vividly remember that wonderful place. Floor-to-ceiling shelves occupied the wall space. The cubbies were filled with yarn of amazing hues and cardboard boxes of incredibly beautiful buttons. The place had a few cozy chairs and a table strewn with knitting magazines.

Mom visited that yarn store a lot. She would take her knitting with her sometimes, especially if she was having trouble with a pattern. There was a woman there—I don't remember her name—but I do remember the half-moon glasses that rode her neck on a chain. She was a yarn whiz, and Mom consulted her often. Women gathered there to knit and talk. And little girls tagged along and learned how to knit on big, plastic needles.

I went back in my mind to that old yarn store when I created the Knit & Stitch, and I have to say that writing about it was almost like spending a little time with Mom, even though she's no longer with us. There is something truly wonderful about a circle of women sharing stories while making garments out of luxurious yarn.

I remember some of the yarn Mom bought at that yarn store, too, especially the brown and baby blue tweed alpaca that became a cable knit cardigan. I wore that sweater all through high school until the elbows became threadbare. Wearing it was like being wrapped up in Mom's arms.

There is nothing like the love a knitter puts into a garment. And writing about women who knit proved to be equally joyful for me. I hope you enjoy spending some time with the girls at the Knit & Stitch. They are a great bunch of warm-hearted knitters.

Hope Ramsay

♥ ♥ ♥ ♥ ♥ ♥ ♥ ♥ ♥ ♥ ♥ ♥ ♥ ♥

From the desk of Erin Kern

Dear Reader,

So here we are. Back in Trouble, Wyoming, catching up with those crazy McDermotts. In case you didn't know, these men have a way of sending the ladies of Trouble all into a tizzy by just existing. At the same time there was a collective breaking of hearts when the two older McDermotts, Noah and Chase, surreptitiously removed themselves from the dating scene by getting married.

But what about the other McDermott brother, you ask? Brody is special in many ways, but no less harrowing on those predictable female hormones. And, even though Brody has sworn off dating for good, that doesn't mean he doesn't have it coming. The love bug, I mean. And he gets bitten, big time. Sorry, ladies. But this dark-haired heartbreaker with the piercing gray eyes is about to fall hard.

Happy Reading!

Erin Kern

♥ ♥ ♥ ♥ ♥ ♥ ♥ ♥ ♥ ♥ ♥ ♥ ♥ ♥

From the desk of Mimi Jean Pamfiloff

Dear Reader,

"If you love her, set her free. If she comes back, she's yours. If she doesn't...Christ! Stubborn woman! Hunt her

down, and bring her the hell back; she's still yours according to vampire law."

Niccolo DiConti, General of the
Vampire Queen's Army

I always like to believe that the universe has an all-
knowing, all-seeing heart filled with the wisdom to grant
us not what we want, but that which we need most.
Does that mean the universe will simply pop that special
something into a box and leave it on your doorstep? Hell
no. And if you're Niccolo DiConti, the universe might be
planning a very, very long, excruciating obstacle course
before handing out any prizes. That is, if he and his over-
bloated, vampire ego survive.

Meet Helena Strauss, the obstacle course. According
to the infamous prophet and Goddess of the Underworld,
Cimil, Niccolo need only to seduce this mortal into
being his willing, eternal bride and Niccolo's every wish
will be granted. Thank the gods he's the most legendary
warrior known to vampire, with equally legendary looks.
Seducing a female is hardly a challenge worthy of such
greatness.

Famous last words. Because Helena Strauss has no
interest in giving up long, sunny days at the beach or
exchanging her happy life to be with this dark, arrogant,
deadly male.

Mimi

♥ ♥ ♥ ♥ ♥ ♥ ♥ ♥ ♥ ♥ ♥ ♥ ♥ ♥ ♥ ♥ ♥

From the desk of Jessica Lemmon

Dear Reader,

Imagine you're heartbroken. Crying. Literally *into* your drink at a noisy nightclub your best friend has dragged you to. Just as you are lamenting your very bad decision to come out tonight, someone approaches. A tall, handsome someone with a tumble of dark hair, expressive amber eyes, and perfectly contoured lips. Oh, *and* he's rich. Not just plain old rich, but rich of the *filthy, stinking* variety. This is exactly the situation Crickitt Day, the heroine of TEMPTING THE BILLIONAIRE, finds herself in one not-so-fine evening. Oh, to be so lucky!

I may have given the characters of TEMPTING THE BILLIONAIRE a fairy-tale/fantasy set-up, but I still wanted them rooted and realistic. Particularly my hero. It's why you'll find Shane August a bit of a departure from your typical literary billionaire. Shane visits clients personally, does his own dishes, makes his own coffee. And—get ready for it—bakes his own cookies.

Hero tip: Want to win over a woman? Bake her cookies.

The recipe for these mysterious and amazing bits of heavenly goodness can be traced back to a cookbook by Erin McKenna, creator of the NYC-based bakery Babycakes. What makes the recipes so special, you ask? They use *coconut oil* instead of vegetable oil or butter. The result is an amazingly moist, melt-in-your-mouth, can't-stop-at-just-one chocolate chip cookie you will happily burn your tongue on when the tray comes out of the oven. Bonus: Coconut oil is rumored to help speed up your metabolism. I'm not saying these cookies are healthy...but I'm not *not* saying it, either.

Attempting this recipe required a step outside my comfort zone. I tracked down unique ingredients. I diligently measured. I spent time and energy getting it right. That's when I knew just the hobby for the down-to-earth billionaire who can't keep himself from showing others how much he cares. And if a hero is going to bake you cookies, what better place to be served *said cookies* than by a picturesque waterfall? None, I say. (Well, okay, I can think of another location or two, but admit it, a waterfall is a pretty dang good choice.)

As you can imagine, Crickitt is beyond impressed. And when a rogue smear of chocolate lands on her lips, Shane is every bit the gentleman by—*ahem*—helping her remove the incriminating splotch. Alas, that's a story for another day. (Or, for chapter nineteen...)

I hope you enjoy losing yourself in the very real fantasy world of Shane and Crickitt. It was a world I happily immersed myself in while writing; a world I *still* imagine myself in whenever a certain rich, nutty, warm, homemade chocolate chip cookie is melting on my tongue.

Happy Reading!
www.jessicalemmon.com

Jessica Lemmon

Find out more about Forever Romance!

Visit us at
www.hachettebookgroup.com/publishing_forever.aspx

Find us on Facebook
http://www.facebook.com/ForeverRomance

Follow us on Twitter
http://twitter.com/ForeverRomance

NEW AND UPCOMING TITLES

Each month we feature our new titles
and reader favorites.

CONTESTS AND GIVEAWAYS

We give away galleys, autographed copies,
and all kinds of exclusive items.

AUTHOR INFO

You'll find bios, articles, and links to personal websites
for all your favorite authors—and so much more.

GET SOCIAL

Connect with your favorite authors, editors, and
other Forever fans, and share what's important to you.

THE BUZZ

Sign up for our monthly romance newsletter,
and be the first to read all about it.